THE RACING
HEART OF FEAR

ALSO BY B.A. CHEPAITIS

The Fear of God
The Fear Principle
The Green Memory of Fear
Learning Fear
A Lunatic Fear
A Strangled Cry of Fear
The Voice of Fear

THE RACING HEART OF FEAR

B.A. CHEPAITIS

WILDSIDE PRESS

PROLOGUE

Planetoid Three, Zone 12, Toronto Replica City

Immediately after Alex left the Planetoid, Jaguar stood in his living room and listened to his absence.

Quiet. The room was quiet.

No voices argued or praised or grieved here. No breath joined hers, no pulse beat within these walls except her own.

She walked to his bedroom and stared at his empty bed. If she lay down and buried her face in the pillows, she would still catch the scent of him, and her skin would remember the pleasure of his body against hers in their lovemaking. She backed away, moving out of the room. She did her best not to feel anything as she crossed the living room, then walked out the door.

Once she was on the street she clipped quickly down the sidewalk, bright autumn sun at her back and traffic humming by as if this was any other day. She heeded neither sun nor traffic, not sure where she was going until she realized she was on her own block. Like any wounded animal, she had merely followed an instinct for home. When she got to her building she entered, ascended the three flights to her apartment, opened her door and went inside.

She stood in her own space and looked around. There was her rocking chair, inherited from her grandmother. There were the herbs that hung from her ceiling—mint and sagebrush to cleanse and heal all shadows she walked through. There was the west facing window that let in its own particular slant of light, casting it over the objects resting on the sill: the jawbone of a big cat, wind-smoothed stones from the mesa, a sage scented candle. Everything here spoke of the choices she'd made; her work as an empath, her work on the Planetoids, Alex as her lover. Now she faced another choice.

She considered. No matter what he'd done or would do, she'd made promises to him, to his son, to herself. She would keep them.

"In grief and praise, I wait for you," she whispered. "In life and death, I wait. Mountains will melt and seas burn before I fail you in this."

The words caused painful motion in the region of her solar plexus. She shook it off and pushed the button to flip out the red glass knife she kept at her wrist. She brought it to her long dark braid, sliced it off cleanly and let it drop to the floor. She raised the knife again and kept cutting until her hair was shorn as short as possible. The clippings fell around her, shards of self scattered here and there. She eyed them without regret.

"Okay," she muttered. "Let's do this."

She walked a circle around the room, starting in the east and moving south, west and north, stopping to speak to those who lived in each direction. She touched the floor, reached skyward, and did the same. She put her hand to her heart and spoke again.

"I myself, spirit in flesh, speak," she said. "Now I stand between the stars. Now I live in the eye of the deer, in the heart of the jaguar who carries all through night toward day. And here I'll stay, until death or the river brings me to my journey's end."

She let a few moments pass while the reverberations of her voice traveled where they needed to go. Having officially notified her spirit guides of her intent, she moved to her couch and knelt on it, pushing the tip of her knife into the wall behind it. Taking her time, she carved out the image of a winged creature. It was large, and had the dual aspect of predator and angel. As she worked, she intoned an ancient chant, going careful and slow because she hadn't sung this one in a long time, and she wanted to get it right.

Soon, she became aware of her door opening, of someone entering, but whoever it was remained quiet, so she ignored them. She kept chanting until the image on her wall was complete. Then she carved one feather within the left wing.

She crouched back on her couch, regarded what she'd done. She spoke the words necessary to call this creature into life.

After that, only silence.

She let her arm drop to her side and was still.

CHAPTER ONE

New Manhattan—Home Planet

Alex Dzarny, former Supervisor on Prison Planetoid Three, walked the streets of New Manhattan, the concrete jungle of his own *selva oscura*, and experienced a strange awakening in this place where his true path was lost. He'd left the Planetoid and Jaguar, his work and his love, only to find himself here, where everything that drove him to leave had begun so many years ago. He pulled his jacket closer against the cool October night and peered around, appreciating the irony.

He'd been stationed here to do rescue work as a young soldier at the tag end of the Killing Times. During his stint he'd had a brief affair with a woman who ran like hell when she found out he was an empath, an Adept, a freak. He didn't know he'd gotten her pregnant, and that their son was already written disastrously into the world.

That son grew up to be rock star Springer Todd, who was sentenced to Prison Planetoid 3 after he opened fire on his audience at a Madison Square concert, killing many. Alex assigned him to Jaguar, and she was expert enough to discover it wasn't Springer, but his grandfather, billionaire Ron Schulman, who planned the crime. But they had no proof, and all her skill couldn't save him. When it looked like Springer was about to kill her, Alex intervened, destroying the only human being he was ever likely to create. Only Schulman walked away clean, with no evidence against him except Jaguar's sure knowledge. Now, Alex had returned to the place where it all began, to New Manhattan, to determine what he needed to do next.

For most of his adult life he'd worked on Planetoid 3, in the prison system created after the Killing Times, where the worst criminals were rehabbed by making them face the fears that drove their crimes. He'd been passionate about his work, felt it added greatly to the store of good in the world. Planetoid programs were more effective than any previous system of incarceration, but working there had made him into the kind of killer he was supposed to heal, and now the thought of going back to it made him physically ill. That door of return was closed, but what door was open?

He stared up at the skyscrapers and saw them as an option. Easy to get to the top of any of them and dive off, and why shouldn't he? In killing his son he'd destroyed his own future, and so his life was forfeit. And he had no fear of that final plunge, in fact felt relief at the thought. But that was too easy. He didn't want to waste his death, and he'd promised his son he'd do something about Schulman. A better way to die would be by killing that man, who would never pay for his crimes unless he saw it done.

He could do it simply enough, since he didn't mind being caught, and all the gods knew Ron needed some killing. The main offices for Schulman Enterprises were just a few blocks over, and he needed no weapon beyond his own hands. Ron would take an appointment with him, just to gloat, and if all went well, Alex could dispose of him pretty quickly.

But there were two problems with this scenario. First, as Jaguar told him before he left, he was in no condition to make big decisions right now. Going after Ron when he was operating from his grief might be a trap, and he'd only have one chance at it. Second, even if he was successful it would be nothing other than an execution, which went against everything he believed in.

But he'd promised Springer, so either he'd do it, or he'd join his son in death. Was it worse to dive off a building, or commit suicide by murder? Worse to fail at a promise you made, or fail your own sense of integrity? That he was even considering the question said something about who he'd become. Someone he didn't want to be.

He was mulling all this when he felt an imperative warmth at his back. Because he was an empath and an Adept, such a strong sensation compelled him to turn around. When he did, he saw something he hadn't anticipated; a scruffy man, with long straggly hair and a torn denim jacket. His eye were rimmed with red, as if he'd been drinking heavily, or would like to be.

"Give something for boys in trouble?" he asked, holding out a can with shaking hands.

Alex winced, thinking of Springer. "What?"

The man shoved a brochure at him. Alex took it, put money in the can. The man thanked him and walked away. Alex stared at the brochure, which was stained and frayed, probably picked up from the streets, and being used to get drinking money. But then, Alex saw a photo of horses, mountains, a big blue sky.

The brochure advertised a horse ranch in Wyoming called *Free Range*, which offered a Western experience to city dwellers. They also ran a program for troubled teenage boys, teaching them to manage their own issues as they dealt with the immense power and wild fear of horses. The brochure said they welcomed volunteers.

Alex crumpled it, then stopped himself and pressed it back to its original shape. He read the phone number, pulled out his cellcom and dialed. A man in cowboy hat and denim shirt appeared on his small screen and he said, "I understand you're looking for volunteers."

The man blinked in surprise, recovered himself. "Sure," he said. "Always are."

"What do you need?" Alex asked.

"Someone with horse experience. And someone who can deal with crazy boys."

"I can do that," Alex said.

He gave a brief *precis* of his resume, which included growing up on a horse ranch and work on the Planetoids. The man's eyes lit up like a Christmas tree. He explained apologetically that all they could offer in return was room and board, along with a very small stipend.

"I'll take it," Alex heard himself say.

He wasn't sure why he did so. A need to make amends, or maybe the warmth he'd felt at his back. And beneath all that, he heard Jaguar's voice, who advised him to take his time in deciding. She had an almost 100 percent average of being right.

Whether he killed Schulman or himself, he'd do so with full clarity, full knowledge of the right way to go. He didn't have anything near that yet. He'd do his penance with troubled boys in Wyoming first and wait for discernment.

CHAPTER TWO

Six months later: Planetoid Three, Zone 12

Dr. Jaguar Addams, Teacher on Planetoid Three and occasional vocalist for the techno-poet band *Moon Illusion*, stood on stage at the Crab Nebula pub, dressed in her best black silk dress, slit up one side, showing her black stockings and black high heels. She sang an old blues tune, her voice a sultry character stalking the patrons, licking and nipping at the back of their ears.

She hadn't done a gig with *Moon Illusion* since Alex left six months ago. She wouldn't have done this one except that Gerry Wallach, lead guitarist and Planetoid team member, bribed her with the offer of a torch and blues night. He even said he'd play sax. She agreed.

She started with *Hit Me with a Hot Note*, just to get things jumping, then moved into her own version of *Blues in the Night*, which had quite an edge. After that, *Whipping Post* let Gerry use his guitar to good purpose, while she let loose with her lower range. Then she'd added a hot and easy version of *Fever*. She was closing the set with *The Man that Got Away*, done slow and sad, her crooning dark and smokey as the whiskey in her glass. Long ago Judy Garland had put it over with feeling. Now it was Jaguar's turn, and she did justice to the tune.

In the audience, her friend Rachel Shofet occupied a table with Marie Camposi, who ran the zoo in this replica city of Toronto. They sipped their drinks and sat in thrall to Jaguar's voice, an electric circuit connected inexorably to loss. Even Gerry, who preferred his technopop, swayed soulfully as he worked his sax.

But when Jaguar got to the line "the man that won you has run off and undone you," her voice broke. Rachel sat up and paid more attention to the singer than the song. She'd never heard that happen before. Not ever.

Marie, who knew Jaguar almost as well as Rachel did, also sat up. "That's not good," she said.

"Yeah," Rachel said. "Really not."

They waited for what might happen next and were both relieved when Jaguar grabbed it back and kicked it out in force, something extra in her voice as she sang that it was all a crazy game. She gave extra clarity to the line that said fools will be fools, scorched the phrase asking where he'd gone to, and moved on, with feeling. She made it almost to the end, but the last line defeated her.

"Ever since this world began, there ain't nothing sadder than," she sang, full voice, and then she stopped completely.

The music kept going. Jaguar closed her eyes, and in a piercing whisper spoke instead of sang, "A one man woman, waiting for the man that got away." She kept her eyes closed and let the band carry the rest.

The sharp touch of it, the authenticity of the mood, made everyone but Jaguar's best friends think she meant to do that. The audience applauded wildly. Marie and Rachel cast concerned looks at each other. Jaguar picked up her whiskey, gave a nod to the audience, and walked off stage.

Gerry took the applause that kept coming, but he made faces at Rachel and Marie to ask what that was about. At the set break that followed he went down to their table and asked it out loud.

"What the fuck," he said. "She didn't even get the words right. It's *looking* for the man that got away. She said *waiting*. I mean, what the fuck?"

"Give her a break, Gerry," Marie said. "You know that's gotta be a tough one for her."

"She picked it," he pointed out. "I wanted *Black Coffee*."

"Glutton for punishment," Rachel said. She patted Marie, stood, and headed toward the green room.

"Remind her we got another set coming up," Gerry called after her. "We're doing *Bob's Blues*. Maybe she can handle that."

Rachel ignored him. She had other things on her mind.

* * * *

She found Jaguar sitting on the beat up old couch in the cluttered storage space that served as green room at the Crab Nebula. She was staring at nothing, looking as hollowed out as the empty liquor cartons scattered around the room. Rachel made her way through them and stood in front of her.

Long ago, Rachel had rebelled against her orthodox Jewish family's restrictions, stole a car and ended up in a high speed chase with a cop who was killed in the ensuing accident. She'd been sentenced to Planetoid Three and assigned to Jaguar, who led her back to herself, helped her realize that her attraction to women wasn't a sin. Jaguar had, quite literally, saved her soul.

After her program was deemed successful she stayed on to work as a researcher and team member. Now she was not only the best hacker on all three Planetoids, but also the best friend Jaguar had. She couldn't have read her any better if she was, like Jaguar, an empath. Her friend was feeling too much, and trying like hell not to.

"Hey. That was great," Rachel said, staying casual. With Jaguar, indirection was often the wiser part of valor.

"Thanks," Jaguar said. She sipped at her whiskey, pulled a cigarette from the pack on the end table, lit it and smoked.

"You're not supposed to do that here, are you?" she asked.

Jaguar shrugged. "Moon Illusion brings in the best business they get. Nobody'll complain."

Rachel plunked down on the couch next to her. She waited a moment, then made herself deliberately cheerful. "So I had an idea the other day. I'm taking some R and R time, maybe like at a spa, and I want you to come along."

Jaguar raised an eyebrow at her. "A spa?"

"Sure. You know. Saunas and seaweed wraps and mani-pedis and fine food. I've got some time coming."

Jaguar shook her head. "I'm working."

"I cleared your schedule with Paul and Junius," Rachel said.

Junius was interim Supervisor, filling in for Alex. Paul Dinardo, board Governor for their zone, wouldn't hire anyone permanently until Alex's leave of absence was up. He'd also gone out of his way to pick an interim Jaguar wouldn't find objectionable. He was being very careful with her, making sure Junius gave her easy cases, nothing she could get in trouble with. And for once, Jaguar wasn't complaining.

She blew smoke out, sipped whiskey. "I appreciate it, Rachel, but I'd rather not."

"C'mon. It'll do you good."

Jaguar eyed her, said nothing.

"Okay then," Rachel amended. "It'll do me good. And you'll have fun. You'll see."

"I don't want to have fun," Jaguar pointed out. "I'm not into fun these days."

Rachel sighed. She knew that. The day Alex left she'd gone to Jaguar's apartment and found her using her glass knife to carve an image into the wall behind her couch. Her long dark hair was shorn, her braid and clumps of loose hair scattered around the room. Rachel had stayed quiet and watched as Jaguar's knife created a winged creature—part human, part bird, and not at all angelic. Then she'd cut a single feather into one of the wings, breathed on it, said some words in her own Mertec language. Rachel had let some time pass before she spoke.

"Your hair," she'd said at last.

"What about it?" Jaguar replied, daring her to say more.

Rachel didn't have to. She knew what it meant. Cutting her hair was a sign of grief beyond words. She'd gestured toward the image on the wall. "What's that?" she asked.

"A Mertec thing," was all Jaguar said.

She didn't elaborate, and Rachel didn't ask for more. But every time she went to Jaguar's apartment after that the wings had more feathers. Now one of them was filled in entirely, the other gathering a new feather each day. 137 feathers, by current count.

Rachel could add and subtract. 137 feathers, one for each day of Alex's absence. Jaguar was a powerful, complicated, and high maintenance woman, and while she could get sex wherever she wanted, a true partner for someone like her wasn't easy to find. In Alex she'd found the best one possible, and he got away. Not fun at all, and it was taking a toll on her.

She'd never been sick before, but in the last three months she'd had a bad bout with the flu, an inexplicable problem with her back that left her flat, and bronchitis. Her concentration wasn't anywhere near as sharp as normal, and she went through her cases in a perfunctory way, closing them efficiently and without appearing as if she gave a damn. Before tonight, she'd refused to sing. That, even more than being sick, was a sure sign for Rachel she wasn't doing well.

But she'd gone underground with her feelings, which made it difficult to help her. In fact, when Alex first left she told her and Gerry and Marie, her three closest friends on the Planetoid, that she didn't want anyone to talk about him at all.

"Don't give me any sympathy, don't try to fix it, don't say a rat fuck word," she instructed them. "Don't even use his name in my vicinity. And if you hear anyone else about to do so—well, you're all trained in restraint procedures. Use them."

Gerry, taking her literally, had thrown himself at a guy at the Silver Bay pub who approached Jaguar while calling out, "Hey—I hear Alex—"

Before the sentence was complete the man was on the floor, under Gerry's formidable form. Jaguar, sitting at the bar, glanced over at them and said, "Good work, Gerry." Then she continued her conversation with the bartender.

The only person who had braved her walls was Alex's assistant, Scott White, a former Navy SEAL. He and Rachel were in Alex's office going over case files when Jaguar stopped in to drop off a report. Scott stood as she entered the room. He didn't salute, but he might as well have.

"Hullo, Scott. How are you?" Jaguar had asked politely.

"Ma'am, can I speak with you?" he'd requested.

She waved a hand, inviting him to continue.

"It's about Supervisor Dzarny," he said.

Jaguar tensed, but at least she didn't kill him. "I really can't talk about that," she said.

"You don't have to. I'm offering my assistance."

She looked mildly curious. "In what way?"

"Guard duty," he said. "I can go to the home planet. Keep an eye on—on things."

A small smile came and went. "You'll watch over him?" she asked.

"I'd be discrete," he noted.

"I've seen how you do that," she said. He'd been watchdog for her and Alex on a difficult case, and he was exceptionally good at it. "I appreciate the offer, but we can't clear you for it. He's on leave by choice."

"I'll use my vacation time," he said. "Quit work if I need to."

Jaguar's face had moved in a confusion of emotions. "I'll let you know if it seems warranted. In the meantime, he's covered."

She didn't explain, but she and Scott exchanged some heavy eye contact, a signal for Rachel that they were speaking telepathically. Scott nodded, gave her a look both coolly appraising, and warm with respect.

"Yes, ma'am," he said. "Let me know if I can be useful." And they all went back to work.

SEALs, Rachel thought. Tough, tough young men, with very soft hearts.

Even Board Governor Paul Dinardo was feeling Alex's absence. When he'd told Rachel his plans for an interim, he stopped and shook his head forlornly. "Alex was the only supervisor who can handle politicians *and* Addams. You think she did this to him?"

"Don't even go there," Rachel replied, glaring at him. Paul had allowed Springer's grandfather, Ron Schulman, to interfere with the case, which was one reason Springer ended up dead.

"Listen," Paul said, "if you think of any way to make him come back, I'll give it all the support you need, bar none."

"He'll come back," she said, meaning it. Her natural optimism made her hope he'd return once he got through his grief. In the meantime, she was using her own intimidating skills to track him. That wasn't easy, because staying invisible was one of his empathic gifts. But once she found out he'd gone to New Manhattan she'd set up a complex program that relied on face recognition from public surveillance cameras, and was lucky enough to catch a view of him staring at a brochure for a horse ranch in Wyoming.

The picture was clearer than usual and gave her the website. From there, she was able to track him on payroll, in occasional photos on the ranch. Her daily checks told her he was still there, which increased her hope. He'd grown up on a horse ranch. Maybe it was the best place for him to heal.

She maintained her positive stance about him, but grew increasingly worried about Jaguar. She always waited hard, but where Alex was concerned, waiting might be the most difficult thing she'd ever done. For that reason, Rachel had arranged a respite. Now she patted Jaguar's shoulder, one of the few people who could get away with that gesture.

"You need a break," she said. "You're not yourself lately. Well, not *all* yourself. Like, you're not all here."

Jaguar gave a slow smile. "That's one way of putting it."

"What?"

"Nothing. I'm just—I'm tired, Rachel. That's all."

"Then a few days at a spa will do us both good. You think I want to hang around and miss Pinkie?"

Jaguar looked more like it. Rachel's girlfriend, Pinkie Horton, former drummer with *Moon Illusion,* had recently taken a job on the home planet. They'd broken off their relationship, knowing it was impossible to maintain at that distance. Jaguar, of all people, understood what that felt like. Rachel saw this and worked the advantage.

"C'mon, Jaguar," she said. "Do it for me. I don't want to go alone."

Rachel watched her maneuver this slippery slope. Jaguar was intensely loyal, willing to do just about anything for someone she cared about.

"When?" she asked grudgingly.

"Next weekend," Rachel said. "Sunday to Monday. Almost a full week."

Jaguar tamped out her cigarette, slugged down the rest of her whiskey. "That'd include the 23rd, right?"

"Yes. Does it matter?"

For a moment, Jaguar tilted her head to one side, as if she was listening instead of considering. She looked far beyond Rachel, far beyond the room. A twitchy smile came and went, which Rachel recognized as Jaguar, working her empathic arts. She didn't have Alex's precognitive abilities, but she was clairvoyant and could see what was necessary in the present. Rachel pressed her lips together to keep from asking about it. This was a delicate moment, and she wouldn't disturb it.

"Did you have anywhere specific in mind?" Jaguar asked after a while.

"I was thinking Colorado, up past Pitkin. They've got a great hot springs place. Mud baths and so on."

"Not too fond of that state. How about Montreal?"

That was a surprise. "Montreal? Why there?"

Jaguar shrugged. "It's nice in the spring. And there's a lot to do in the city, besides mud baths. Good restaurants, music, the circus, racing."

Rachel knew the sound of Jaguar working out a personal agenda, but she was in no position to press the point. "Sure," she said. "They'll have spas. So you'll do it?"

Another moment passed. When Jaguar looked to her again her eyes were sparking.

"Okay," she said. "I'm in."

CHAPTER THREE

Free Range Ranch, Wyoming, Home Planet

Alex's horse, a blue-eyed appaloosa called Wolf, took the trail over this ridge of the eastern Rockies swiftly and surely. She could be skittish, but he was good with skittish creatures. Behind him Ryan, a fourteen year old boy with gangly limbs and thick black hair that hung over his eyes, rode his more sedate bay, looking to Alex for direction.

They'd come to check the fencing at the base of the ridge, but Alex figured Ryan would appreciate extra time out so they took a side trip, justifiable because they'd had reports of a cougar prowling around. They rode further up, looking for scat or a cache.

Whatever they found or didn't find, the ride was good, the sky over their heads big and blue, the air redolent with sweetgrass and sage. At the crest of the ridge Alex reined Wolf to a stop and looked around.

"Let's take a break. The horses can rest," he said to Ryan.

"Sure," Ryan said. He dismounted, eyed Alex from under the fringe of hair that hid his eyes, and saw he wanted to be on his own. He had good instincts about that. He was here in a program for troubled boys that paired them with horses to train and care for. He'd been abandoned by drug addict parents and went through a few abusive foster homes before he hit back and landed in the criminal justice system. He'd spent much of his life reading the signals people put out, for his own safety.

Alex got off Wolf, dropped the reins and let her graze. This ranch and the land around it reminded him of where he'd grown up. Being here was like stepping back to a time before the Serials, before the Planetoids, before Jaguar was anything but a vision of beauty and confusion in the mind of an unwilling Adept. Here, he'd found a temporary respite from the warfare of his soul. He was aware of something almost like peace.

No. Not peace. A truce of sorts. A moment when his attempts to discipline himself beyond feeling actually worked. It might not last long, but he was grateful for it.

Since he'd come here, on his best days he felt only a dull ache in his solar plexus when something triggered a memory of who he'd been before he killed his son. It was an emotional phantom limb, gone but still aching. He'd learned to bear it in quiet, while he continued his work with the boys, and sought clarity for his own next best move.

Now, as he looked down from the ridge where he stood, he wondered if this was a better place to cast himself down than the skyscrapers of New York. He considered the idea without passion or prejudice. He wasn't deciding, only wondering, calm and contemplative, when a commotion of hooves beat the ground behind him. He swiveled around to see Ryan's horse rearing wildly as the boy struggled to catch hold of him. Alex moved to him quickly, took the reins.

"Quiet," he said to Ryan, who looked terrified. Then he turned his attention to the bay, put a hand on its face and made empathic contact.

It was an instinctive move. He hadn't done any empathic work since he left the Planetoid, but Jaguar had taught him how to reach animals in wordless communication, sharing pure energy, calm and assurance held against fear. In short order the bay lifted her ears and snuffled around, quiet again. Alex lowered his hand, thought about what he'd just done. Not a good idea, really. Empathic energy carried too much of his former life. He wiped his hand against his pants, as if to remove contamination.

"Thanks," Ryan said. "I don't know what I did wrong."

"Nothing," Alex said. "Something spooked her. Horses smell things we don't."

Ryan, a city boy, looked apprehensive. "Like a cougar?"

"Could be. Or coyotes, maybe a bear." He lifted his head, looked around. "Nothing too close. Let's head back anyway."

They remounted and moved down the ridge. Parts of the path were steep and they went slowly, Alex in the lead. At a bend he stopped, stared down at the drop below him. At least 5 thousand feet, he thought, with jagged rocks at the base.

"What're you looking at?" Ryan asked.

"Options," Alex murmured.

"What?"

Alex turned to him. "Go slow," he said. "It's tricky through here."

They went on without stopping, and when the main house came into view Alex felt himself moving toward resolution. Tonight, when everyone was asleep, he'd go back up the ridge, find a cliff. Maybe a cougar or a pack of coyotes would find him. Or maybe a wolf, his spirit animal, would take him home. If nothing found him, he'd go kill Ron. If something did, the decision would be made beyond him. The idea appealed to him. He still didn't know what was right, but larger forces of nature might be able to tell him. He'd settled his mind on it when he felt warmth at his back, the same as in Manhattan. He turned to it.

Kelby, a young ranch hand, stood behind him. His thick glasses looked strange under his cowboy hat, and though he rode like a real horseman, he talked like a geek. A boy genius, in high school he'd done soft juvie time for hacking into NASA's system, a crime he committed because he wanted more than anything to be an astronaut. Instead, he ended up here and found the sky big enough to encompass his dreams.

"Hey," Kelby said. "I was looking for you. You got a telecom."

Alex frowned. Nobody knew he was here. "Who is it?" he asked.

"Some old guy. Name of Jake. I told him you were out riding and you'd call back but he said he'd wait. Said you were close by. Don't know how he figured it."

Alex felt his heart thump hard, then return to normal rhythm. Jake and his wife One Bird were Jaguar's mentors in the empathic arts, two of the most powerful empaths he'd ever met, practical and magical as salt. They lived in New Mexico, in a village called 13 Streams, near the sacred site of Chaco Canyon, and he'd spent time there when he and Jaguar first became lovers. That memory dredged up a slashing pain, which he asked to subside. He owed Jake in a big way. He had to respond.

"I'll take care of it," he said. "Can you get Wolf settled in the stable?"

Kelby took the reins as he dismounted. Alex walked slowly toward the house.

* * * *

Jake's narrow face showed a scowl when Alex sat in front of the telecom screen, and his long, thin nose twitched as if he was trying to sniff the air for information. He shifted uncomfortably, rubbed at his balding head. Alex knew none of that indicated anger. He just didn't like telecoms.

"Jake. How are you?" he asked.

"My knees hurt like hell but everything else seems to be working," he shrugged. Then he got right to the point. "I'm calling because you need to come here."

Alex pulled back from the screen. Go there, where Jaguar's presence was part of the earth itself? He couldn't. He tried a smile, and an elide.

"Sure," he said. "We're pretty busy from now through the end of summer, but I'll have time to visit in the fall."

Jake's scowl deepened. "I'm not inviting. I'm *telling* you. You need to be here. Now."

Alex could think of only one reason why Jake would say that. "Is she—is something wrong? With her?"

One of Jake's eyebrows raised high over his bright, dark eyes. "Can't say her name?"

Alex had no answer. He continued silent.

"Yeah," Jake said. "That's one reason you have to get here. There's a few more."

Okay, Alex thought. He should know better than to underestimate the power of those who taught Jaguar, but that only made him want to go there even less. "Jake, I'm good here. There's nothing you can do right now."

"That don't matter," he said. "Not to Maya. She says you're coming for a visit."

Maya. A little girl who claimed Jaguar as her spirit mother. He and Jaguar had saved her from a Greenkeeper and brought her to live at 13 Streams. Alex sighed. In his philosophy, when you saved someone's life they didn't owe you. You owed them. If you kept them on the planet you had to make sure they remained well. And though she was only 12, she was already a skilled empath, getting better every day. Maybe she'd seen something important.

"This was her idea?"

"Her and One Bird. They told me call you. Right now. Brought me in from the cornfields for it."

Well, he thought. Oh well. "I have a few things to wrap up," he said. "I'll be there day after tomorrow."

"Good enough," Jake said, and signed off.

Alex sat for some time staring at the blank screen, feeling much more ready for the ridge than a trip to New Mexico. He'd worked hard to close down feeling. He'd have to work a lot harder to maintain that where he was about to go.

CHAPTER FOUR

Montreal, Canada—Home Planet

Jaguar and Rachel lay on separate tables, in a semi-dark room that smelled of lavender and soap. Both women were slathered in seaweed and wrapped in warm blankets, while a droning chant from a didgeridoo played over the sound system. Rachel had cucumbers on her eyes, buttermilk, honey and oatmeal on her face. Jaguar sported a mask of green tea and clay.

"This feels pretty damn good," Rachel murmured.

"Mmm," Jaguar replied, the only sound her constricting mask allowed her to make.

Since they'd gotten here on Monday, they'd had massages and whirlpools, taken advanced classes in yoga and Tae Kwan Do, strolled the city shopping for shoes, and ate good food in a few restaurants. Today was facial day.

The door opened, and a demure woman dressed in white approached Jaguar's table.

"Doctuur Addamz?" she asked, her thick French accent spoken in a voice that was professionally soothing.

"Mmm," Jaguar said again, keeping her eyes closed.

"I have confeerm your 'air cut appointment. Tomorrow at ten."

Jaguar was about to say 'mm' one more time, but Rachel sat up and spoke with feeling. "Absolutely not," she declared. Her cucumbers fell off her eyes, onto her blanket.

"What?" Jaguar asked, and felt a fissure form in the drying clay around her mouth.

"You're *not* getting your hair cut again," Rachel said. She turned to the demure woman in white. "Cancel the appointment. No 'air cut. Comprende vous?"

The woman cast confused glances between the two of them. Jaguar sat up. "Why the fuck not?" she demanded, her mask cracking tectonically and irrevocably.

"Because," Rachel said. "We're on vacation. And—and I *miss* your hair."

Jaguar's eyes went still as cool water in a resting pond. She kept them on Rachel for a moment, then turned back to the woman in white. "Keep the appointment on the books. I'll call in about an hour to let you know."

"You mean to cancel," Rachel cut in.

Jaguar ignored her. "You can go," she told the woman. You don't need to hang around listening to us bicker."

The woman gave a professional smile and left. Jaguar turned back to Rachel. "I wanted to take karate tomorrow morning, but you said I should do something more relaxing."

"We're here to relax, not kill people," Rachel said.

"I wouldn't even hurt anyone. Well, not much."

Rachel rolled her eyes. Yesterday, in the Tae Kwon Do class, she'd sent a young man whimpering from the room. "You say that *now,* but when you're in the class—"

"That's why I made the hair appointment." Jaguar said. "It's relaxing."

Rachel made a tsk sound. Here at the spa, where everyone exuded well-being, she was even more aware of the circles under Jaguar's eyes, the blank look within them that gave her an almost ghostly appearance. She needed some activity that involved neither killing others, or a renewal of her grief ritual.

"There must be something else you could do," she insisted. "Sauna, steambath, massage?"

Jaguar let out a long sigh. "None of that interests me much. I don't know. Maybe the race would be okay. As it happens, it *is* a race weekend. First practice is tomorrow."

That was totally out of left field. "What race?" Rachel asked. "Horses? I didn't know they did that here."

"Not horses. Formula One."

"What's that?"

"Cars. Or really more like rockets on the ground. They've got so much down force you can drive them upside down on a ceiling. Theoretically, anyway. The Gs are incredible"

Rachel leaned up on an elbow. She hadn't forgotten that Jaguar asked specifically about the date of the weekend, and specifically requested Montreal. Because she knew there was a race? "You like car racing?" she asked. "You never mentioned."

"You never asked. You'll like it, too. The drivers are really good looking."

"Please. Why should I care?"

"I mean, good looking women. They've got women drivers. Alicia Senna and Meris Grant. Also, some fine young women on team management, test driving, engineers. The Boy's Club thing is gone for good."

Jaguar nattered on, telling her how Formula One had resisted women in racing longer than any other sport, but that was over now. A few years ago Alicia Senna, great-grand niece to the revered Ayrton Senna, got on the Terra team. They were backrunners, but she kept moving up front, proving she had as much skill as her ancestor. She'd worked her way onto the GM team, where she earned a driver's championship, and got her team close second for constructor's championship. She was promptly sought by Ferrari, but she only signed their contract after they agreed to take on another female driver. They hired U.S. driver Meris Grant, making Ferrari the first all-female Formula One team.

Rachel smelled a scam. Jaguar had never once talked about car racing, yet she knew all this. "Fascinating," she said. "Now tell me what you're up to."

Jaguar widened her eyes in a paltry imitation of innocence. "I don't know what you're talking about," she said.

"Don't even try," Rachel said. "I saw your face when you suggested Montreal. You're here for the race, or I'm a—a hedgehog. Tell me why, or we won't go."

Jaguar slewed her eyes, lifted a hand. "Then I guess I'll get my hair cut instead," she said.

Rachel groaned, gave it up. She had absolutely no weapons in her arsenal. She'd have to get some before she found out what the real agenda was.

"Okay," she said. "Off to the races."

* * * *

The next morning, they took the metro to *Ile Notre Dame*, and walked the last mile with the rest of the crowd. The skeleton of the Biosphere, partly dismantled during the Killing Times and now a memorial, was still visible to those who made their way toward the race track. As they jostled their way through an increasingly thick pack of spectators, Jaguar offered information.

"Montreal lost the race during the Killing Times," she said. "The guy that owns F1—Larry Engle—moved all the races off North America, the wuss. But the city spent a gazillion dollars to rebuild the track and seduced him back. Good passing, fast corners. They even moved enough earth to create elevation shifts. They kept the Wall of Champions, where everyone crashes sooner or later, and they added replicas of some really cool corners. Parabolica from Monza, 130R from Suzuka, even the

Senna S from Interlagos. Then they put in a tunnel, like the one at Monaco, but made it better. There's no guard rails because it's all tritanium rubber. Drivers can bank around it. Very cool."

"Great. I really wish you'd tell me why the hell you know all that."

"I told you. I like racing." Then she gasped, and fell hard on one knee.

"Jesus," Rachel exclaimed and knelt next to her. "You okay?"

For a moment Jaguar stared blankly ahead, her hand clutching pavement as if it was a boat rocking badly on a stormy sea.

"The stars," she said, her voice hoarse and low. "They're so close."

Rachel repeated the phrase to herself, trying to make sense of it. "What?" she asked. "What stars?"

Jaguar looked down at her hand, lifted it, moved it around. Then her gaze came into focus. With some effort, she pulled up a sheepish smile and showed it to Rachel. "Ouch," she said, putting a hand to her foot. "New shoes."

She wiggled her heel, a black stiletto sandal that zipped up the front she bought just yesterday. She believed heels should either serve as weapons, or be nonexistent.

"How long do you think you can get away with this?" Rachel asked curtly. Jaguar was surefooted as the cat whose name she bore, heeled or barefoot.

"What? I'm fine. See?" Jaguar stood, balanced on one foot and waved her hands around to prove it. "C'mon. Let's get to our seats."

Rachel filed it, along with a bunch of other similar episodes, for use when she had something to blackmail Jaguar with.

They worked their way to their seats in the bleachers. Not as many people came to watch practice as the race, but it still seemed pretty crowded to Rachel. Their seats, Jaguar said, were on the straight just before Parabolica. "It's a great spot," she told Rachel. "Lots of passing on the straight, and we can still see them make the turn."

"If you say so. But we can't see much else, can we?"

Jaguar lifted a hand toward the big screens across from them, which showed what the TV and internet audience saw. Announcers with British and Australian and vaguely Latin accents—Dave and James and Memo—kept up a constant patter about the drivers, the track, the city, the technical developments of various teams. It meant little to Rachel, but Jaguar listened carefully, as if it mattered to her.

"Look," Jaguar said, pointing to a red car as it whizzed by. "There's Meris Grant. Alicia Senna's team mate. Number two driver, and she don't like it much."

"You say that like I know what you're talking about," Rachel said.

"Teams have a number one and number two driver. The cars are set up for the number one, and you know what they say about number two. Watch—you'll see. Here comes Alicia, right behind her."

Jaguar pointed toward the track where one red car was closely followed by another. The one in back drew even with the first, almost bumping it as it went around.

The announcers made whooping noises. "Well, that proves it," James said. "Anyone who thinks women are less competitive than men never met those two."

"Not that different from Ayrton's battle with Prost," Dave agreed.

"I heard they tried to get Eileen Prost, but she's a model and doesn't even have a driver's license," Memo added, and they all laughed.

"What are they talking about?" Rachel asked.

"Ayrton Senna. I told you about him. Alicia's great grand uncle. He had this thing going with another racer, Alain Prost. They were teammates for a while, but Ayrton was always trying to take him out, and vice versa. Made for some great races."

"Oh," Rachel said. "Then it's like—race gossip?"

"Something like that."

The announcers carried on. "Prost and Senna—That got ugly at times. You think this will? I mean, Alicia almost slammed Meris into the wall."

"Aah, but she didn't, did she? I think Alicia knows *just* how far she can go."

"She can go as far as she wants." Jaguar commented. She turned to Rachel. "She's really hot. So is Meris, in a different way. You want me to figure out a way for you to meet them?"

"I'd rather you didn't, since I know the kind of things you tend to think of. Who's that man?" Rachel asked, pointing at the screen.

Jaguar looked up, and on screen she saw a smallish man, with wispy blonde hair, cut as if someone had put a bowl on his head and trimmed around it. He was accompanied by a very tall and curvy blonde, and press microphones pointed at him from all directions. "Larry Engle," she said. "I told you about him, too. He owns F1."

"You can own this?" Rachel asked, but Jaguar hushed her, listening to the announcers.

"Pete Newton, our man in the pits," Dave said. "What's Larry say about the rumors that he's selling out?"

The smiling face of a young blonde man appeared large on the screen. "Not much, Dave," he said. "The rumor mill keeps churning, but he's not confirming or denying."

"Hmmph," Jaguar said.

"Can you—or should you—explain?" Rachel asked.

"Larry inherited F1 from his mother, who got it from her mother, who got it from the original owner. There's talk that he wants out, and he's selling to the highest bidder."

"Oh. Who might that be?"

"Someone with more money than any god," Jaguar replied.

The announcers whooped again as a Lotus zipped past, swerved, wiggled hard to right itself, and went on. When it was gone, they saw what made it lose control. A black dog, sleek and intent, trotted along the side of the track.

"Whoa!" James exclaimed. "Did you see that?"

"Very dangerous," Memo tsked. "Looks like Alicia's dog, doesn't it?"

"It can't be," Dave said. "I met her a few times, and she was absolutely obedient."

"Could be a stray."

"Either way, it's a huge hazard—for drivers and the dog. You think they'll red flag it?"

They continued to discuss this prospect while the dog crossed the track, found a crack in the fence and disappeared behind it. Rachel returned to watching cars zoom by, until she heard Jaguar groan.

"No," she said distinctly. "Not me."

Rachel turned, saw Jaguar staring at the bleachers to their left. A black dog was heading in their general direction. When it spotted Jaguar it stopped and aimed liquid brown eyes toward her. Ignoring the rest of the crowd, the dog walked unswervingly to Jaguar and rested a chin on her leg. Rachel surveyed the scene.

"That's, um, interesting" she said. "I wouldn't peg you for a dog person."

"I'm not," Jaguar answered. "I just have that affect on animals sometimes."

"They recognize close kin?"

"Something like that." She glowered down at the animal. "Really?" she asked. "I mean, do you know who I am?"

The dog's tail batted back and forth. Rachel had the impression that if it could nod, it would. It shifted and sat at attention, staring at Jaguar calm and alert, waiting for commands to obey.

"What's it want?" Rachel asked.

"It's a retriever," Jaguar mused. "I think it's retrieving me."

"Why?"

"No idea. Gimme a minute." She leaned over, put a hand on the dog's head and was silent. Rachel waited. The dog went perfectly still. After a moment Jaguar shivered lightly and released her hold. She closed her eyes, opened them again, and to Rachel she looked a little pale around the lips.

"You okay?" Rachel asked.

"Sure," Jaguar said, though she didn't sound it.

"Did you, um, learn anything?"

"Hard to tell. Zen mind, Doggie mind. I saw an abiding interest in chasing sticks, and in me. Also a sense that it's lost and wants guidance." She bent and looked at the tags hanging from the collar. "Not it. Her. The announcers were right. She's Alicia Senna's dog. Luna."

At the sound of her name the dog stood and began tap dancing on all four feet, flicking a tongue out toward Jaguar's face, which showed a broad grin.

"What're you smiling at?" Rachel asked.

"*Not* the dog," Jaguar said. "I just figured out how to get you a meeting with some very hot racing women."

CHAPTER FIVE

Montreal, Home Planet

Luna sat quietly throughout practice, not once moving her focus from Jaguar's face.

"You sure that dog's okay? She looks like she wants something," Rachel said.

Jaguar peeled her attention away from the McLaren that just sped past and cast a glance at the dog. "She wants to watch me," she said.

"Okay. But why?"

"Dogs are genetically predisposed to seek information from humans."

"Um—what?"

"I don't know. She just does. Hey—you see that?"

"See what?"

"Williams just took Mclaren for third. Rachel, stop watching the dog watch me. Just enjoy the cars. We'll take care of Luna after practice."

Rachel found the noise of the cars disturbing, and most of what happened on track either baffling or inconsequential, but she hadn't seen Jaguar this interested in anything since Alex left, so she bided in patience. When the announcers said it was over, Jaguar stood and gestured to Luna, and the three of them walked to pit lane.

Between Jaguar's Planetoid ID and Luna's ambassadorship, they were waved on to the Ferrari pit without any trouble, though Rachel was surprised that Jaguar gave her identity away so easily. Usually, Planetoid workers on vacation were careful to hide who they were, what they did. But she supposed in this circumstance it was necessary, so she didn't question it.

Quite a few people stopped to greet Luna, and she wagged at them furiously, giving small whinnies of joy as one person and then another patted her, took her face in their hands and talked to her. They moved on to their destination, the Ferrari paddock, which was buzzing with motion and sound, all business. It was the only place where no one paid attention to them. They stood at the entrance, unnoticed, casting about for Alicia.

Inside, mechanics fussed over vehicles. Beyond where they worked were closed doors to other rooms, and an open door with trailers beyond it.

"Can you see her anywhere?" Rachel asked.

Jaguar shook her head, and Luna nudged a nose against her hand. Jaguar looked down at her. "Okay," she said. "You lead."

They'd only taken one step forward when Jaguar, her eye on the dog, saw feet on the ground directly in front of her. She stopped short and lifted her gaze to stare at the bright blue eyes of a dark haired man, lean and fit and just an inch or two shorter than her. He offered a courteous smile, and moved a practiced gaze over both women.

"Bon jour," he said. "Puis-je vous aider?"

Jaguar pulled out some of the little French she knew. "Ju suis American."

"Ah," he said. "Then may I help you?" His English had just enough of France in it to make it interesting.

"We've got something that belongs here," she said, and gestured toward the dog.

"Luna!" he exclaimed, said something French and reached down to pat her. She backed away, made a low growl at the back of her throat.

Jaguar looked from dog to man. "She doesn't like you," she noted.

"Nonsense. She just knows she's in trouble." He wagged his finger at the dog, and Jaguar noted how fine and smooth his hands were. Well kept, she thought. Then again, Ferrari crew and drivers could afford to be well kept in all ways.

"Naughty girl," he told her in mock sternness, and the fur at the back of her neck rose. Jaguar put a hand on her head, spoke in her Native Mertec. Luna licked nervously at her lips, but subsided.

The man turned a bemused expression to her. "I think you are good with wild things, yes? You understand them. Where did you find her?"

"She found me. In the grandstands."

"How strange. She never wandered before, and she's been around the world with us. In fact, she's the most intelligent dog I ever met. Sometimes you think she's going to break into speech."

"I got that impression," Jaguar agreed.

"You were kind to return her. Alicia has been very worried." He stuck his hand out. "I'm Didier Picot. Test driver."

Rachel saw the glint in Jaguar's eyes, and wondered if he saw it as well. If so, he didn't recognize the way a cat's eyes gleam when it spots prey. Rachel marked it in her mind, to ask about later.

Jaguar took his hand, let him hold hers for a few seconds longer than necessary before she released it. "This is Rachel Shofet," she said, gesturing toward her. "And I'm Dr. Addams," she said. "Jaguar Addams, from Planetoid Three."

"The Planetoid?" he said, and shifted nervously. Most people on the home planet were nervous about Planetoid workers, assuming they were freaks and empaths, or dangerous in other ways. "You're not seeking prisoners, are you?"

"Not a hunting expedition, unless you count shopping for shoes," she clarified. "Just a little R and R."

He went back to his smile. "Perhaps I can help with that. I know the better places in Montreal."

"That might be nice," Jaguar said.

Rachel, watching, could tell nice was a euphemism. What she really meant was useful to her agenda. She sighed audibly. Jaguar and Didier turned to her.

"Something wrong?" Jaguar asked.

"Just wondering when we can get some lunch," she lied. Everyone else was, so she might as well join in.

"Of course," Didier said immediately. "You're here to enjoy the city. I can bring Luna where she belongs."

"I'd like the honor, if you don't mind," Jaguar said.

"Ah. And you deserve it. Alicia's in the meeting room. I'll show you." He led them to the doors at the back part of the paddock, pressed a button on one and it opened a crack. Didier and someone on the other side whispered to each other. From within, Jaguar heard a female voice speaking regally, rising above theirs.

"Meris and I understand each other," she said, her mild accent and careful grammar signifying that English was her second language. "We are teammates, but we are also racers, and we race. That is so, is it not, Meris?"

"Sure," a more strained female voice replied, sounding pure American. "But I'd like the engineers to pay as much attention to my set up as yours. You get that, right?"

At Jaguar's side, Luna wriggled and made whining sounds. "Yeah, girl," Jaguar said. "It's time. Go."

She moved her hand in a small gesture and Luna pushed forward past Didier. Jaguar followed close behind, grabbing Rachel's arm and dragging her along. As soon as they were in the rather crowded room Luna bounded ahead, rushing Alicia, who sat at a stool on the right side of the room, her minions around her and at her back.

At the sound of Luna's delighted whinny she turned, made her own sound of delight and opened her arms to the dog, who lapped furiously at her face. "Luna, you silly one! Where have you been?" she exclaimed, and took the dog's head in her hands. When she emerged from her love fest, she lifted her face in Jaguar and Rachel's direction.

Alicia, seen full face, was even more beautiful than in profile. Her dark shoulder length hair curled around wide, dark eyes. Her features were strong, but in absolute harmony with the frame that bore them—high cut cheek bones, a roman nose and a flower of a mouth showing her both imperial and sensual. Then, across the room from her, Meris Grant heard the commotion and turned to them, showing her fair face, fresh as a morning in May. Leggy and blonde, she was beautiful in an entirely different way.

Rachel, viewing them, flapped a helpless hand at Jaguar. "Oh, God," she said, louder than she meant, and eyes turned toward them.

"Hi there," Jaguar said to those who stared at them. "Good practice today."

Didier intervened. "Alicia, these kind women found Luna and brought her back. Jaguar Addams and Rachel Shofet."

"Jaguar?" Alicia questioned. "An unusual name."

"They're here on vacation from the Planetoids," Didier said.

"Ah," Alicia said, as if that explained all oddities. Then, moving quickly to what concerned her most, she addressed Jaguar. "But my Luna—where was she? Why did she run? She never runs."

"I think she wanted me here," Jaguar mused. "Though I don't know why."

Alicia's head tilted about an eighth of an inch. Her dark eyes stared directly into Jaguar's, not something most people did. Empath? If so, she didn't want the others to know about it. She glanced at Didier. "Didier, you may return to what you were doing before we interrupted," she said.

"As you wish," he said, though he didn't look it. He touched Jaguar's elbow, offered her a card. "If you need anything while you're here, call me," he said. "It would be my pleasure to assist you." He gave a bow and left them. Alicia turned back to Jaguar.

"Thank you so much for bringing her back to me," she said. "I had all the Marshals out looking. She's a very special dog. How can I repay you?"

Jaguar grinned. "Let me drive your car."

Alicia laughed. "The race car, or my Berlinetta?"

"Both," Jaguar said.

"My team would be very angry at me if I let you drive the race car," she said. "Maybe the Berlinetta, though. We'll see. But I can at least treat you to dinner. Tonight? Seven o'clock? We have only more practice tomorrow, so this is our best night. At Estoril. It's on Rue St. Paul. Meris, you'll join us, won't you?"

Meris cast her gaze over Jaguar and then Rachel, but lingered longer over Rachel. "That'd be great," she said.

Jaguar looked to Rachel, who continued to stand one step away from gaping. "What do you say? We're free, right?"

"Absolutely," Rachel said. "Free and easy. I mean, easy in the sense that we're free."

"Then we'll meet you there." Jaguar took Rachel's elbow and led her away. Once they'd put distance between themselves and the paddock, she stopped.

"Free *and* easy?" she asked.

Rachel pressed a hand to her chest. "Be still my beating heart," she said.

"See?" Jaguar said. "I told you."

CHAPTER SIX

Home Planet, New Mexico

Alex stood in the circle of adobe houses that comprised the center of 13 Streams. They surrounded him warmly, pieces of tawny-hued earth, molded into human habitation. They meshed so completely with the landscape of sand and mesas, it seemed they grew of their own volition rather than having been built. He moved his gaze over them and waited, letting the warmer air of spring in New Mexico penetrate his skin. He knew the protocol. Let the land and its creatures adjust to you. Wait and see if you were welcome.

In little time, the door to Jake and One Bird's house was flung open and Maya tumbled out. He imagined she'd been straining at the bit, waiting for Jake to release her. Patience was not her strong suit. She raced to him, her hazel eyes brilliant with happiness.

Since he'd seen her last, she'd grown to the gangly length of a colt. She wore her light brown hair in one long braid now, like One Bird, like Jaguar. And her face was more open, filled with light. He was glad to see that.

When he'd brought her here she was broken, and they'd healed her. Of course they did. They'd done the same for Jaguar, when she escaped Manhattan during the Killing Times and showed up at their door, deeply wounded in body and soul. But both Maya and Jaguar were young when they arrived, and what happened to them was against their will. What he'd done was very different. He doubted even their medicine could cure his ills.

He shrugged that off, and moved toward Maya, ready to greet her. She stopped short a few feet away from him, lowered her arms, looked at him hard. Then she burst into tears.

No amount of discipline could keep him from responding. Pity coursed through him, and he went to her quickly, gathered her in.

"It's not that bad," he murmured, patting her back as she sobbed on his shoulder. "It can't be that bad."

"Yes it is," she sobbed.

"Tell me about it. Did someone hurt you?"

"It's not me. It's *you*. I don't want you to die. You *can't* die."

He pulled back, put his hands on her shoulders. She could sniff the truth from a stone. Did she smell death in him? Had he already chosen that? If so, it was in a state of numbness, allowing himself only thought in the absence of emotion. Besides, choosing and doing were two different things, and here he was, still alive.

"I'll try not to," he said.

"Really?" she asked.

"Really. I promise."

"But you *might*. You're not sure. You haven't made up your mind."

"I haven't," he admitted. Nothing but complete honesty would do with Maya. She was like Jaguar in that. Jaguar, her adopted mother. He supposed that made him her adopted father, a disconcerting thought right now, when he was working hard to relinquish ties.

But he couldn't let go of her easily. She'd tugged at his heart from the first time he'd met her. She was, like Jaguar, so strong and so vulnerable to pain, fragile and enduring as light, a quality they both shared with his son, who was strong as music and brittle as thin glass broken by a scream. It was a combination that always inspired his best instincts of protection and admiration, in equal measure. Something else to know about why he'd loved Springer, and part of his horror at what he'd done.

Maya wiped at her eyes, drew in breath and blew it out. Then she lifted a hand, ran it over the air around him, reading his energy just like any empath would.

"Somebody you love died," she said. "And you're sad. *Really* sad."

He nodded, said nothing.

"I knew you were sad because I dreamt about it, but I didn't know it felt like *this*. I hate being sad, but I was worse when you found me, and you helped. Now I can help you."

He pushed himself to standing. The last thing he wanted was for her to think she was responsible for his choices. "Maya, it's not your job to take care of me."

"I know that," she said impatiently. "I'm just doing what my dreams told me. Jake says I'm good with dreams. And it's only fair, isn't it?"

Maya had known enough unfairness in her short life to appreciate the value of equity. "Okay," he agreed, "but what I choose isn't up to you. You get that, right?"

She thought about it. "It might be," she said judiciously. "We'll see." She took his hand, led him solemnly to the house.

Inside, Jake and One Bird were putting plates on the table. One Bird turned to him, watching him with eyes that weren't very different from

Maya's. Worried eyes. Jake lifted his head. "Have a seat," he said. "It's time for supper."

Maya led him to the table, sat across from him. The smell of corn-bread and lamb stew filled the room. Alex remembered it from his last visit here. He'd been hungry then. Now he ate because it was necessary, and expected of him. Jake and One Bird sat, they all gave thanks to the plants and animals that provided their food, and dug in.

Conversation would have been difficult without Maya, who chattered at a mile a minute. She'd made up her mind what she was going to do for Alex, and had no doubt she'd accomplish it, so she felt free to move on to more important topics. She was attending the school at 13 Streams, and had a lot to say about her math class, which she loved, and her history class, which she found boring, and her classmates, whom she loved and disparaged with equal intensity.

"You wouldn't have so much trouble if you didn't try to be better than everyone," Jake said to her curtly.

"I'm perfectly compassionate with my classmates," she said, lifting her chin.

"And they know it," he said. He turned his gaze to Alex. "She thinks she's got something on them because she can travel—even though she's not allowed to until she's 16." He turned a glare back at Maya.

"I'm *not* traveling." She spoke to Alex. "I know it's best. Not because he says so, but because it's very draining," she confessed. "When I'm better at other things, it won't be so hard. And I'm a fast learner. Even Jake says so." She looked at him, and he sniffed, said something in Zuni, and Maya replied in kind.

"See?" Jake told Alex. "She already knows the language."

Alex smiled. "I'm not surprised."

"It's because I take after my mother," Maya said with pride. "My *real* mother, I mean. Jaguar."

"You're almost as bad as she was," Jake said. "At least you haven't—"

One Bird reached over and touched his arm. "Don't give her any ideas," she said.

Jake chuckled, and One Bird subdued a smile. Alex kept his face on straight, negotiating pain. A child who called Jaguar her mother. A child of his heart if not his body. But she wasn't his son, whose spirit stirred restlessly within him. Springer was supposed to come here for his own healing, and Alex was very aware of why he hadn't.

He attended to his food and let the talk flow over him. Conversation moved from Maya to local matters. Crops, the rains, recent ceremony. They wouldn't broach anything important until after dinner. When they'd cleared their plates One Bird stood and took Maya's hand to lead her back to her adopted family. Jake and Alex were left alone. Jake's sharp, dark eyes glittered like bright pebbles under a running stream.

"How'd you know where I was?" Alex asked.

"We keep track of our people. Especially when they're in trouble."

Our people. Jake still saw him that way. "How much do you know?"

"The important parts," Jake said. "You killed your son, and left Jaguar."

Stated so bluntly, it should hurt, but it didn't. In fact, it was a relief. Jake named it out loud, and still called him one of his people. He didn't have to run from it here.

"I did," he said.

"So now you're not sure you want to keep living. Maybe you're too dangerous to have around. You don't need a weapon because you *are* a weapon."

Alex studied his hands. They were trained to be lethal, and he was exceptionally good at using them. "It's more than that," he noted.

Jake nodded, hearing what Alex didn't say. That he despised himself for his failure, because his job was to save people, not kill them. That he was angry at Jaguar, because of all the criminals she'd dragged through darkness into light, she couldn't save his son, a boy he'd known only briefly, and loved beyond all reason. That he'd breathed in his son's last breath, taking his grief and pain, not wanting him to bring that with him when he left. And he'd carry it to the ends of the earth, or the end of his life, which seemed imminent one way or the other.

"Yeah," Jake said. "A lot more. And it's all wrong." He pressed his hands against the table and stood. "Get some sleep. You'll be with us a while. We'll sweat you. And you can spend some time with Maya."

Alex stood with him and moved toward the door. Jake cast him a glance. "Where you going?" he asked.

"I'll sleep in my airrunner," he said.

"There's a room for you in the house."

"I don't think that's a good idea."

"Because it's Jaguar's room?"

Alex shrugged. That seemed pretty damn obvious to him, and he figured it was just as obvious to Jake.

"You think she's any less present out there?" he asked, nodding toward the land around them.

"I can only hope," Alex said, and made his way to the airrunner.

Once he was outside, he bent his head back, looked up to the sky with its infinite supply of stars. Immediately, he caught sight of the Planetoid rim and started asking himself where Jaguar was right now, what she was doing. None of the answers he came up with were good, and not ten thousand miles or ten thousand years of self-discipline could keep his yearning at bay. He lowered his head and moved forward. He'd worked hard not to feel. Not pain, or joy or hunger or thirst. Not anything. He wouldn't throw all that away because of the night sky in New Mexico.

He got himself into the airrunner quickly as he could, lay down on the bunk in the back and turned his face to the wall. He wanted to reach sleep before he felt anything else, because Jake was right. Her presence was palpable in the clarity of this air, under the depth of this sky, her flesh contiguous with the land that surrounded him.

As he tried to coax himself toward unconsciousness he sensed warmth at his back. A sheltering, as of wings. It was the same warmth he'd felt in New York, and at the ranch. By now it was familiar. A calm, protective watchfulness, warm as a whiskey coated voice singing in a smoke-filled bar.

He'd theorized it was the part of himself that wanted to stay alive, but right now he wasn't so sure. In this clear air it felt like an outside force. Could it be from Maya, who dreamt about his sorrow and wept at the possibility of his death?

No. Not her. She was an old soul, but not this old. And she got in your face, while this presence kept a distance, made itself known only through the events that followed in its wake. Maybe something of One Bird's protective magic? If so, he wasn't comfortable with the gift, undeserved since his own protectiveness had failed at a crucial moment.

In spite of that the warmth smoothed over him like water, and this time offered him the sweetness of sleep, a dive into darkness, which he wanted more than anything. Against his will his body relaxed, begging him for this small respite.

"What are you?" he asked the darkling night.

A voice clear and subtle as moonlight, almost human female, spoke into him, using words that made no sense.

Nahuak. I wait with you.

Then, silence. More warmth. He'd never heard the term Nahuak, had no idea what it meant, nor did he have a clue where the voice came from, but he didn't have the energy to grapple with anything beyond his own heart right now.

"I'm tired," he whispered.

Sleep, she said. *I'm here. By your side.*

A blanket of warmth and darkness flowed over him, and he let go of resistance. Maybe it was a hypnogogic dream. A moment of random vision between waking and sleep. And she caused no harm. She only stayed.

He slid into the darkness, the easiest place to be.

CHAPTER SEVEN

Home Planet, Montreal

Estoril, the restaurant on Rue St. Paul, was a study in understated elegance, all black and white, with plenty of waitstaff to keep an eye on customer needs the way Luna had kept an eye on Jaguar. And when Jaguar and Rachel entered, they saw that Luna was one of the guests, laying near Alicia's feet, at a table in the back of the room.

"Interesting," Jaguar muttered as they approached their hostess.

"What is?" Rachel asked.

"The dog," she said, but didn't elaborate. She moved forward, then stopped again.

"What now?" Rachel asked.

Jaguar tilted her head toward Alicia's table. A tall, lean man with dark hair stood next to her seat, his hand on the back of her chair. Luna picked her head up, and Alicia touched her, keeping her still. She spoke to the man, flashing a smile. He leaned down and kissed her cheek, then moved away. When he was gone, Luna lay back down. Meris spoke, and Alicia waved her words away, her smile gone, her face brooding.

"Huh," Jaguar said. "More interesting." She walked to the table. Rachel noticed that her eyes were glittering like glass in bright sun. She braced herself for trouble, knowing the signs of a hunting cat.

When they got to where Alicia and Meris waited, Luna lifted her head and batted her tail back and forth. Jaguar leaned down and gave her a few pats. "I didn't know dogs were allowed in restaurants," she said.

"She's a service dog," Alicia said. "They can go anywhere. Please, sit. We've just ordered a Barca Velha—a lovely Portugese red wine."

Jaguar took her seat across from Alicia, and Rachel took hers next to Meris. "What kind of service?" Jaguar asked.

Alicia turned to her. "The best. This restaurant is known for its fine service."

"Dog service," Jaguar corrected. "What kind is she certified for?"

"Ah, that. Protection. She protects me."

A silent waiter arrived with wine, and presented it to Alicia, uncorked it and poured a small portion into a glass for her. She sipped, swirled it in her mouth and swallowed.

"Yes," she told the waiter, and he filled their glasses and left.

Alicia, clearly ceremonial leader, raised her glass to the others, who did likewise. "To good people, who care for dogs," she said. Everyone drank, and put their glasses down.

"Do you need it?" Jaguar asked.

Alicia smiled brightly, falsely. "We all need good wine now and then."

"Not that," Jaguar said bluntly. "The protection."

Alicia's fine, dark eyes considered Jaguar, taking in a great deal more than someone else would. "You ask many questions," she noted.

Jaguar lifted her glass, swirled the wine inside it, drawing translucent red curtains over the inside of the crystal. "I do," she said, "You got a problem answering them?"

Meris laughed nervously. Rachel stifled a groan. She'd been looking forward to a social evening, rather than a hunting expedition. "Jaguar," she remonstrated, "you'd think we were at work."

"You would, wouldn't you?" Jaguar answered, then turned back to Alicia. "Is it a problem?"

Alicia waved a hand, dismissing trouble of all kinds. "No. I'm glad to answer. I had some threatening messages last year—during this very race. Insurance companies insisted I have a bodyguard, and Luna allowed me to escape the indignity of being followed around by a large man with a gun. This year, they asked that I continue the practice."

"What kind of threats?" Jaguar pursued.

Alicia closed her eyes, opened them again. Her hand moved an inch toward Jaguar's, and though she didn't touch, Jaguar felt the motion of empathic contact. She blocked it politely as possible, at the same time letting Alicia know she also had gifts. A small smile lifted and left Alicia's lips. She turned to Meris.

"You remember, don't you?" she asked. "The usual nonsense."

Meris, her lips pinched tight, shrugged. "Rumors were going around about Alicia leaving GM. They accused her of killing her engineer—Dave Tempe, and said they'd get revenge. As if she would. He was one of the best, and ready to go to Ferrari with her. It's stupid, but we have to pay attention to these things."

"Sure you do. How'd the engineer die?"

"Heart attack," Meris said. "Couldn't take the stress, and the party life."

Jaguar, still in pursuit, turned to Alicia. "They ever find out who sent the threats?"

"The police said it was untraceable," Alicia said. "Not that it mattered. I wasn't afraid. More wine?"

"Absolutely," Jaguar said. "It's wonderful. And maybe you can tell me where to get good boots in Montreal. I'm on the prowl for that."

Alicia filled her glass, and Jaguar receded, though Rachel noticed her eyes kept their glittering watchfulness, even while the conversation moved to the pleasures of Montreal, where they were staying, what they'd seen so far. And Alicia kept watching Jaguar, her eyes asking questions. They were both so involved in surveying each other that Alicia didn't notice the man approaching her from behind until he put a hand on her shoulder. Then she gave a small yelp, startling hard and turning fast.

"Didier!" she exclaimed. "Is it courteous to frighten a lady?"

"I'm so sorry," he said, and pulled his hand away. "Certainly that wasn't my intent. I saw you and thought, how lovely—I come out for dinner at one of my favorite restaurants, and I find some of my favorite women. May I join you?"

Luna picked up her head and snuffled at him, but at a word from Alicia she subsided back into her doggy doze.

"What if I say no, Didier? Won't that be embarrassing for you?" Alicia asked lightly.

"Not at all. If you're here for a—what do you call it—girls night out? Then of course, I must leave you alone."

Alicia's mouth twitched into irritation, but she waved him to a seat, and he took it. The waiter came over, and they ordered their food, Jaguar choosing the grilled sardine, the others opting for Paella and Caldo Verde.

When the food arrived, Jaguar cut away the head of her fish and picked it up with her fingers, crunching at it. Didier stared at her with a combination of desire and repugnance.

"Do you always eat the head?" he asked courteously.

"Of course," she said. "Otherwise, what's the point?"

Alicia laughed. "That is the best part." She leaned to Didier, tapped his arm. "My friend, you must get over your fear of wild women, if you want to be comfortable in F1 these days. Isn't that right, Meris?"

Meris gave Rachel a sideways glance and a smile. "We're all pretty wild," she agreed. "That must be true where you work, too."

Rachel felt a new interest in racing, and everything to do with it. "Some of us are more wild than others," she acknowledged.

"Are you allowed to talk about it?" Meris asked. "What you do, I mean."

"Not a lot," Rachel said. "Besides, to us it's just work. I'd rather hear about what you do, since I know next to nothing about racing. Jaguar told me something about—about Ayrton Senna?"

"My great grand uncle," Alicia chimed in. "He won three championships, and was known as the master of driving in wet conditions. He was also very outspoken. When Jean-Marie Balestre put him on the dirty side of the track at Suzuka, after promising he wouldn't, he refused to yield the corner to Prost, and said exactly why. And he risked his life at the Belgian Grand Prix to help another driver in a crash."

"You've answered that question many times at press interviews, Alicia," Didier said. "Don't you ever resent living in his shadow?"

She brought her majestic gaze to rest on his face. "I don't live in his shadow," she said. "I live in his light."

There was no appropriate response to this except applause, and Jaguar gave it, clapping her hands slowly. "Brava," she said. "Good for you."

Alicia inclined her head in acknowledgement, a staged move, but her eyes sparked with fire, appreciating someone who understood what she said. "I hope to live up to his legacy, though I'd rather avoid his particular end."

"What was that?" Rachel asked.

"Killed in a crash at San Marino, in the bad old days," Meris said.

"Everyone remembers his death, but he was not the only martyr," Didier noted. "There were other accidents that weekend. Rubens Barichello, who survived, and Roland Ratzenberger, killed when his car went into the wall at the Villeneuve corner."

"No one forgets them, Didier," Meris said. "But fortunately, racing is much safer now."

"Largely as a result of Ayrton's death," Alicia noted. "Still, there's always a chance of, well, mischance. Or mischief."

"What's that mean?" Jaguar asked.

"Teams will do what they can to capture the Constructor's title, which gives them a great deal of money. Creating accidents, stealing information—that's mischief. Mischance—well, we are all subject to that."

"I'd caution against paranoia, Alicia," Didier said. "Mischief is the exception. For the most part, we all just do our jobs."

"Is that what you call it?" Alicia asked.

"Certainly. What do you call it?"

She offered a smile. "My life," she said.

The phrase, and the energy contained in it, hung around the table like smoke from a recently extinguished candle. Everyone took it in, and then Jaguar spoke. "Some of us love our jobs more than others," she said.

"Are you among that group?" Alicia asked.

"You bet. Though I'll admit I'm enjoying a break, and looking forward to qualifying tomorrow."

"Are you? So are we, yes, Meris? And here's something you might like—I'll get you passes for the club house. You'll be right on the start-finish line, and have a good view of the pits and the track. Also, you'll be with the rich people rather than the—what is the term? The madding crowd?"

"Alicia, you've been reading," Didier said.

"I often do," she said. "Didier, could you pass the bread? It's too good to let it sit uneaten.

Didier offer her the basket, then moved it to Jaguar. "Bread and circus," he said to her. "Isn't that what we all want? And speaking of that, Cirque du Soleil is premiering a new show this week. Do you like the circus?"

"Always wanted to run away and join one," she replied.

"Then let me take you to a show," he said, and put a hand on her arm lightly.

"Sure," Jaguar said, and was about to say more, but instead pulled in a gasp and jerked away from him.

"You okay?" Rachel asked her.

"So far away," Jaguar answered, her voice wistful.

Meris and Alicia exchanged glances. Rachel smiled briefly, turned back to Jaguar. "Um—what?" she asked.

Jaguar stared at her, but clearly wasn't actually seeing her. Rachel reached over and tapped her hand, which was clenched into a fist. Jaguar startled, composed her face.

"Wow," she said, speaking only to Rachel. "That hurt like hell."

"What was it?" Rachel asked quietly.

"Not sure. What did I say?"

"Um—so far away?"

"Far away?"

"Yeah."

Jaguar ran a hand through her hair. "Okay. Well, then."

"Are you ill?" Alicia asked politely.

Jaguar turned as if seeing her for the first time. "Just coping with interesting circumstances." Then, back to Rachel. "Maybe you can explain to these people what I do for a living, and how I do it. Either it'll help, or it'll scare the hell out of them so they won't ask any other questions.

Meantime, I'll go use the facilities." She rose and headed toward the restrooms, leaving Rachel to manage.

"Your friend is rather—unusual," Didier said politely.

"Yeah," Rachel said.

"I like that in a woman," he noted.

Rachel looked from Didier to Alicia and took a chance. "I think she wants me to tell you she's an empath. A big one. I mean, she uses it a lot. And I guess she just got some kind of message. She usually doesn't give that away, but maybe you're special. And if that's not what she wanted, I'm in deep shit."

"Hell," Meris muttered. "Not another one."

"She's devoted to her work," Alicia noted. "I can appreciate that."

"Right," Rachel said. "I better go see what unusual thing she's up to now." And she rose, following Jaguar into the restroom.

* * * *

The women's room in Estoril had all the amenities, including an ante room well stocked with tissues, hand cream, hairspray and combs in a sterile solution. When Rachel entered it she heard a sound that seemed out of place with the fresh flowers, gold-framed mirrors, and cushioned seats. Someone in the bathroom proper was retching.

"Jaguar?" she asked, moving toward the sound. "Are you sick?"

More retching, followed by the toilet flushing. Jaguar emerged from a stall, and she was white at the lips. She moved to the sink and stuck her hands under the faucet. No water came out. "Fucker," she told it. "Give me water. Now."

A brief spurt came out, and she gathered it in her hands, splashed it on her face. "I hate these damn faucets," she said. "They give you a drop of water and you have to keep dancing with them to get more."

"Dinner didn't agree with you?" Rachel asked.

"I don't agree with me," she muttered, and put her hand under the towel dispenser, which didn't dispense a towel. "God *fucking* dammit," she growled.

Rachel put her hand to another dispenser and got a paper towel, folded it and and wet it under the faucet, then pressed it against the back of Jaguar's neck. "Try this," she said.

Jaguar leaned against sink. "Thanks. That helps."

"I hope so, because now you're gonna tell me what this is all about."

Jaguar opened one eye. "Empathic blowback from an unresolved situation. It happens sometimes. Sorry."

"What situation?"

"An old case."

"What old case? Is it about—"

"Don't say it," Jaguar growled.

"I wasn't going to. I was just hinting broadly."

"Don't even do that. Did you tell them about me?"

"You said I should, right?"

"I did. How'd they react?"

"Okay."

"Details, please."

"Meris was irritated. She said 'not another one.' Alicia took it in stride. Didier looked sexually excited, but I think he always looks that way."

Though Rachel wasn't an empath, she had great people skills, and Jaguar trusted her reading. "Thanks. That's helpful," she said.

She tossed the paper towel in the garbage and moved to the door, but Rachel grabbed her arm. "Not leaving," she said. "I want in. Like, right now. Tell me why that's helpful."

"Maybe I'm checking Didier out," Jaguar said. "He could be fun."

"Ha," Rachel said. "Ha ha ha. Try again because you already told me you're not into fun lately. And if I don't get the truth, I'll start rooting around."

"We're here to relax, Rachel."

"That's what I thought, but apparently I was wrong. You wanted Montreal. You're here for the race, and you're about to tell me why. No bullshit about you just like racing either, unless you want me hacking a variety of systems until I find out on my own."

"You wouldn't."

"Watch me," she said, and dug through her purse, pulled out her cellcom, which was equipped with all manner of interesting applications, some of which she'd invented.

Jaguar put a hand on hers. "Put your weapon away. I give."

"Smart," Rachel said, and tucked her cellcom back into her purse. "Now talk to me."

"Alicia's former team is GM," Jaguar said.

"Okay. So what?"

"We happen to know their money man."

"We do? Who is it?"

"Ron Schulman."

A long pause followed, while Rachel put all this information together. Jaguar, who never mentioned a race before, wanted to be here, in Montreal, for this race. Her face tightened into anger. "That's why you asked for Montreal? You dragged me to the races because of—of *Schulman?*"

"Maybe," Jaguar said, and tensed for more tirade. She didn't get it.

Rachel's expression went feral. "Can you nail the son of a bitch? In the crotch? Can I help?"

Jaguar relaxed, laughed. "And you look like such a nice Jewish girl. I don't know what I can do yet. I'm just poking around."

"Well, how do you know about him and GM?"

"I've been poking around him for a while."

Of course. This piece of game meat was something she longed to sink her teeth into. "But is this special? I mean, do you, like, see something?"

"I'm not an Adept, Rachel."

"But you're other things. Do you have a feeling about it?"

"I have a feeling I'm doing exactly what I'm supposed to do. Listen, when you gave me dates for a vacation, I thought of the race, and since I knew about Schulman's interest in racing, it occurred to me he might show up if he knew I was here. It's the first chance I've had to make anything happen, though I haven't got a clue what that might be. So right now, I'm just observing and reflecting on what I observe."

"You're a real pain in the ass, you know that?"

"So I've been told," Jaguar admitted.

"Just tell me how I can help, okay?"

Jaguar put a hand on Rachel's shoulder. "You'd do just about anything for him, wouldn't you?"

Rachel knew who she meant. Alex. The name she wouldn't say, or let anyone else speak. She felt honored that she'd go this far. "Of course," she said. "So would you."

"Right. So there's a few things you can do. Find out anything you can about Tempe. Anything. He was Alicia's engineer, and pretty young to die of a heart attack. Also, there's rumors about Schulman increasing his interest in F1. Maybe buying it out, or at least grabbing the media rights. You can track that, see if he's acting on it. Also find out where he is right now, what he's up to. And don't mention his name outside this room. I don't want anyone else to know about my interest."

"Got it," Rachel said, her face scrunched into determination.

"Good," she said. "Now let's get back to the table. I think I need more of that very very good wine."

Home Planet, New Mexico

Early the next morning, Alex was wakened by a knock on the door of his airrunner. When he opened it, he saw Jake staring at him.

"Time to sweat," he said, and walked away.

Alex dressed quickly and followed him. By the time he caught up, he saw Jake's figure receding some ways ahead, outside the circle of adobe houses. He jogged to catch up, and they walked together toward the base of a mesa crowded with giant stones that stood guard like a huddled family. Here, a deerskin-covered dome stood near a rock lined pit dug into the ground. Jake crouched down and addressed the stones briefly, dropped some sage onto them, then turned back to Alex.

"Let's get the fire going."

Alex had done sweat lodges here with Jaguar, and he knew the routine. They worked together, covering the rocks with dead pinyon pine branches and lighting them. As the logs burned down to red coal Jake remained silent and Alex did the same. Then Jake grabbed a pitchfork leaning against the lodge and handed it to Alex, who brought two of the stones inside, placed them in the pit dug at the center. He put the pitchfork back outside and Jake joined him inside. He drew the canvas over the opening to the lodge, leaving them in total darkness except for the red of the rocks.

He dropped sage onto them and let it burn, the scent cleaning out any lies that might try to live here. Then he poured a dipper of water onto them. Steam and heat rose in the tight space like a living animal. It entered them, licking at their blood.

Alex opened himself to the incursion as best he could. Running away was not an option, and he had too much training in the spirit world to disregard what he might learn here. As his body adjusted, he and Jake honored the spirits and ancestors of the east. Then, another round of rocks and they honored the South. More heat, gnawing its way through his veins, like nanobots seeking infection to consume. Another round of stones for the West, another round of words and more heat, digging deeper. So far so good, Alex thought. A physical sweat. Nothing here to disturb his truce.

Then, the final round, in the North. When Jake addressed the spirits in this direction, he spoke of grief. "You bring the burden of pain that cleanses us," he said. "We welcome you."

A rush of air, cooler than what should exist in this intemperately heated space. Alex felt the spirits crowding him, with something to say. Instinctively he pushed himself back against the wall of the lodge, put up all his personal boundaries.

"Listen," Jake hissed at him. "You gotta listen."

Alex took in deep breath, tried to relax. "I'm listening," he said.

The clamoring of the spirits called by Jake's entreaty moved over his skin, through his veins. He wavered between acceptance and rejection. He'd relinquished his empathic arts, which were not enough to save his son, and what could they tell him that he didn't already know? But he was here to learn, seeking clarity, seeking direction. He spoke the necessary words.

"Find me," he whispered. "Guide me. Open the doors I need to enter, and close the doors of all places I need to leave."

What happened next surprised him.

Immediately, he saw an image of himself, driving a car, and driving it fast. He couldn't tell where he was, or when, but he knew he was careening toward purposeful disaster, about to crash into something, and it was the right thing to do.

"What?" he demanded. "What?"

No answer. Just the image, followed by the darkness of the lodge. Then, against his carefully built boundaries, he felt something like breath brush over the place where he held his son's grief.

"No," he gasped. "Leave it alone. It's mine."

Whatever moved around him made an exit. Jake spit out a word in Zuni that probably had no place within this sacred space. And that was all. The energy of the spirits Jake had invoked breezed away, and Alex relaxed. He'd gotten through it, his truce intact. Jake led him out of the lodge, and they sat on the earth, under bright sun.

"How was that?" Jake asked after a while.

Alex considered. "I guess it went well."

"But you chased it away at the end. The rest—you didn't feel it."

"I know it's right," Alex said.

"Knowing lives in your head. That's nothing. Meantime, you got something to do, and you can't do it while you're hanging on to what you don't own. You gonna let it go?"

"No," Alex said.

Jake didn't look surprised or perturbed. "I'll ask you again," he said. "Another sweat tomorrow." He stood and started to walk away.

"Wait," Alex called after him, and he stopped, turned back. "What if I can't?"

"You can," Jake said with confidence. "Because you're the kind of man who'd let Jaguar stick a knife in you when it mattered most."

Alex winced. "Don't," he said.

Jake kicked at the dirt, rubbed at his nose, then turned and shuffled away.

CHAPTER EIGHT

Montreal, Home Planet

Rachel did her research, and by morning, brought a report to Jaguar's hotel room.

"Schulman's in town," she said. "Been here for a few days. He's staying at digs he owns—255 Rue St. Paul. His office space, his apartment."

Jaguar, still tucking her knife up her sleeve, paused. "Is he now?" she murmured. "I'd guess he knows I'm here, too."

"I didn't see any signs of him messing with your stuff, but he'd hide that. What I did find out is that he's meeting with a lot of F1 folks. A few of the stewards were at his office yesterday for most of the day. He had dinner with Larry Engle—in a private room at the Moroccan restaurant—then lunch with Meris Grant at a diner a few days ago. Guess we know who's low on the food chain. And dinner at *Du Jour* with our friend Didier, along with some of his legal eagles.."

"Nothing with Alicia?"

"Not a sign of it."

"Huh. Maybe he's too busy," Jaguar said. "What about Tempe? Anything on him?"

"Nothing with Schulman. Tempe died of a heart attack, in the paddock at Nurburgring, just before practice. One of the pit crew found him. Autopsy showed what they called extreme damage to the muscles of the heart."

"Is there any video of his death?"

"Should be. There's cameras all over the paddocks. You want me to get it?"

"I do," Jaguar said. "ASAP. I'm guessing his body's not available anymore."

"He was cremated, but I can probably get the full autopsy report."

"That'd be good."

"You think Schulman had something to do with it?"

"It's worth poking at. Right now, let's see if we can poke at qualifying."

"Qualifying. What is that, anyway?" Rachel asked.

"Were you raised in a cave? Never mind. It's a series of short races to see who gets to start up front at the real race. My money's on Alicia for pole position."

* * * *

This time when they got to the track, instead of barreling through the bleachers to uncomfortable seats, they ascended to the club house, a glass enclosed structure with a balcony on either side, and easy access to both the garage, and the pit wall. Rachel, peering around at people who wore expensive jewelry and designer clothing, felt not at all at ease, until she spotted the computers in the Ferrari paddock.

"What's that?" she demanded, her nose twitching like a bunny's in clover.

"The crew watches the telemetry there," Jaguar said.

"Can I watch, too?" she said.

Jaguar eyed her. "Do you know what telemetry is?"

"Um, something to do with the cars?"

"Something," Jaguar agreed. "They track everything—brakes, aerodynamics, tire pressure, fuel load. Everything."

"Cool," Rachel said, already moving in that direction.

"You've been good enough to put up with my obsession. I'll give you yours," Jaguar said generously.

They descended the stairs at the back of the building, and made their way along pit wall, back to the paddock. Rachel, peering up at the computers on pit wall as they passed, grew restive. "Can't we stop and see what kind of programs they use?" she whined.

"Yes, when we get to the Ferrari paddock. Heel, girl. Heel."

They clipped forward and moved into the paddock area, toward the computers occupied by red uniforms with a yellow shield and prancing horse on them. Jaguar spotted Didier sitting in front of one of them, and waved for his attention. Seated at his computer, talking to someone through an earpiece, he waved back.

"Hello," he said. "Why aren't you in the clubhouse?"

"Rachel's fascinated by anything to do with computers. She wanted to see yours. Is that okay?"

"For you? Certainly." He indicated an empty seat next to him, and Rachel grabbed it. Didier's face curled into disappointment.

Jaguar shrugged. "Sorry. This is her thing. I know little and care less about technology."

"What's this?" Rachel demanded, pointing at the screen. "An algorithm?"

"Um, yes," Didier said, surprised at her vehemence. "It measures track use against tire wear. How you drive affects how fast the tires wear down, so—"

"—so after the race, you can tell your drivers what they need to change. Oh, cool. And this?" She pointed to a small personal notebook, open, and showing graphs that meant nothing at all to Jaguar. She peered down at it. "Another algorithm—something to do with sound values?"

Didier laughed nervously, swept the notebook away, pressed a button to turn it off. "Actually, I'm ashamed to say it's my investments. I track their movement, too, if the race gets slow."

Rachel's brow knit, a small line forming between her eyebrows. "Oh. But…"

"Here," Didier said. "Let me show you how we code for wind velocity."

Rachel leaned in, totally absorbed. Jaguar patted her shoulder, told her she was going to the clubhouse, but doubted that Rachel heard her. She went back up to mingle with the rich folk, and watch the action.

* * * *

As the first round of qualifying started, Jaguar stood on the balcony, watching the racers on the track, and on the big screen just across from the clubhouse. In this round, they wouldn't push too hard. They wanted to make it to the next round without wearing out any of their parts. Meris clocked in ahead of Alicia, but not by much, and GM managed to get around them both for time. The announcers kept up their talk about that, and about how close the two teams were in points.

Jaguar, looking around, noticed that Enzo Imaldi, currently Pope for Ferrari, was standing a few yards behind her, a glass of champagne in one hand, and a leggy blonde about twenty years his junior in the other. Nearby, Bernadette Culper, who got famous for her role in the latest remake of King Kong, stood chatting with Larry Engle, and Jaguar wondered if rumors about their affair were true, and if she saw anything in him beyond his money.

The second round of qualifying started, and the announcers went wild when Meris almost clipped Alicia as she came out of pit lane. Once again, Meris had the better time, and once again, GM superceded them both.

"I think Meris is growing irritated at being second driver, don't you?" David asked his compatriots.

"Growing?" Memo laughed. "Did you see her at the last race? Alicia put a hand out to her after she won and she turned her pretty head and walked away."

"Girl fight," Jack said.

"No," David said. "Racer fight. There's some talk Meris will go to GM."

"The silly season. People will say anything. But it would be a coup for old Ron Schulman, wouldn't it?"

Overriding their chatter, Jaguar heard a male voice booming behind her. "He'll be *thrilled*," it exclaimed.

She turned to it, saw a robust, red-faced man in suit and tie, smacking Larry Engle on the back. Jaguar recognized him from internet photos—a billionaire CEO named George Haliday. Larry didn't look thrilled to be smacked, even by someone with that much money, but he made a smile. "Yes, I suppose he will, if it's true," he agreed, and took a step away, putting himself out of range.

"Where is he, anyway? I thought for sure he'd be here today."

"He never comes to the races," Larry said. "Too much work to do."

"So that's how he got so rich. He works. Ha! But I thought he was buying you out, so isn't this work now?"

"Time and place, George," Larry said, curt and sharp. "We don't talk business here."

Larry swiveled on his heel, put a hand to Bernadette's elbow and started to walk away. George got in front of him, but they were out of range of hearing. Jaguar saw George making apologetic gestures, as another man stepped close to them, also observing

Tall and lean, with a shock of straight dark hair falling over his forehead, his hazel eyes had a sharply observant quality, which he brought to bear on Larry. And she knew him. He was the man who greeted Alicia at the restaurant. She scanned him, noted a regulation issue belt sensor, noted that he was wearing a weapon. She looked to her left and saw a track security guard, wearing a badge and a different kind of sensor, carrying a taser rather than a gun. Whoever the lean man was, he wasn't track security. Discreet police protection for Alicia? Could be. If so, she wanted to make his acquaintance.

She stared at him openly until he returned her gaze. He moved his eyes over her, but not as Didier had. Didier was checking her for possibilities. He was checking her for weapons. She slid her arm back just enough to reveal the tip of the red knife she carried up her sleeve. He noted it, brought his gaze level with hers, then lowered it slightly, his eyebrows shifting down just enough to tell her he was checking his memory banks for information on her.

Then, he raised his eyes again, his eyebrows elevated slightly. He took one step forward. As he did, a female voice called her name.

"Hey—Jaguar—there you are. Oh my God, it is so cool, what they do down there."

Rachel, approaching fast, her face alight with enthusiasm.

"I guess you'd think so," Jaguar said. "So why are you here?"

She sighed. "Someone needed my seat. But listen, they have a program to capture derivative motion in response to correlative blue tones. I mean, really. They do."

"That's great," Jaguar said. "Just great." She craned her neck around Rachel to find the man who'd been watching her watch him, but he was gone. She gave her attention to the race, while Rachel chattered on about things Jaguar would never understand.

When the third round of qualifying started Alicia went out early and put down some fast laps. But when she went in for a tire change Meris put in a faster lap, and with less than ten minutes remaining, Alicia came out again. Then, as she was going around the hairpin, the GM car driven by Daryl Holser spun out, smashed into the barrier and bounced back onto the track in front of her. Alicia's car spun, righted itself and went on. Cameras showed her hand lifted out of the cockpit in a rude and meaningful gesture.

The track was yellow flagged, forcing all drivers to slow as it was cleared, and the broadcast of Alicia's radio communication with her team had to be bleeped out.

"Wish they let us hear that," Jaguar grumbled. "I like a woman who can curse well."

By the time the yellow flag was lifted, there were only three minutes left. Alicia and Meris were both on track, putting in hot laps, and it ended with Alicia less than a half second ahead of her teammate, and a Lotus close behind her. The announcers were beside themselves with ecstasy. Alicia, on the big screen, looked angry rather than triumphant as she got out of her car and tore off her helmet. Meris looked equally angry, but probably for different reasons. Ferrari owned the front row, the ideal for any team, though at the interviews afterward, Alicia didn't seem thrilled.

The media asked all the usual questions—How do you feel? What about the race? With such a narrow margin, are you disappointed? The racers answered circumspectly, but when they were done, Alicia took command.

"I want to say something about the GM accident," she told them. "There have been similar incidents in the past, when teams tell a driver to cause an accident in order to garner a win. In each case, the stewards investigated and it was dealt with, but now—well, the money grows more important than the race, and bigger names are involved, so I fear it will be overlooked. But team owners should know that drivers are aware of the politics going on at a higher level, which affects us, affects our safety and integrity, and we won't be quiet about it. The stewards should not be quiet either. I've mentioned all this to a friend of mine who works on the Planetoids. She will understand."

She was immediately hammered with questions. Was she implying the accident was staged to take her out? Did she think Ron Schulman's interest in Formula One played a part? She raised her hand and stopped them all. "I'm just saying it should be investigated. That is all." And she would say no more.

"Hecate," Jaguar said.

"Yeah," Rachel agreed. "That's not good is it? I mean, she practically named you."

"She's either pissed as hell, or scared shitless, or both," Jaguar said.

"Scared?"

"It's her way of letting Schulman know there's Planetoid people here. That she's got more protection than Luna. Which means she suspects he's behind the threats." She shook her head. "She doesn't know him well enough. My presence won't stop him."

"What do we do?" Rachel asked.

"Give her fair warning, if she'll listen."

They were invited back to the Paddock after the interviews, and when they got there, they saw Alicia standing with a hand on her hip, all her body language expressing rage, as she spoke with her team manager. Luna sat at her heels, at full attention. Meris stood nearby, chewing nervously on a fingernail.

"Why should I keep my mouth shut?" Alicia demanded. "Is anything I said untrue? GM is second to ours in points, by not very much. They had the incentive to act badly. The crash should be investigated."

The team manager muttered something about lawyers, and Alicia raised an aristocratic hand to wave his words away. "Their lawyers can go to hell," she said. "Or worse. They can speak with mine."

Jaguar thought it was time to make her presence known. "Helluva crash for GM," she said, and everyone turned to her. "I didn't think you'd get around it. I'm guessing GM thought the same thing."

The hard lines of anger in Alicia's face dissolved and she laughed, gestured toward her team manager and then Jaguar. "There," she said. "Other voices speak with mine." Then, to Jaguar, "You see too much. I'm surprised you live to tell about it."

"I could say the same," Jaguar noted. "But you also say too much." Then, in a move that surprised Rachel, she put a hand out and grabbed her wrist. It was risky, trying empathic work here, when it might tumble her into a chaos of unmanageable responses, but she had to. She didn't try for subtlety, though. She let her presence be known, and found what she could. A quick dip into Alicia's thoughts revealed her fear, well contained, and her determination, unbounded.

Jaguar spoke into her. *We need to talk*, she said simply.

The response was just as simple. *I know about you, and you know about me. What else is there to say?*

Jaguar released her, broke contact. This was as much as she could do for now, and as much as she'd get. Alicia knew about her, which meant she knew trouble was ahead.

"Sorry. Just checking your pulse," she said out loud. "I hear it gets really high when you drive."

Alicia eyed her coolly, nodded once. "Heart rate can go as high as 200 beats per minute," she said. "We spend some time learning to keep it lower than that."

"We train for that on the Planetoid too," Jaguar said.

"Do you? I'd like to hear more about that."

"So would I," another voice joined in. Jaguar turned and saw Didier, just behind and to her left. "Though my impression is that nothing would break your cool."

At the sound of his voice Luna laid her ears back and growled softly. Jaguar touched her head, took a moment to read her lightly. She sensed defensive aggression, but nothing more specific. At her touch, Luna calmed.

"You're good with dogs," Alicia noted.

"I'm good with nonhumans," Jaguar amended. She looked to Didier. "I was right. Luna really doesn't like you."

"Perhaps because I'm a cat man myself," he said. "There's nothing like a kitten curled up in your lap to make you smile."

Jaguar tilted her head, spoke with a purr that might become a growl, something Rachel recognized as her version of flirting. "Kittens, yes. But cats—I'd guess they're too independent for you."

"I like independence."

"When it doesn't interfere with your pleasure," she noted.

"Nothing should ever interfere with pleasure. That's something all cats understand. If you like, we can meet for dinner and discuss it further."

"Not tonight," Alicia cut in. "We've got a race tomorrow, and some work to do. The weather forecast says it will rain, but I do not believe it. The set up will have to be discussed. And I am not at all happy with the braking ratios. They must be changed."

Didier showed a carefully controlled anger. Much as he liked kittens, he did not like big cats telling him what he could and could not do. "Of course. After the race, Jaguar?"

"I'll give it some thought," she said. Then, to Alicia, "We should talk more about how to keep a pulse low. Maybe later tonight?"

"I focus only on the race the night before. Tomorrow, after I've won," Alicia replied.

Meris made a sound that might have been clearing her throat. When they all looked to her, her fair, fresh face gave them a bright smile. "Or after I win," she said.

Alicia laughed. "That's the spirit," she said.

Jaguar ducked her head down, brought it up. "We'll talk tonight," she said to Alicia.

That woman lifted her chin and regarded Jaguar like a queen ready to castigate an unruly subject. But when their eyes met, she backed off.

"I have work to do," she said. "I don't know when I'll get to my room."

"Whenever you do, I'll be there," Jaguar said. "Call me."

She gave her cellcom number and Alicia gave her hotel name and room number.

"Nobody else. Just you," she said.

"Sure," Jaguar said. "See you later."

CHAPTER NINE

Home Planet, New Mexico

The second sweat was done at night, after a day of fasting, a sweat of ancestors and memory. The spirits of the west were predominant, his ancestors offering him the grief they shared with him. They'd also longed for their legacy to continue through his son.

Under the weight of their presence, Alex bowed his head and acknowledged his failure. It was part of the penance he owed. When they were done, he thanked them, and asked again if they wanted anything from him. The answer returned, clear as air and cryptic as his life right now.

Listen, they said. *Follow what you hear.*

Listen to what? The voices in his head that said his life was over? Jake, telling him to move on? The air, the stars, the wind? "Tell me what to do, and I'll do it," he said.

He sensed small laughter. He sighed, and let it be. His first mentor, Sophia, told him long ago that when you were in the middle of a lesson, the spirits wouldn't give you the answers you had to learn yourself. He found the notion irritating, but it had proved true at every important juncture in his life. But Sophia also told him if the lesson went on too long, you could always request a hint. He did so now.

"Give me a sign," he said, "because I'm not getting it, and I need to."

Small whisperings, and once more, the image of him driving fast on an unknown road, toward disaster. A rushing of wind, a heavy pressure of sound, and the impact of his vehicle against another.

"That doesn't help much," he muttered, when it dispersed.

He heard Jake making a noise that sounded like a chuckle. "Sweat's over," he said. "Open the door."

When they exited the sweat lodge and Alex looked up to the starry sky, Jake cast a glance over him. "You wanna sleep inside tonight?" he asked.

Alex shook his head. "Not yet. Thanks for asking."

"Yeah." Then, unexpectedly, "Where's the wolf?"

At first Alex didn't know what he meant, but then he saw Jake staring at his throat. When he came here with Jaguar to dispense with a Greenkeeper, Jake had given him an obsidian fetish, its face half wolf and half jaguar. Jaguar's grandfather made it, and it was meant for the man who would partner her. He'd taken it off before he left the Planetoid and meant to leave it on his nightstand, but at the last minute he grabbed it, unwilling to leave it behind. He'd shoved it into his pocket, and continued to transfer it from one pocket to the next. Occasionally, his hand would reach for it, feeling the cool stone under his fingers, finding calm in the gesture.

He put a hand in his pocket, took it out and showed Jake.

Jake grunted. "Okay," he said, sounding relieved. He turned and walked away.

* * * *

As Alex lay down to sleep, he mentioned once again to the spirit world that he didn't have a fucking clue what they wanted, and he'd like to know, quickly. Being here was more difficult by the day, and he longed for resolution. And in his mind, the options were simple: Should he kill himself, or kill Ron Schulman and then die? Either one would do, and he saw no possibility beyond that. For a brief moment, it occurred to him that death might be the easy way out, merely an escape rather than a solution, but he waved that away. What else could he do? Nothing. Nothing at all.

He shifted, uncomfortable with his own ambiguity, and became aware of a familiar presence, watchful and warm, resting at his back. What had she called herself? A word he didn't know. She spoke into him, longing and sorrow in her voice.

Where are you going? she asked.

The question echoed within him as if she called across the vast expanse of the canyon, her voice ringing against ancient walls of stone, against the geography of his soul. The image of a nearby mesa appeared in his mind, the sky beyond it melting into infinite blue. It was the place where he and Jaguar had learned to love each other. He imagined himself at its rim, looking out toward forever. He asked if it was ready for him, because certainly he was ready for it.

"There," he said, and showed her. He could go there and be emptied of the crashing, jagged motion of his heart, a motion he couldn't subdue in spite of all his discipline.

The presence studied this. *I go with you,* she said, her voice speaking within him.

He frowned. "You can't," he said aloud, though he didn't know what he meant or who he spoke to.

I see your road. I walk with you, she replied.

He'd done two sweats without breaking the walls that stood between him and emotional chaos, but eight words from this voice made nothing of his discipline. Grief pierced him, suddenly and thoroughly. He pulled himself together. He wouldn't allow it.

"It's my road, not yours," he reasoned. His fate was his own. It belonged to no other. Whatever she was, surely she knew this.

The voice returned, rich with a yearning he did not have the courage to feel. *I dare that road with you. I can dare myself.*

A decision reached beyond his will. Nothing he could do about it. Sorrow seeped into him, deeper than the blue of the far horizon. "What are you?" he whispered.

Nahuak, the answer returned. *I go with you.*

"Nahuak," he repeated. Yes. That was the word. An energy he'd never encountered before. "Why?" he asked her.

I wait with you. By your side.

The pulsing love in her voice was too much for him. Too much to feel, and his walls were already breached. He groaned, rolled away. The presence drew back. She wouldn't impose herself on him. That was not her goal. Instead, she breathed soft sleep onto him.

Rest now, she said. *I'm here.*

He fell into the warmth, soft as her breath, beautiful as the face of love, and he slept.

CHAPTER TEN

Home Planet, Montreal

Alicia's call came shortly before eleven, saying she was in her room. It didn't take Jaguar long to get to her because she'd parked herself in the hotel bar from nine o'clock on, where she'd been sipping coffee and fending off drunk men. She made her way to the penthouse floor, knocked on the door.

It opened, and Jaguar stood where she was, while Alicia, shorter than her by a few inches, peered up. "I was hoping you'd fall asleep and forget," she said.

"I don't sleep much these days," Jaguar replied.

Alicia sighed. "Come in," she said.

Jaguar did so, and stood in the suite living room, gathering her thoughts and her words.

"I know why you're here," Alicia said, anticipating her. "You fear for me, and want to give me warning."

Jaguar lifted a hand, let it fall. "All that and then some," she said.

Alicia eyed her, and Jaguar felt the sensation of another empath entering her thoughts. She allowed it. After a few moments, Alicia shivered.

"You have lost someone you love," she said.

"More than one person," Jaguar admitted. "All through the same man. And you know who that is."

Alicia nodded. "Ron Schulman. He is—I am not sure of the right words in English. A persistent evil?"

"That works," Jaguar said. "And he's in town. So we have to make sure he doesn't do anything to perpetuate his evil with you at the race. Like maybe he tried today."

"And you are Kanima to his evil?"

Jaguar startled at the word, a South American term for a werejaguar who hunted murderers. The last time it was applied to her, Springer had used it. Either Alicia had plucked it from her mind, or she knew it herself, which was entirely possible. She was Brazilian, after all. Either way, she used it accurately.

"Is that a problem?" Jaguar asked.

"No," Alicia said. "For my part, no." She moved toward the kitchen area of her suite. "I am pouring some wine. Would you like a glass?" she asked.

Jaguar laughed. "Not enough wine in the world to cover this one," she said.

"I don't care to cover it," Alicia said. "I just want to taste the good wine."

"Sure," Jaguar said. "Pour me a glass, too."

She did so, and brought it to Jaguar. "Please, sit," she said, indicating the couch and Jaguar did so. Alicia curled herself into the deeply upholstered chair across from her. A Ferrari driver, she got all the perks, including the best hotel rooms.

"I'd like to protect you if I can," Jaguar said. "But I need more information. David Tempe—you suspected his death wasn't natural, and you talked to someone about that, didn't you?"

"I spoke to the Montreal police about it. They found nothing."

"But you continued to suspect. Why?"

"His death occurred so close to my decision to leave GM, and he was going with me to Ferrari," she said.

"There was something else," Jaguar said, knowing this was true.

Alicia stared down at her hands. "Nothing I could—what is the phrase—pin down? A sense of sound. A feeling of heaviness."

"Show me," Jaguar said, and opened herself to empathic contact. Alicia raised a hand, touched Jaguar lightly on the arm, and did so.

Jaguar felt rather than heard the sound, and experienced the sensation of something heavy pressing her down, like being under too much water. When Alicia lifted her hand from contact, Jaguar felt the blood leave her lips, felt the room spinning. She waited for it to pass.

"Is something wrong?" Alicia inquired politely.

"Quite a bit," she said. She couldn't name what Alicia showed her, but she sensed the menace in it. "Maybe," she said, "you should sit out the next race."

Alicia laughed. "In what universe would you believe that is possible?" she asked. "You know about Ayrton, who left it all on the track so other drivers would be safe. Would I relinquish that—that mission?"

Jaguar caught a scent of how Alicia got as far as she did in F1. "He—he communicates with you?" she asked. "He taught you to race?"

She inclined her head. "Our ancestors always want us to continue their legacy, don't they? Continue their story, take it to the next chapter?"

Jaguar took a long sip of her wine, lowered her glass and put it on the small table in front of the couch. That was a philosophy she espoused as well, but not at the expense of someone she was trying to protect. "He wouldn't want you to die for Ron Schulman's pleasure," she noted.

"He would want me to take a risk, if it meant ridding the world of a—a persistent evil. And isn't it possible that if I do not take the risk, he will never be caught?"

Jaguar tilted her head, eyed Alicia. "Adept?" she asked.

Alicia shrugged lightly, sipped more wine.

Fucking Adepts, Jaguar thought, not for the first time. They always thought that just because they saw something, they could manipulate events to their ends. "I'm here to prevent harm, not wait for it to happen and then use it," she said. "And I can't do my job if you're playing Spider Magus games, so just tell me what you see. Really."

Alicia smiled, gracious and calm. "Jaguar, please don't waste your strength in worry. My statement was merely conversational. I see nothing except my race tomorrow, which I intend to win. And I am not afraid. Not of Ron Schulman, or Meris, or Lotus or GM. I am doing exactly as I was put on this earth to do. And now, I think you should leave. I want to rest, and be ready for the track tomorrow."

Jaguar stood, thinking of all the risks she'd taken because she was doing exactly what she was put on earth to do. Because she saw nothing beyond the goal she was trying to reach, which left no room for fear. She put out her hand and Alicia took it, held on for one warm moment.

They were two warrior women, with different agendas but the same soul. Jaguar would have to leave Alicia to deal with hers, while she dealt with her own.

* * * *

The morning of the race dawned under a grey sky, but the rain held back. Jaguar and Rachel once again viewed the event from the clubhouse, but this time Jaguar kept her eye glued to the racers, and answered Rachel's questions briefly or not at all. Rachel tried to be interested, and mostly failed.

Alicia stayed up front at the race with some help from Meris, who kept the GM car from worrying her back. The announcers discussed this with interest, noting that Meris was being a good team player, which was unlike her. As Alicia extended her lead to five seconds, then ten and twenty, it looked clear she was heading for a victory, while Meris held onto second place.

"This oughta make you happy," Rachel noted.

"Well," Jaguar said, "I'd like to see more racing rather than driving, but it *is* satisfying to watch the bad girl wipe out the competition."

"Sure it is," Rachel agreed.

They continued watching, Jaguar remaining tense, when a small wave of laughter rose behind them. Jaguar turned to her left, saw people pointing, then parting and making an open way. Soon she saw why. Luna was weaving through them, heading toward Jaguar, her leash dangling behind her.

"Shit," she said. "No."

Rachel stared at her, saw she'd gone pale. Luna reached her and nuzzled her hand, whining. Jaguar's face took on the focus Rachel recognized as empathic work, but in short order she groaned, put a hand to her head. "Goddammit," she whispered fiercely, "let me *do* this."

Alicia's car sped past them, then inexplicably slowed.

"Oh, no," Dave announced. "Something wrong with the Ferrari?"

"Gear problems?" Memo asked.

Then, a voice over her radio, transmitted over national television. "Box box, Alicia," it said. The pit crew wanted her in, now.

"Leave me alone," she snapped back, her voice high and wild. "I know what I'm doing."

While the announcers guffawed over that, she got her car going at speed, made the next sector at top speed, then spun wildly, careening into the barricade, her car flipping once, twice, and bursting into flames.

Luna put her head back and howled.

* * * *

As soon as it happened, Jaguar grabbed Rachel by the arm with one hand, and took hold of Luna's leash with the other. Luna tugged hard, whining and coaxing them on.

When officials tried to stop them Luna yanked at the leash, turned on it and grabbed it in her mouth, worrying it. She led them inexorably to the crash site, where medics and the ambulance were already in attendance, but a cement barrier stood between them and the car, and race marshalls pushed her back, paying no attention to her Planetoid ID.

Luna, frantic, tore the leash from Jaguar's hand and leaped the barrier, rushing to the stretcher where Alicia lay, her eyes closed, her face calm. Once there she paced and sniffed and whined.

"Jesus Christ," one of the marshall's said. He called to another official. "Get that dog out of here."

Jaguar grabbed his arm. "Don't. She's trained for protection and she'll bite. Let me get her. She knows me."

The race marshall scowled, then waved her on. "Go," he said.

"Wait here," Jaguar told Rachel, and moved to the stretcher. She took hold of Luna's leash, put a hand to her head and spoke softly to her. Luna continued to whine, to move back and forth. Jaguar stared down at

Alicia. Blood trickled like tears from the corners of her eyes. Her helmet was off, but her balaclava was still on, and Jaguar saw blood seeping through it, from her ears. She took a chance and listened empathically, hoping to pick up on whatever she'd last felt.

First, a shock of dread, the sense of an ominous presence. Then heat, like fire burning inside her suit. Finally, a determined continuation of action, as she kept racing. The only words Jaguar heard were about that. *Don't lift. Hit the apex. Engine good, brakes good. Go.* Then, unexpectedly, *tell Jaguar*.

A moment of exigent rage roared through Jaguar. "Tell me *what?*" she demanded, but no answer was forthcoming. Dizziness washed over her, as if she stood balanced precariously on a high place. She hung on to Luna, got her bearings. Too late. She was too late.

She turned to the paramedics who were lifting her into the ambulance. "Cover her face," she said.

One of them gave her a panicked look. "The cameras. Everyone will know."

"That she's dead? She is, isn't she?"

"Meris is still racing," he whispered. "She can't know."

Jaguar reached over and jerked the sheet up over Alicia's face. "Tell the fucking truth, can't you?" she snarled.

The medic glanced around for cameras, pulled the sheet back down and quickly got the stretcher into the ambulance. A marshall touched Jaguar's shoulder.

"Ma'am, you'll have to take that dog out of here."

Jaguar glared at him, but made her way back over the barrier, to where Rachel waited.

Rachel touched Jaguar's shoulder. "Jaguar—is she okay?"

"She's dead," Jaguar said dully.

"You're sure?"

"Yeah," she said. Luna, panting nervously, tugged at the leash, pulling Jaguar toward Alicia's car, still billowing smoke and covered with the fire extinquisher's foam. She got as close to it as she could from her side of the barrier. Two men were guarding it, waiting for the crane to take it away.

"Hey," she yelled at them. "Don't touch a fucking thing on that car."

She flashed her Planetoid ID at them fast enough that they couldn't tell if she was a cop or a steward. "What the hell?" one of them said.

"You heard me," she said. "That's evidence for what killed her."

The men shuffled uncertainly. She spoke with enough authority that they didn't know what to do next.

"Killed?" Rachel gasped. "You don't mean, like, murdered?"

"Yes I do."

"Mother of God," Rachel said sincerely.

"Not currently available, or she would've prevented this," Jaguar said. "Hold the dog. I'm going over there." She handed the leash to Rachel, and moved to cross the barrier, but a hand on her shoulder made her whirl around, her own hand raised in defensive posture. She confronted a large security guard, with Larry Engle right behind him.

"You'll have to leave, miss," the guard said.

Rage still twitched at her neurons, and she spoke from it. "It's *Doctor* Addams. And I"m not going anywhere until I call this in." She jerked away from him, saw she was surrounded by other tall men with thick necks.

Larry stepped up. "Miss—Doctor Addams, I don't know what you think you're doing, but this is not your purview. We're getting Alicia to proper medical treatment."

"They got treatment for dead?" Jaguar shot back.

"We don't know her condition yet."

"You think I can't tell dead when I see it?"

"The medics might revive her."

Jaguar's face took on an aspect Rachel had seen before—when she was about to lay out her Tae Kwon Do partner, about to say exactly the wrong thing to an Administrative official, about to let loose. She held her breath.

Jaguar made a fist and swung at Larry's jaw, catching it hard. He flew back, tossed into the arms of his various minions while two guards moved in to grab her arms. Luna leapt up, barking furiously. Rachel hung on to the leash.

"Pig shit bastard," Jaguar spit at Larry as she struggled against those who held her. "Somebody *killed* her. And when did Schulman buy you? How much did he give for your puny little soul?"

Larry regarded her with distaste, and turned to the marshalls in attendance. "The race goes on. We wait for a report from the hospital. And keep this girl restrained. Get a muzzle on her."

"Girl?" Jaguar made a move that defied Rachel's comprehension and broke free from those who held her. She threw herself at Larry, wrapped her arms around his neck and got him in a headlock. Luna jerked her leash out of Rachel's hold and lunged at the security detail, bared teeth latching onto the nearest arm.

One of the men yelped and another tugged him away, and for a brief moment Jaguar owned the field. She held onto her prey and Rachel could see she was reading him. By the time Rachel got Luna under control and security pried Jaguar away, her eyes were glinting with triumph. She'd gotten what she wanted.

"You're an idiot *and* an asshole," she told Larry

"You can't behave this way here," Larry said, striving for dignity.

"I already have," she said, cool again, in charge of herself.

"Deal with her," he told security. He straightened and left the field.

The guards took hold of her and she let them take her away. Rachel followed, keeping a tense Luna in check as they made their way to the security trailer beyond the grandstands. At the door, the largest one turned and shook his head at Rachel. "No room. You can wait here," he said, and slammed the door shut.

Once inside they put Jaguar in a chair and stood staring down at her.

"Look, guys," Jaguar said. "I'm Planetoid, here on vacation, and I didn't want my race weekend ruined any more than you did. So how about you just let me go, and we can all get on with our day?"

"Right," one of the security men said, desultory and disinterested.

She sighed. Normally she'd have them call Alex, but she couldn't do that anymore. She decided to go higher up on the food chain, and hope for the best. "Call Paul Dinardo," she told them. "He's Board governor for my zone on Planetoid Three. He'll tell you who I am, and why you have to secure the scene." She gave them his home phone number, his cell com, his office number.

The guard knit his thick brows over this, torn between his track duties, and his own nervousness about anything to do with the Planetoid. He turned to his compatriot, who rubbed at his nose. "I don't know," he said.

"Yeah," the other guard replied, and pulled out his cellcom, walked out of the room.

Jaguar sat kicking her heels against her chair until he returned, looking subdued. "You'll be getting a call," he told her, and as he spoke, her cellcom buzzed.

She answered it, prepared for a good long fight with Paul, but instead she saw the square, dark face of Junius on her small screen, his expression undecided whether it was irritated or amused.

"Junius? What the hell do you want?"

"I'm your supervisor, Dr. Addams," he said dryly.

"You plan on scolding me?"

"No. I don't like exercises in futility. I'm giving you your next assignment. Preliminary research, concerning the death of Alicia Senna. You've got full access to information and people, at Governor Dinardo's direct order."

"Paul did that?" she asked.

"You know any other Dinardo?"

"Okay. But—why?"

Junius shook his head. "That's why I said I'd never be your supervisor. You get what you want, and you still question it. Listen, try this. Maybe he wants to make it right."

Jaguar's faced moved through a variety of expressions. "I'm guessing no on that."

"Then maybe he saw a brief but vibrant clip of you plastered all over the internet, where you're calling someone—what was it? Pig shit bastard?"

"Oh. That got out quick."

"Yeah. It did. And it got viral, under the title Girl Beats Man."

"And now Paul wants me to make it okay for him? Save his ass again?" she said.

"You can take it that way," Junius noted. "Or you can just use the opportunity. Which one you want?"

She didn't answer. Junius nodded at her. "Anything else I can do for you?"

"You want a dog?"

"What?"

"Never mind. Tell Paul I get to keep Rachel, and he'll send any other back up I want. And someone has to let the local cops know. We'll need to keep people here, have access to the track, the car and so on. Can you take care of that?"

"Yeah," Junius said. "I don't think you'll get any argument."

"I better not," she said, and closed her cellcom.

She turned a smile to the security detail. "I'm on the job, boys," she said.

* * * *

When she exited the trailer, she found a tense Rachel waiting, a nervous Luna at her side. "Are you okay? They didn't hurt you or anything?"

"Of course not. They acknowledged we're legit. And we're on assignment. Prelim research into the death of Alicia Senna, by Planetoid orders."

"Oh," Rachel said. "That's strange. What's it mean?"

"It means," Jaguar said, "I'm stuck with a dog."

CHAPTER ELEVEN

Jaguar sent Rachel to the paddock to keep an eye on events there, "There's another fifteen laps left, so you keep Luna and go get some things for me from the paddock."

"What things?"

"Gloves, socks, balaclavas—anything with the scent of Didier or Meris or Alicia on it. Get some bags. Pack them separate."

"Sure," Rachel said. "That man—Larry—is he involved? I saw you reading him."

"All he had on his mind was PR. No joy there. Listen, stay at the paddock until Meris gets in. Let her know what happened."

"Won't she know already?"

"No. They'll keep it from her. Tell her, and watch her reaction."

"Jaguar, you can't possibly mean—"

"—I mean, do it now, before the stewards get to her," she said, and took off.

The race continued to its conclusion, and Meris took first place. When she came into the paddock she was all smiles, and greeted Rachel with a joyful whoop and a kiss on each cheek. "Nailed it," she said. She looked around. "Where's Alicia? I want to gloat."

Rachel chewed at her lip. Clearly Jaguar was right, and no one had told her. "Meris," she said gently, and put a hand on her arm.

"She's out, right? My crew told me. Her car did a bunk and she bashed into the tire wall. So where is she?"

Behind her, Rachel saw a variety of stewards and the Ferrari team manager moving toward them with determination. They didn't want Meris to know yet. Wanted her to stand on the podium and cheer her victory and guzzle champagne so nobody else would know. They were using her, to create their happy PR moment. Suddenly, she understood Jaguar's anger.

"Meris, it's bad news," she said quickly. "Alicia was killed."

Meris stared at her blankly. Her head moved in a quick negative. "Killed? No. She had engine trouble and crashed out. The crew told me."

"I saw her," Rachel said. "She's dead."

Meris lowered her head, shook it, then raised a face full of rage to Rachel, moved to her quickly and hit her hard in the arm. "No," she said, her voice guttural and low.

Rachel stayed very still, said nothing.

Meris lowered her arm to her side. "No?" she asked.

"I'm so sorry," Rachel whispered.

Then, the stewards reached them, grabbed Meris's arm and pulled her away. When Rachel tried to follow, one of the larger ones blocked her. She wasn't Jaguar, wouldn't take a swing at him, but she saw Meris looking over her shoulder, and nodded at her grimly.

Soon after, Meris stood on the podium while the national anthems were played, but she remained stony faced, and walked away before the traditional champagne spraying and interviews that would normally follow. She believed Rachel.

"I must say, that's odd," Memo noted. "What's going on?"

"Not sure, but it doesn't look good," Dave agreed. "Let's see if our man down in the pits knows. Peter, what's with Meris?"

When the cameras moved to him, he showed a solemn face. "No official announcement, Dave," he said, "but we've got this—a clip that went viral."

The screen showed footage of Jaguar, jerking the sheet over an unconscious Alicia's face. The medics jerking it back. Then, Jaguar screaming that someone killed Alicia, and throwing herself at Larry Engle.

Rachel, watching it on the screen in the paddock, sighed. Jaguar couldn't avoid controversy if her life depended on it. She waited a while longer, but Meris didn't reappear. She took her store of gloves and socks, got hold of Luna's leash, and went back to her hotel.

* * * *

It was another hour before F1 stewards held a press conference, informing the world about the regrettable death of Alicia Senna in what they called a racing incident. By then, Jaguar had used her Planetoid clout to secure Alicia's car for forensics, and moved on to the hospital where they'd brought her. She went right to the morgue, flashed her ID, and asked to speak with the ME who'd be doing the autopsy.

"Auwtopsee?" the clerk repeated. "Alicia Senna? Zere is no auwtopsy."

"There is now," she said. "Get the ME."

It took an hour for that personage to show up, on a Sunday night, for a death that wasn't even classified as suspicious. When she walked into the morgue Jaguar was waiting. "You speak English?" she asked.

"I speak Brooklyn," she said, and brushed her long dark hair back from a heavily made up face, then snapped her gum. "Dr. Mitchell, doing my residency here."

"Good. I know Brooklynese. And I want to know cause of death," she said.

"Really? She hit the barricades at about 200 miles an hour. You need something else?"

"Drivers survive a lot worse. So you'll autopsy, and tell me exactly what killed her."

Dr. Mitchell looked at the clock. "That might take a little time, and I got a date."

"Had a date," Jaguar noted. She sat down on a metal folding chair. "Get to work."

"Christ," she said. "I shoulda taken the residency in Queens, like my mother said. If you wanna stay, you better suit up."

They both did so, and Jaguar helped to turn Alicia over, while Dr. Mitchell put a scanner to her perfect spine. They watched the image appear on the screen behind them, viewing the road of her bones which should have carried her through many more years.

"Shame, ain't it?" Dr. Mitchell said. "I mean, look at her. Best condition, all around. But you're right about one thing. The crash didn't kill her. No sign of head injury, nothing high up enough in the spine. Look here, though." She pointed to a disjuncture in the lower spine. "That would've given her some trouble."

"How bad?"

"Unclear right now. Probably some stem cell work would repair it."

"Okay. So what did kill her?"

"She was bleeding from the eyes and ears, so maybe internal organ damage. Gotta look around more to know for sure. Help me turn her again."

Jaguar did so, and Dr. Mitchell used her scanner again. She hadn't gotten far before she stopped, and said with feeling, "Holy crap."

Even Jaguar, viewing the scan, could tell something wasn't right. "Her heart," she said.

"Yeah. I gotta open her up. I didn't want to. I mean, look at her breasts. They're as perfect as her spine." She sighed, picked up the laser scalpel and put it to Alicia's sternum. Right before she cut she turned to Jaguar. "If you pass out, I'm not catching you. Or picking you up."

"I work on the Planetoid," Jaguar said.

"Yeah. Okay."

Once she'd opened her up, Dr. Mitchell whistled long and low. "Now that's something I never seen before."

Inside her chest cavity, Alicia's heart was crumpled into a small knob of flesh, shredded at the edge. "What did that?" Jaguar murmured.

"I haven't got a friggin' clue. From the looks of it, she—well, her heart melted. Like, she was melted from the inside out."

"Melted? How the hell would that happen?"

"You been listening to me? I don't know. I'll have to do some cellular work."

"Do it," Jaguar said.

"I'll need the lab," she said.

"Then get them."

"At seven on a Sunday in Montreal? Not a chance. I won't get them until tomorrow morning. If you got a hotel room, you should go find it."

"What can you do tonight?"

Dr. Mitchell put down the tools of her trade and pulled off her gloves. "I can write a preliminary report on a suspicious death, set up the lab work, and still make my date," she said. "And you can get out of here. Leave a number and I'll call when I know something. It'll be a few days. That kind of work ain't easy, or fast."

Jaguar said a few words, but they got her nowhere so she left, but she didn't return to her hotel. Instead she made her way to the forensics lab on Catherine Street, where she found two young men, one short and round and the other long and lean but both dedicated geeks, going over the car.

"What do you see, boys?" she asked them.

"A really cool car," the round one said.

"Sure. Anything unusual in it?"

"Oh, yeah. This suspension set up is incredible," the lean one replied. He moved his hands as if they were on a steering wheel and made vroom noises.

"I was thinking of something more incendiary," Jaguar cut in. "Like a laser gun, rigged to shoot her in the heart, maybe."

The two of them turned blank stares her way. "What?" the round one asked.

"Stay with me, fellas. The ME says her heart was damaged. Anything in the car that might have caused it?"

"Nothing we can see," the lean one answered. "But it'll take a while to know for sure. I mean, if you want details.

"Was there anything wrong with the car—gear problems, that kind of thing?" she asked.

"We got the telemetry, and it didn't show anything like that. The fire wiped out a lot of the physical evidence, though, so we might never know for sure."

"Fuck me," Jaguar said with feeling. They both swiveled around and gave her a good long inspection. "Not an invitation, boys," she said, and left.

On the way back to her hotel, she left a message for Junius, reminding him to inform the local police of their involvement, and to keep all of F1 in Montreal for the time being. She wanted all people at her beck and call, and she knew Planetoid clout could make that happen. No matter what aspersions she cast on the administrative body that ruled her, when they wanted something, they got it.

When she got back to the hotel she went first to Rachel's room, and as soon as she entered, Luna stood and moved toward her fast, snuffling with need and joy. Jaguar put a hand on her head, spoke to her softly.

"She okay?" she asked Rachel.

"I don't think so. She keeps whining and pacing, then sitting down and licking her paws."

Jaguar made brief empathic contact, and felt the swirling of tension, like wolves howling on a lonely night. Dogs knew when something irrevocable happened. Luna's world was in tectonic motion. Alicia had been her human, her job in the world, her stability. Without her Luna was tossed into a void, and Jaguar felt this directly, without the mediation of words. She considered going deeper, looking for anything like memory, but empathic contact with animals wasn't easy at the best of times, and these were less than that by a lot. She drew back. Rachel didn't need to see her throwing up again.

"What do you think?" Rachel asked.

"Not much," Jaguar answered. "Dogs react to death. She's reacting."

"So am I. You find out anything useful in your travels?"

"Forensics saw nothing suspicious, but I doubt those guys could find suspicious unless it was parked up their asses, where they mostly keep their heads. The ME says—well, Alicia's heart melted, from the inside out."

"What?"

"You heard me. And she doesn't know how, but it happened before she crashed. She just kept driving."

"With her heart melted?" Rachel said.

"Yeah. I know how that feels," Jaguar mused. It would take a few seconds for the blood to leave her brain, a few seconds for her reflexive instinct to keep driving, keep driving, to dissipate. And so she died, with her hands on the wheel.

"But that means she really was—was—"

"Murdered," Jaguar finished for her. "Though who did it and how is beyond me." She ruffled up her hair. "We'll need full background on

Meris, Didier, the rest of the crew. If you can follow up on their meetings with Schulman in any way, do so. And I'll want security footage from the paddock, from practice on. We can review right there. Make a thing of it. See you there later?"

"Jaguar, nobody's there."

"Oh. Right. Sunday night in Montreal. Tomorrow morning?"

"Not too early. I'll need a few hours to get it together." Rachel agreed.

"Around eleven, then." She made a hand gesture to Luna, who stood and went to her side. "I'll take her with me."

"Really?" Rachel asked surprised. "You sure you don't want me to keep her?"

"Not tonight," Jaguar said. "We've got a few things to talk about."

CHAPTER TWELVE

Luna continued to tremble lightly and pant, licking at air, at her lips, as Jaguar tried to settle her down in the hotel room. When offered food or water, she turned her head away. Frightened dogs won't drink or eat, so no surprise there. But when Jaguar ran the microwave to make tea, she tucked her tail between her legs and tried to crawl behind the couch. Jaguar turned on the radio, and the music made her whine piteously. She turned it off again, went and knelt next to the dog.

"What gives?" she asked quietly. "You *heard* something you didn't like?"

She lifted her hand, clenched and unclenched it. She had no idea if she'd be able to get anywhere, or what it would do to her to try, but she had to. Clearly this animal was carrying information she needed to know.

And though she wasn't drawn to dogs as a species—their subservience troubled her, asking her to hold a power over them she didn't want—Luna was, as everyone said, special. Intelligent, empathic, and right now, pitiful. Her loss resonated against Jaguar's grief like a struck bell, and she wanted only to relieve it, as if doing so would make her believe she could relieve her own.

She took a breath, put a hand to the soft fur at the back of her neck, and opened contact, waiting for whatever might emerge.

At first, all she got were scents. Something sweet, and something acrid. Something perfumed and something sweaty. She let them flit around, hoping they'd translate into images she could interpret later. Then, an overwhelming dread and awe, the same as she'd felt in Alicia. She brought herself into the quiet necessary to soothe this animal, worked to draw away the fear, but she felt herself pressed into the ground by heaviness, followed quickly by a sharp ringing in her ears, and a blazing heat. She heard Luna howling, the sound as big as a sledgehammer, smashing into her skull. Dizziness moved through her with a vengeance, and the next thing she knew she was down on the floor, her world going dark.

Luna's whining woke her, and now she was frightened of something else, lapping at Jaguar's face, her feet moving in a dance of anxiety. Jaguar let the the world come back into focus and sat up.

"Yeah," she said. "Silly humans, right?"

Luna trembled and licked the air. Jaguar sighed. "Okay, moon doggie," she said. "Let's try something else."

Jaguar pushed herself up, got Luna's leash and put it on her, then led her out of the room, onto the streets of Montreal. Once there, she started a jog, gradually increasing her speed until she and the dog were both running, Luna's tongue flapping out the side of her mouth, her body stretched taut in motion. One block, two blocks, and she kept the pace up. Three and four blocks, five and six, and Luna was panting now from energy expended rather than fear. Four and five more blocks passed quickly, and then Jaguar slowed her pace slightly, went back to a jog, then to a walk.

Luna, still panting, trotted beside her, her tail up and her head held high, her chemistry shifting into a more normal doggie zone. Jaguar continued to walk her at a good clip for a few more blocks, and then she stopped, crouched down next to her, gauged her energy.

"You're okay now," she said softly. "You're okay."

She stood and continued walking back to the hotel, back into the room. This time, Luna drank water greedily and ate the food Jaguar offered with gusto. When she was done, she let out a doggie sigh, and laid down. Jaguar considered trying for empathic contact one more time, but in truth she was as exhausted as the dog, and knew she'd get nowhere. They both needed to rest.

"Maybe tomorrow," she told Luna. "We'll see what we see. With any luck, events will occur."

* * * *

The next event occurred first thing in the morning, and it wasn't one she was hoping for. She got a call from the Montreal Police, requesting her presence at the cop shop. Specifically, from Detective Francois Thei. Cursing exigently, she got dressed, called Rachel to come get Luna, and went there, anticipating obstacles.

As she approached the building, she was stopped by a sight she hadn't expected. Didier pushed his way out of the cop shop and stood in the middle of the street. Soon he was joined by a man Jaguar thought she recognized, tall and lean, with dark hair. She backed into the doorway of a storefront, not wanting to be seen. From where she stood she couldn't hear them, but she had other means of eavesdropping and she used them.

They spoke in French, and she understood none of it, but she'd remember, and try for translation at a later date. In the meantime, she caught the feeling tone—anger from Didier, reassurance from the other man. Didier, not placated, walked away fast.

She waited a moment, then stuck her head out. She saw Didier's back, receding. The dark haired man was not in view. She went to the cop shop, and entered.

Once inside the offices, which were clean and quiet, she went to the front desk, gave her name and title, and asked for Detective Thei. The desk sergeant, a large, fair haired man, sniffed at her, pressed a button on his board, and muttered in French.

In short order, another man appeared. He was tall and lean, with a thin, angular face and sharp hazel eyes that took in everything. He brushed away a shock of straight black hair that fell across his forehead. And she knew him.

"It's you," she said. "You were at the clubhouse, and the restaurant. And you were just talking to Didier." He stared at her blankly, and she tried again. "Vous. C'est vous," she said, with bad accent.

"Parlez vou Francais?" he asked dubiously.

"That's about all I got. But if you don't speak English, we can try Tzutujil Mayan. Or Mertec."

"English is fine," he said, and inclined his head politely. "Dr. Addams, yes? I understand you're conducting preliminary research for the Planetoids, regarding the death of Alicia Senna. I'd like to know why the Planetoid feels it necessary to have a presence here."

"And I'd like to know why you were in the clubhouse and the restaurant," she replied. "Also what Didier had to say to you."

"Perhaps I'll answer your questions, after you answer mine." He gave her a smile, courteous but cool. Home Planet police didn't like Planetoid interference any more than Planetoid liked a home planet presence.

She grinned, thinking of similar interactions she'd had with Alex, the two of them stalking the edges of trust. Then, too late, she remembered it was a bad idea to think about him, especially after she'd shot her wad trying far too much empathic work. Her world started to spin, darkness creeping in around the edges of her eyes.

"Hell," she said, gasping for breath, struggling to pull the room back into focus. She felt pressure at her elbow.

"Sit," a voice said, and she did. She wasn't sure how long the world was gone, but when it came back, a glass of water was in her hand, and dark hazel eyes regarded her solicitously. "Are you ill, Dr. Addams?" Detective Thei's smooth voice enquired.

She lifted the glass, drank, waited for vision to fully return. "No," she said, when the room became lit and ceased to tilt. "Just—I haven't slept much in the past few days."

"Have you eaten anything today?" he asked.

She thought about it. If she had, she didn't remember. "Maybe?" she tried.

"Yesterday?"

"Not sure."

He grunted with disapproval, stood and called to a uniformed cop who was passing through the room. He spoke to him in rapid French, then returned to Jaguar, took a seat next to her.

"They'll bring a sandwich. It will not be the best food you'll eat while in Montreal, but it will do. Drink more water."

She did so, appreciating his courtesy. She'd done without anything as straightforward as courtesy for some time. Then he was putting a sandwich in her hand, insisting that she eat it before they talked. He left her alone, giving her just enough time to finish it and feel its sustenance, then he returned and took a seat next to her.

"Well," he said, looking her over. "You now have the color of a living human instead of a ghost. How do you feel?"

"Better," she said. "Thank you."

"What happened to Alicia—you saw it. Perhaps the shock still disturbs you?"

"I've seen worse," she noted.

"Of course. You work on the Planetoids. But you knew her. You have been spending time with her, yes?"

"Her dog got lost and I found her, brought her back. Then, yes, we spent some time together."

"And you thought well of her?"

He was interrogating her as politely as possible, and she chose to be polite in response. "I did," she said. "She was a remarkable woman, and I'm pissed as hell that I didn't prevent her death."

"As I am," he agreed. "Then are you sure this investigation isn't more about your anger than any real cause to think it's murder?"

That, she thought, was a nice slide. "Someone threatened her last year at the Montreal race. Your people investigated, didn't they?"

"We did, but the threats were untraceable, and they said only the usual—that she'd abandoned her team, and her disloyalty earned a punishment. That sort of thing."

"And that she killed David Tempe, GM's engineer," Jaguar noted.

An eyebrow elevated. "She told you?"

"She did."

"That's interesting. In general, she wanted it kept quiet as possible."

"I can be persuasive," Jaguar noted. "I'd like to see those emails."

"I may let you. But those threats don't constitute reason for a Planetoid investigation."

"Not alone. But when I saw her, after the crash, she was bleeding in a way not consistent with any possible injury. And later, the ME agreed the crash didn't kill her."

"I know. I spoke with her."

"Then you know damn well I'm not saying it's murder just because I'm feeling petulant."

A smile tried to emerge, and he subdued it. "Even so, I understand the Planetoid schedules preliminary research *after* an arrest, once a trial has been set. You have not even a suspect."

She shrugged. "This is different."

"Yes. Exactly. And, once again, I'd like to know why."

He was, she thought, persistent as Alex could ever be. She surveyed him, considered how much to say and not say. She didn't know enough about him to make a rational decision, so she went with winging it.

"Because," she said. "I requested it."

He nodded as if this confirmed something he already suspected. What he'd wanted wasn't the information so much as finding out if she'd be clean with him. "You would not have requested it unless some larger issue was involved. I'd like to know what that issue is, and if it has anything to do, for instance, with Mr. Schulman."

"Good old Ron," she said. "You after him too?"

"Not right now," he said. "But let's talk about it. My office is this way."

CHAPTER THIRTEEN

Jaguar noted that Detective Thei's office, was clean and uncluttered, reminding her of the office she spent the most time in on the Planetoid. He sat behind his desk, listening without comment, while she sat across from him and talked.

She was judicious in choosing what to say and what not to say, sticking to information he could easily get from an official report, without embellishment. She was willing to let him know that Ron Schulman had interfered with a Planetoid case, but not willing to tell him that the case involved her lover, and her lover's son. She emphasized that the board governor of her zone continued to resent Ron's interference, and suspected him, without proof, of interfering in larger ways. Therefore, he was amenable to any investigation she might make that involved him.

When she was done, Detective Thei rose from his chair, moved to a map of the city he had on one wall of his office, and stared at it. She waited, staying quiet and still. After a while, he ran a hand over his hair, and turned to her.

"You're very good at silence," he said.

"I don't waste air."

"Yes. You don't waste your air or your time. That means this is important to you, perhaps in more than an official way?"

She lifted a hand, let it fall back onto her lap. "Does that matter?"

"It might. I don't know unless you tell me."

"Detective Thei, I've answered all your questions. I'd appreciate it if you'd answer mine. Why were you at the clubhouse, and at the restaurant?"

He paused, and she saw him work to deliberately keep his face smooth and official. "Alicia invited me," he said.

"Business or personal?"

His mouth lifted in a smile. "Does that matter?"

She smiled back. "How about this—we'll keep our private lives private, and you can let me go do my job."

"Leave me alone, I know what I'm doing?" he asked.

She ducked her head down, brought it up again. "You heard that?"

"Yes. I understand it's becoming a t-shirt, for sale. An appropriate legacy for Alicia. I'd be happy to leave you alone, but your work is more than a Planetoid prelim. You're investigating, and that's my job."

"I have a different protocol, and it'll help yours, if you let me use it."

"What do you plan to do next?"

"My assistant is getting all the video footage from the paddock, to see if we can find any interference with her car. I'll watch it, along with the other people in the Ferrari paddock who might be involved. She'll also get the footage from David Tempe's death for me to watch, in case I see anything you missed. I can send it all your way after, with my report, but I'd rather the police weren't present at the viewing."

"Because it might stifle their reactions, and their reactions will tell you as much if not more than the recordings, yes?"

"That's the idea," she said. "A great deal of my job is—well, disturbing people."

He returned to his seat, sat back and relaxed. "And you have some specialized gifts for disturbance, don't you?"

"As it happens, I'm rather good at it," she said.

"I have heard that about you. But you're aware that evidence gathered from use of psi capacities is not admissible in our court system?"

"I am," she said. Montreal was cagey about the empathic arts. Though they didn't persecute practitioners the way some cities did, they were clear that it was to be used purely for personal reasons. Psychologists, law enforcement, doctors—those on the Planetoid who used it regularly in their work—were not permitted to do so here. If they were reported for doing so, they could be fined, lose their license to practice.

He was being direct with her. She decided to do the same. "I think it's stupid, but it's not my city, so I won't make trouble about it. I'm also guessing you don't use them, professionally or personally. Though I don't doubt you could easily learn how."

This put tension in his jaw. "You are not the first person to say so."

"Who was?"

"Alicia was one. Before I met her, an old man I arrested for vagrancy said the same. It was winter, and our shelters were full, but he needed somewhere warm to sleep. He was grateful, and wanted to instruct me. He said I had natural gifts, which I should cultivate."

"But you chose not to. Why?"

He put his elbows on his desk, leaned forward. "You move toward risk, as part of your nature. I prefer to gauge the risks I might face, and work to limit them."

She did a scan of his energy, moving smoothly across the placid surface of his mind. Even there, she caught the scent of fear. "There's other reasons," she said.

He could have denied it, but instead he caught her gaze and held it, his forest shaded eyes intent. "I see a great deal without using psi capacities, Dr. Addams," he said. "For instance, I see that you are very beautiful, and very sad. Grief moves through you like a river. And I suspect it grows in part from your willingness to use what you call your gifts. For myself, I prefer gifts that bring joy rather than pain."

Though his answer surprised her, it was probably the best reason she'd ever heard for avoiding the arts. But if he was naturally gifted, not using those gifts also exacted a price. She wondered why he was willing to pay it. "Someone you cared about was hurt using the arts?" she asked bluntly. If he was getting personal, so would she.

He turned his head down, examined his hands. "Is that your business, Dr. Addams?"

"Not at all. But that answers the question, so you might as well tell me who."

He continued his examination of his hands. "My father," he said. "He was murdered during the Killing Times, when empaths were unmoving targets in a shooting gallery."

"I'm sorry," she said, meaning it. She'd heard that kind of story many times, and knew she'd only avoided that fate through better fortune.

"Thank you," he answered, and raised his face to hers. "Now tell me, have you never considered leaving off what you do, for an easier life?"

An odd question, and one that caught her up short. "I don't see what that has to do with this investigation," she said.

"My father's death is also irrelevant," he noted. "I'm getting acquainted with you, to ensure my decisions are well informed. As you are doing with me."

She inclined her head, acknowledging this. They were circling each other, with purpose. She drew her lower lip through her teeth, considered how to answer him. She'd relinquished an easy life, a normal life, long ago, or it was relinquished for her by nature of her birth, her people. And during the Killing Times she had to dig deeply into worlds others never knew in order to survive. Was that a blessing or a curse? As she weighed the balance, she thought it was both. And either way, it was hers. Her way. Her life to live.

"I come from a Mertec heritage," she said. "My people say that grief and praise are the same. To praise something is to know you value it enough that you'll have to grieve it sooner or later. To grieve something is to give it praise. If you refuse either, you lose your passion, and that's something I can't do without."

"Yes. That is what makes you beautiful as well as sad. Alicia was the same."

"She was," Jaguar said. She debated pursuing the topic. Did he care about Alicia? Were they lovers? If so, he must be grieving, though he didn't look it. Then again, people showed grief in different ways. His way might be about work, as hers was. And she had more pertinent questions on her mind. She moved on.

"Why did you mention Ron Schulman? If you've got an interest in him, I'd like to know what it is."

"There was the incident at qualifying, which the stewards will investigate. And he's a very powerful man, accustomed to getting his way. When Alicia received threats, we considered he might be involved, perhaps in anger at her leaving GM."

"And?"

"We found nothing, though he has a great deal of experience in self-protection. We keep an eye on him, in our own way."

"That's a good idea," she said. "He's skilled at creating disaster for others, then sidestepping the flak."

"So you say, but you have no proof, do you?"

"None that's admissible in your courts," she said. "That doesn't mean I don't know."

He kept his gaze on her, gave a short nod, as if he'd learned something. "That worries me, Dr. Addams," he said. "You already said his name in a moment of anger, which the whole world can watch."

"That," she said. "I was...out of sorts."

"Is that what you call it? Even so, Mr. Schulman is a friend to our city. One reason I wanted to speak with you is to make sure you do not bother him for a personal obsession, or for Planetoid interests which range beyond our own. He is not to be disturbed unless we have evidence against him. Do we understand each other?"

She lifted her hand, held it palm up. "I understand you," she said, emphasizing the last word.

He showed her an official smile. "I'm glad. Is there anything else you need to know?"

"Just what Didier had to say to you. It seemed pretty urgent."

His jaw twitched, and he shifted too quickly. That caught him off guard, but he recovered himself. "You saw that," he noted. "Did you hear as well?"

"Not really," she said. "The little I caught was in a language I don't own."

"Yes. He spoke in French. Well, it was urgent for him, though not for us. He protests being kept here. He is nervous about that. In fact, he threatened me, if I tried to hold him against his possibilities of getting a seat with a team. I am keeping an eye on him."

"Are you? That's good. So am I."

He relaxed his expression into something less formal. "We'll work together on this, Dr. Addams," he said. "You can disturb people, but you'll report to me on a daily basis, and if I find you are becoming a nuisance to Mr. Schulman, or holding back important information, I'll see to it that your job becomes difficult."

"Fine by me," she said. "Is that all?"

He hesitated, opened his mouth as if to say more, then closed it and started over. "Yes," he said. "That is all, for now."

She rose, and left his office, with a great deal more to consider than she'd had before she got here.

* * * *

Jaguar took the time to mull what Detective Thei had said, and what he hadn't. He also suspected Ron Schulman's involvement, but if any boats were to be rocked, he'd do the rocking. He was someone who believed in protecting the suits, for as long as he could. He knew Alicia, perhaps in a biblical sense, and cared for her as deeply as he was capable of caring. She wasn't sure how deep that went with him, however. He liked the light on the water, rather than what lay beneath. And yet, he was drawn to someone like Alicia, drawn to empaths like Jaguar, as well.

She sensed fear in him, but didn't dare make contact to explore exactly what that signified. She'd have to wait and let it unfold. In the meantime, she was grateful for his willingness to speak and listen to her with courtesy and kindness. And she went on to the next task, at the Ferrari paddock, on the Montreal race track.

When she got there, most of the crew was milling around, not sure what they were supposed to be doing. As soon as she hit the garage entrance, Meris got in her face.

"What's going on? A bunch of cops told us we can't leave, but we've got a Texas race coming up. You can't possibly mean to keep us here, can you?"

"Yeah, I can," Jaguar said. "This is an ongoing investigation, and you're all required to hang around until we say otherwise, so get comfy. Is Rachel here?"

Meris ran a hand through her long blonde hair. "She's in the trailer, with Luna. Doing something with video footage, she said, but she wouldn't say what. Will you tell me?"

"Sure. It's movie day. Wanna watch?"

As she spoke, Rachel entered the space, carrying a thumb drive. Jaguar looked to her. "Ready?" she asked.

"Everything I could get for now," Rachel said, and set up her own computer, started pressing keys.

"What is it?" Meris asked, agitated.

"Camera footage from the crash, from the garage before the crash, from David Tempe's death. It'll be a long flick. You want popcorn?"

"What?"

Jaguar moved her hand. "Sit, or leave. We're working."

"Here it is," Rachel said and pulled up a chair. Jaguar did likewise and sat next to her. Meris tapped an impatient foot, then joined them. As she watched, she chewed on the end of her thumbnail.

What they saw at first was footage from Tempe's death, which showed a finely built man in his prime clutching at his chest, gasping and falling. Jaguar made Rachel play it once, twice, three times. Then she twisted her face around.

"Do you hear that?" she asked Rachel.

"Hear what?" Rachel replied.

"That—never mind. Let's move on."

Rachel pressed a few buttons, and they saw the initial footage of Alicia's race. They were no more than ten minutes in when Didier came on the scene.

"I heard there's something going on," he noted, and Meris shushed him.

"Don't ask," she said. "Just—stay or leave."

He stared at the screen, took a seat and was silent.

Audience footage didn't show anything revealing, so they moved on to security camera footage from inside the garage. That also showed more of nothing, except for one brief section, no more than a minute long.

"Stop," Jaguar told Rachel, and she hit pause.

"Go back," Jaguar told her, and she did. They watched again. It was an apparently neutral bit, showing crew moving about the paddock, but then there was a blip of white.

"There it is," Jaguar murmured. She swung around to Rachel. "Do you see it?"

"I do," Rachel said, her eyes wide.

"Can you recover it?"

Rachel bent over the screen, pressed buttons on a keyboard, then shook her head. "Sorry. It's gone."

"Rat fuck," Jaguar said with feeling. "Well, at least we know it's there."

"What is it?" Meris asked.

"A blank spot. Someone erased part of the footage. Less than a minute, probably."

"Who would do that?"

"I think that's what we need to find out. Rachel, play it again."

She did so, three more times, and Jaguar shook her head. "Move on. Show me Alicia, from the time of her radio message, to the crash."

Rachel hit keys until they were there, hearing Alicia say "Leave me alone, I know what I'm doing."

"Again," Jaguar said, and Rachel replayed it.

"One more time," Jaguar said, and it ran again.

Didier shifted in his seat. Meris chewed harder on her thumbnail. "Why are you doing this?" she asked.

Jaguar whipped around to her. "Shut up," she said. Then, to Rachel, "Again."

Rachel did as she was asked. Jaguar leaned close to the monitor. "Stop there," she said. She leaned back in her chair. "Do you hear anything odd?" she asked Rachel.

"Not really. I mean, Alicia's agitated. Her voice is higher than usual. That's all."

Jaguar gave a curt nod. "Okay. Go to the crash."

Rachel did so, and they watched as Alicia's car spun wildly, crashed in flames against the wall of champions.

"Again," Jaguar said, and Rachel replayed it.

Then once, twice, three more times, and the last time Jaguar closed her eyes and only listened. "Did you *hear* that?" she asked Rachel.

"Hear what?" Rachel answered.

Jaguar shook her head. "Play it again."

They replayed it five more times until Didier, his voice tight and high as Alicia's had been in her radio transmission, spoke up.

"Is this necessary?" he asked.

"Yes," Jaguar said.

"You—you torture us. To see if we'll confess to killing a woman we all loved? I did not want her dead. No one here wanted *that*."

She gazed up at him. "What did you want?" she asked.

He moved his hand in a gesture of refutation, but said nothing.

"You don't have to stay," she noted. "Go get a drink. You look like you need it."

"I do," he agreed, and exited.

Meris stayed and kept watching, chewing her thumb, her face twisted in pain. When they'd viewed the crash for the tenth time, Jaguar sighed. "I see a few possibilities, but nothing definite. I'll need more."

"How will you get it?" Meris asked, speaking for the first time.

"Damned if I know," Jaguar replied.

A small commotion at the paddock entrance interrupted them. Jaguar lifted her head, looked back, and saw Larry Engle enter, surrounded by his entourage, his smile working.

"Xipe Totec flay him," she muttered, but it didn't happen. At least, not as soon as she would have liked. He approached her, spoke her name.

"Dr. Addams. Alicia's death is now an official investigation," he told her, as if he'd just invented the notion.

"I think I mentioned that last time we met," she said.

"Yes. Well, I'm sorry it's come to this, but I want to offer my assistance in any way possible, to make sure it's resolved quickly."

"I'm hoping to resolve it fairly, and honestly," she noted.

"Of course," he said. "That, too. I understand some of the teams are required to stay."

"Ferrari, GM, Lotus, McLaren. The top runners. The cops'll vet the rest and send them on their way if nothing's wrong. We'll need to spend more time with the others."

"There's no way around that?" he asked.

"None at all."

Reluctantly, he gave her a nod. "The teams will use the time for testing and practice. Is that within bounds?"

"Sure," she said. "They can do what they want, as long as they stay."

"That's good. Of course, I'll assist the police and the Planetoid in any way possible."

She eyed him, saw ideas moving behind his small eyes. "You got something in mind?"

He glanced down at Luna. "Alicia's dog. Someone can take her off your hands."

"You?"

He laughed lightly. "Hardly. Didier Picot will take her. I ran into him as he was leaving. He asked if he could help, and I mentioned the dog. He'll care for her."

"He doesn't like dogs," she said.

"He likes his job."

Her hand moved at her side, fingers clenching and unclenching. "I'd think Meris would be the obvious choice. And she'd take her." Jaguar turned to her. "Right? You'll watch the dog?"

"Sure," Meris said.

"We thought it might be…painful for her," Larry said. "And Didier's glad to help."

"For a rich man, you're a lousy liar," Jaguar noted. "Was this Didier's idea, yours, or Ron Schulman's?" she asked, watching his face closely.

"It seemed mutually agreeable," he said.

"Yeah? Your face went all twitchy when I said Ron Schulman," she noted. Then, "Oops—just did it again. Why is *he* making suggestions about the dog?"

"Mr. Schulman wants everyone to know he had nothing to do with the racing incident at qualifying, and nothing to do with this tragic accident. He's—he's showing good faith."

"Whoopie for him," Jaguar said. "But he doesn't get Luna."

"Really, miss—Dr. Addams. I'd think you'd welcome the opportunity—"

"You'd be wrong." She waited for what she thought would come next, and got it.

"The dog meant a great deal to Alicia. She should be somewhere where she's safe, and cared for. Somewhere away from all this mess. In fact, I really must insist."

"Must you? Go ahead. See where it gets you."

His face moved indeterminately as he waffled between using power or seduction. He finally grabbed for something in between. "Why do you want her?" he demanded.

She grinned. "Protective custody."

"What?"

"She witnessed the crime. I'm keeping her in protective custody."

"That's—that's—ridiculous."

"So what? The dog is mine." To emphasize her intent, she took Luna's leash in her hand and stood. "By the way, I hear you're selling your F1 rights. To anyone I know?"

She made an effort, and tried a quick dip into his thoughts. Fortunately, they were neither deep nor complex, and before it hurt her, she got the information she needed. But she wasn't anywhere near as smooth as usual, and Larry felt it, put a hand to his head and gaped at her.

"What did you do, you—you bitch," he spit at her.

"Preliminary research," she said. She looked to Rachel. "I've got some errands to run. Walk me out."

Rachel stood and they left, neither woman looking back to see the astonishment on Larry's face. When they were well out of the paddock and headed toward the track, Jaguar spoke.

"The pig shit bastard is selling out, and to Ron, who's got his fingers in this pie already. But he doesn't know anything beyond self-interest.

Hell. I'm heading back to the hotel. I've got to report in to Detective Thei. You take Luna and go back and talk to Meris. Find out what you can from her."

"What? You want me to—to—what?"

"I want you to find out what you can about her. Any way you can. Then bring the footage over to the Montreal cops. And don't let Mr. Rat Fuck Engle near that dog." She turned again and trotted on, leaving Rachel behind her.

Rachel, feeling distinctly unlike herself, went back into the paddock, Luna in tow. Larry was gone, and Meris greeted her nervously. "Listen, what's really going on here?" she asked.

"Planetoid investigation," Rachel answered.

"Yeah, but you aren't like the cops."

"No," Rachel admitted. "Not at all. But when we anticipate a trial that'll send a prisoner our way, we do preliminary research, and we're thorough. More thorough than the cops, really, because we're not gathering trial evidence. We're looking for stuff we can use on a prisoner. Going to the Planetoids isn't like going to jail. We don't want to bring anyone up unless *we* know they're guilty."

"Okay," Meris said. "I get that. But you—are you hanging around because you want to, or because your boss asked you to?"

"Both," Rachel said, honest as the day.

"Which one matters more?" Meris asked.

"Both," Rachel said again.

Meris ran a hand through her hair. "Look, I've heard rumors about her. That she's having an affair with someone she works with. That isn't—I mean, it wouldn't be you, would it?"

Rachel stared at her blankly for a moment, then burst into laughter. "Is that what you thought?" She laughed some more.

"It's not that funny," Meris grumbled.

"It is if you know anything about either of us."

Meris offered a sheepish grin. "Well, for once I'm glad to know I'm wrong. But Jaguar—she's complicated. You trust her?"

"Without question," Rachel said. Then, added more judiciously, "If you want to know if *you* can trust her, that's different. You can trust her to do what she's best at, and she's great at blowing things up. Great at getting to the truth even if it means destroying an entire Planetoid. So, it depends on if you want the truth or not."

Meris frowned. "My world's got lots of politics in it, and nobody much tells the truth."

"Like Larry?" Rachel asked.

Meris shrugged. "Word is he's selling to another team owner. Ron Schulman—GM. But people say shit. There's no telling if it's true. Meantime, I'd like to know who's holding your boss's leash."

Rachel grinned. "She's an off leash kind of woman."

"That's what you think, but how do you know? I mean, Alicia played her cards close, but I'm pretty sure she suspected another team was dirty dealing us. What she said at the interview, right? And for all I know, your boss was paid to frame someone for Alicia's death."

"You'd have more luck making the sun move around the earth than corrupting Jaguar."

Meris gave a small snort. "Everyone's got a price," she said.

"Sure. And Jaguar's price is the truth."

Meris narrowed her eyes. "You mean that, don't you?"

"You bet. I've known her a long time, and that's all there is to her."

"That's why she's so—so—"

"Difficult? Scary? Strange? Yeah. All that and more."

"And you—what do you do on those Planetoids?"

Rachel smiled. "Research," she said. "Not very sexy, but it helps."

"Actually, I think it's incredibly sexy," Meris said. "Tell me more."

She took one step closer to Rachel, and her fresh, bright face showed only hope. Rachel knew all the impossibilities of the situation. She was here investigating a murder, and apparently Jaguar thought Meris might be part of it. She worked on the Planetoid, and Meris drove around the world in fast cars. There was no hope for anything except a fling here, and yet, maybe a fling was just what she needed.

She lifted a shoulder, let it fall, and took a step to match Meris's. "Sure," she said. "What do you want to know?"

CHAPTER FOURTEEN

Home Planet, New Mexico

Jake had the third sweat set up, the fire ready to be lit, early the next morning. When he gave Alex the matches to get it started, Alex hesitated, his hand refusing to do the task he'd appointed.

Jake eyed him. "What's the hold up?"

"I don't think I should," Alex said.

"Why not?"

He wasn't sure. He felt the spirit of his son kicking up dust, and an ethereal female voice telling him things he didn't want to know. "I have to—to figure it out myself."

"Yeah? How'll you do that?"

"Not this way," he said. "It's my problem. I have to *know*, Jake."

"Know what?"

Alex stretched out his hand, stared at the lines etched in it. "With Springer, I saw what I should do, and I was wrong. I need something with a little more assurance of success."

He dropped his hand, which had betrayed him, betrayed his son. Within its lines he'd seen what he believed was truth: Jaguar would save Springer. They would bring him here, and see him healed. But it must have been ego or fantasy, because everything he'd seen in Adept space ended in disaster. He needed a new way of knowing.

"You saw it, right?" Jake demanded. "What happened with Springer—you used your gifts and saw what to do. You think you failed just because he's dead? That makes everything you are not true?"

Alex had trusted Adept space all his life. He couldn't say everything about it was true except this, because it didn't turn out the way he wanted. That made him no more than a child, crying for the moon. But Springer wasn't just dead. He was dead at his father's hands. What did that tell him?

Jake made a noise in the back of his throat. "You keep spinning around, coming back to the same place," he said impatiently. "But it's from your head, not your heart, so you keep spinning. Maybe you should go somewhere else."

"Like where?"

"Like what you're seeing in the sweat lodges. Like where you were led you in the first place."

Where he was always led. To Jaguar, and her complex world of empathic gifts, which had so richly informed his. But where was it leading him now? To crashing cars? It made no sense, and he no longer trusted it.

"It's nothing to do with her. It's just—it's mine."

"And you can't share it with her?"

"He was *my* son." He insisted on this, felt it in every fiber of his being. What he'd done, what he'd promised, and how he might fulfill that promise, was his burden. He had to separate that from her, from any love he felt for her, to get it right this time.

"She gave you everything. Even her knife. Why would you deny her your grief?"

Jake lived in a world where grief, like someone's knife in your chest, was a gift to be shared with those you loved most. Right now, Alex could not eat that truth. Killing himself would be easy in comparison.

"I can't sweat today," he said. "I just can't."

Jake kicked hard at the wood around the fire, and walked away.

Home Planet, Montreal

Jaguar called in to Detective Thei's personal number, and reported to him fully and succinctly, including Larry's interest in Luna, and its source. He nodded once or twice, but asked no questions. When she was done, he said, "You do good work, Dr. Addams."

"If I did, Alicia wouldn't be dead," she answered.

"Surely you know better than to take that on yourself," he chided. "In jobs like ours, and like hers, there are no guarantees of safety."

She raised an eyebrow at him. "This, from a man who likes to limit risk?"

He brushed back his shock of black hair, and grinned. "I am a realist," he said. "And you, I think, are a romantic."

"Maybe," she said. "But you're not as much of a realist as you portray, Detective."

"Realist enough to know that if footage was deleted, something is amiss. When will you have the recordings to me?"

"Later today. My assistant, Rachel, is taking care of it."

"We'll speak tomorrow, after I've viewed them."

"Will you look further into Schulman's sudden interest in dogs?"

"How do suggest I do that?" he asked.

She was about to get testy, but realized he was right. Not much he could pursue there. "Then see what he knows about heart attacks, of any kind. We've got two busted hearts now, so surely there's a connection."

"I'll do my job, Dr. Addams," he said. "We'll speak tomorrow."

When he signed off, she spent a few hours of her own time going over David Tempe's autopsy, which told her nothing, then poking around through her own computer's research program to see if she could find a connection between Ron Schulman and bad hearts. That told her more nothing, so she closed shop for the night.

Her next intent was to crawl into a hot bath, but she only got as far as kicking her shoes off before there was a knock on her door. She looked through the peephole and saw Didier, his hand full of flowers, a cart of food at his side. She opened the door.

"Well," she said. "Bearing gifts?"

He raised a hand, lowered it and showed her a smile. "I think I left, as you say, in a huff. That was rude of me. You've had very difficult days, and perhaps need a little indulgence. So I took the liberty of getting dinner, to make up for my discourtesy. If you like, I'll leave it for you. Or, if you want company…"

The bath held greater appeal for her than dealing with Didier, but she might be able to glean something from him. "Come in," she said.

He wheeled the cart in, handed her the flowers, which were fiery red crocosmia. She put them in her ice bucket.

"What's the occasion?" she asked.

"I think it's always the right occasion to bring flowers to a beautiful woman," he said. "Am I mistaken in that?"

"Not at all. Are you hungry?"

"Only if you don't care to eat alone."

"That would be a waste," she said. "Sit down. What did you bring?"

He pulled metal lids off the plates, revealing filet mignon, baked potatoes, salad. Good food, cooked well. If Jaguar was at all hungry, it would be just what she wanted, but she still felt slightly queasy, not sure how food would settle in her. Regardless, she pulled a chair up and sat, and Didier did the same.

For the first part of the dinner, they spoke only of inconsequential matters—the weather in Montreal, what Paris was like this time of year. Not until they got to coffee, and the chocolate souffle did Dider broach anything else, and then he did so bluntly.

"Tell me," he said, "do you really believe someone murdered Alicia?"

"Yes," she said. "Otherwise, I wouldn't be here."

"That seems so fantastic to me. Like a news story, or a movie. Who would do so?"

"Lots of people, from what I can tell. Including you."

He put a hand to his heart. "Me?"

"Sure. You want her seat, don't you? Or at least, you want someone's seat."

He ducked his head down, brought it up again, and this time showed her a deprecating smile. "There are easier ways to get a ride than murder," he told her.

"You got offers?" she asked.

"Jaguar, you know I can't speak."

"You don't trust me?"

"Well…" he let the sentence hang in the air, unresolved.

"What will make you trust me? You need to see me naked?" She wore a long sleeved sage green silk shirt, button down, over her black leggings. To emphasize her point, she unbuttoned the top button, then the next one down.

His lips parted in a smile. "That would be a good start," he murmured.

She unbuttoned one more button, then stopped. "But how do I know I can trust you?"

He eyed his prospects. "Cara, this isn't a bargaining session."

"Sure it is," she noted. "Tell me what's on your side of the table."

"What do you need to know, my chatelaine?" he asked.

"I am so not that," she said. "Just tell me where Alicia was getting her fun."

He shook his head. "We don't tell tales out of school," he said.

"She's dead," Jaguar said. "It can't hurt her. And I'm not selling it to the tabloids."

He cast his glance over her again, and deemed her more appetizing than the souffle. "When the police helped her with those threats, one detective was particularly attentive."

"Detective Thei?" Jaguar asked.

"Yes. That was his name. How clever of you to know."

"I'm all about clever," she said. "Were they lovers?"

He lifted a hand, let it fall. "I saw them together in her hotel a few times. He had her hand in his. And there were rumors, but there always are."

"Eternal as the grass. Is that why you were yelling at him on the streets of Montreal?"

"What?" he demanded.

"I saw you talking to him outside the cop shop. Want to tell me what that was about?"

"I resent being kept here, against my will. I was voicing that to him."

"Didn't get you anywhere, did it? Speaking of rumors, I hear you're negotiating with Ron Schulman for a seat on GM. True?"

His pupils dilated. "Do you always know everything?" he asked.

"Whenever I can," she replied cheerfully. "So how's it going?"

He shrugged. "Negotiations for contracts are kept quiet until the papers are signed. Let's just say that right now I'm in the happy position of having more than one excellent option to pursue, and I'll take my time deciding which one suits me best."

She considered making empathic contact, but knew she wasn't up to a quick dive and carry he wouldn't feel. All his microexpressions spoke of smug satisfaction, and she'd like to keep him there for now. That would make it easier to trip him up later, if she needed to.

"I'm guessing you'd prefer Ferrari. You like to be on top," she noted.

"For racing, definitely. For other situations, I'm flexible."

She ran a hand along the side of his face. "Someday maybe I'll test that," she noted. "For now, you need to leave."

His face showed disappointment. "Jaguar, must I?"

"No kitten in your lap tonight. I'm working. When I'm done, I'll have more time, and our negotiations can continue. That is, as long as I don't find out you killed Alicia."

His lips became a thin line. Anger, she thought, but couldn't tell if it was because she was right, or because she was wrong. Or merely because he'd wasted a dinner on her.

It took her another five minutes to talk him out the door, and when he left, she collapsed on the bed, not up to thinking further about her conversations with complicated Frenchmen.

CHAPTER FIFTEEN

Jaguar fell into sleep as soon as her head hit the pillow, and she dreamt relentlessly of racing.

In one dream she was in the Ferrari, her body joined to Alicia's as she crashed. In another, Alicia was driving her Berlinetta, Jaguar in the passenger's seat. "Take the wheel," Alicia told her, and became ephemeral, as Jaguar slid into her, suddenly driving on the track, another car ahead of her. She was pushing against it, passing it, pushing it onto the green. In yet another dream, she was racing Didier in the F1 car, and as she drove around him she noticed he was naked, and grinning.

"Fuck this," she groaned, as she woke from this last dream, and gave up on the notion of sleep. She sat up, looked around her hotel room, anonymous and interstitial. She was caught between worlds, visiting Nowhere, in transition, physically and emotionally.

"Waiting sucks," she said out loud. She rubbed at her face, and reviewed her dreams. Keep moving, they all said. Take the wheel, drive the car.

She frowned. "Drive the car," she murmured, and an idea formulated itself for her. Not a bad idea at all, she thought, but she'd need some cooperation, either willing or enforced. And she knew what she had to do to get it. She got up, got dressed, had coffee. It would be afternoon on the Planetoid. A good time to put in a call to Junius.

"My favorite Teacher," he said, deliberately cheerful, when he picked up the call. "Who'd you kill?"

"Nobody yet. But I'm working on something that might be suicide."

"Pardon me?"

"I couldn't save Alicia, so maybe I should become her," she said, and she told him.

When she was done, Junius chuckled softly. "Yeah, okay," he said. "I'll admit it's an idea. What do you need to get it moving?"

"Someone has to make sure the Stewards and that little gnome man who owns everyone don't give me shit about it. I'll take care of the rest."

"Done," he said. "And good luck."

After that, she made her way to Meris's hotel.

When she knocked on her door she heard a muffled response, and another voice speaking. She put a hand to the door and briefly listened in. Then a broad grin spread across her face. "Well, well," she murmured. "At least one of us is having some fun."

The door opened a crack. Meris's face peered at her. Her eyes were sleepy, her hair tousled.

"What?" she asked.

"You have to teach me how to race," she said.

Meris blinked at her. Shook her head. "Are you nuts?" she inquired mildly.

"Only now and then. Is it a driver qualification?"

"Jesus Christ," Meris said.

"Don't call him if you don't want him. I learned that from a holodemon. Get dressed. We're going to the track. And tell Rachel to come along. I need her."

A brief pause. Then, with a poor imitation of surprise. "Rachel? I don't have her number. Shouldn't you call her?"

Jaguar rolled her eyes, pushed the door open. "Rachel," she shouted into the room. "Get up. We're working today."

She looked at Meris. "There. I called her. Now hurry up. I'll go on ahead and meet you at the paddock."

* * * *

Jaguar was waiting impatiently in the garage, ignored by the engineers and team members who milled about, when Meris and a sheepish Rachel arrived. Luna, at her side, batted her tail at Jaguar.

"Hi there," she said. "Let's get the awkward stuff out of the way. I know you two slept together last night, and if you're happy about it, so am I. Now, teach me how to race one of these machines." She gestured toward the Ferrari.

"You really are nuts," Meris said with wonder.

"You say that like you're surprised. Fortunately, I'm in a position for my delusions to be realized. If you check your messages, you'll probably find one from Planetoid officials, ordering you around about this. You want to confirm?"

"Do you know how long drivers train for this? How many years it takes to get here? Do you have any idea what it takes to drive one of these cars?

"Sure," she said. "You punch the brakes with the equivalent of a hundred pounds, and your head weighs about five times what's normal from the helmet, then sustains G forces of 3.5 or more, depending on the corner. You lose up to 3 kilograms of water during a race, and sustain a heart rate of around 150, though it can go higher. Anything else?"

"Well, yeah," Meris said. "There's the car itself, which you know nothing about, and which has all kinds of complications around braking, tire wear, shifting. There's the mental demands for concentration. And there's how much these damn cars cost."

"I'm no stranger to mental demands," Jaguar said. "And the car is worth twenty million, give or take. But I'll have to drive it anyway."

"Nobody would allow it. The stewards would be livid."

Jaguar flipped open her cellcom. "Which one you want to talk to? They all got the same message you did, and approved me driving."

"Why would they?"

"Because," Jaguar said. "I'm Planetoid and I scare the shit out of them. Also there's at least two US senators who owe me, and the stewards would like to retain their standing in US races."

"Christ almighty," Meris said. "Politics."

"I know," Jaguar agreed.

"Why do you need to do this?" Meris asked, pleading now.

"Honestly, I'm not sure. I just know I have to."

Meris grabbed at her hair, made a noise.

"Yeah," Jaguar said. "It's not easy being you right now."

Meris lowered her hands, spread them out, palm up. "I was actually thinking it's not easy being you. I mean, you seem to just do things—crazy things—and you can't even say why. That's how it works?"

"Sometimes," Jaguar admitted. "Was Alicia like that, too?"

"She was," Meris said. "Half an hour before a race, she'd insist on changing her set up. Then, when she won, it'd be because she insisted."

"Bit of an Adept. I know. Well, I'm not, but you'll find me even more difficult. So the sooner we start, the sooner we'll be done. And don't worry too much about my lack of experience. We're going to cheat."

Meris groaned, and stood. She took Jaguar and Rachel to the trailer where a VR track simulator was set up, complete with sensation of G forces, and the rumble in the butt drivers read the road with.

Jaguar looked it over and chewed on her lip. "Do we have to?" she asked.

"Yes," Meris said firmly. "If nothing else, maybe it'll change your mind."

"It won't," Jaguar said, "but you should know, I have a tendency to melt down this kind of equipment."

Meris turned to Rachel, seeking sanity. Rachel lifted her shoulders, let them fall. "She's right," she said. "She does that. It's got to do with her psi capacities."

Meris swiveled back to Jaguar. "On purpose?"

"Sometimes. Other times, it just happens."

"You're just a barrel of laughs, aren't you? Well, you have to anyway, so get in. And put a helmet on. I know—you're not going anywhere, but you need the feel of it."

Jaguar took one of Alicia's helmets and let Meris hook her up to all the monitors for input and output measurement. She was only halfway around the virtual track when lights started blinking, and the thing started shutting itself down. Meris swore with feeling.

"I warned you," Jaguar noted, taking off the helmet. "Let's try it my way. Is the Berlinetta here?"

"Out back. Why?"

"I'll take it around the track, with you next to me, and you can show me the corners and so on. Then we'll come back here and you'll drive the Ferrari, while I watch."

"The Berlinetta sounds good. That'll help some. But you can't learn by just watching."

"I watch better than most," she said. "Let's just start with the other car, and you'll see."

They did so, Meris talking her through the braking times and apex for each corner, letting her get a feel for which ones were fast and which ones were slow. She liked Parabolica, but found the tunnel disturbed her, the sudden shift to less light throwing her off, and the bend at the exit when she went back into the light giving her pause.

"You gotta come out fast," Meris told her each time they approached it. "This is a fast tunnel. You can't lift at all."

"So you say. I think the curves bug my eyes," she said. "I get the feeling I should be driving right up the side."

Meris grinned. "Theoretically, you could. Also go over the ceiling and come back down the other side. Not in this car, but in the Ferrari."

"I've heard that," Jaguar said. "You ever try it?"

"Not me. Alicia wanted to, but the team had a shit fit and for once, she let it go. But look—dammit, you're lifting. *Don't* lift."

By the tenth time through, she'd gotten that under control, and by the fifteenth, she'd cut five seconds off her track time, and was satisfied with her progress. They brought the Berlinetta in, and she told Meris, "Okay. Now you drive the Ferrari. I'll be watching."

"That still doesn't make sense to me," she said.

"Because you're not an empath," Jaguar noted.

Meris shied away. "Oh. You mean *that* way. Like Alicia. I'm not sure…"

"I am," Jaguar said, not feeling quite as certain as she sounded. She'd be using a particular kind of contact, intended to get Meris's moves into her on a visceral level, and she thought she could manage it without trouble, or at least, hoped she could. She'd be dealing with muscle memory, visual memory, nothing emotional about it, so perhaps it wouldn't disturb her equilibrium the way other kinds of contact did right now. Since Meris knew about it, she wouldn't have to make the effort of a surreptitious dive, nor would she have to share experience of her own, which was deadly right now.

"Are you sure this won't—like, mess me up?" Meris asked.

"Alicia taught you this way, didn't she?"

"A little," Meris admitted grudgingly.

"Did it mess you up?"

"No. It—it helped. But that was different. She was showing me, not eavesdropping."

"Even though you were reluctant to listen. You wanted to do it your way, not hers."

"How'd you know that? Never mind. Don't tell me. Just—how do we do this?"

"Like this," Jaguar said. She touched Meris lightly on the forehead, focused on entering this specific physical realm and staying there. It wasn't easy—nothing was these days—but she felt the hum and buzz of another consciousness flowing through her, and she nodded at Meris. "Go drive," she said.

Meris made an exit, and Jaguar took a seat in the garage. Rachel plunked down next to her and Jaguar turned to her.

"You're staying?"

"Yup," Rachel said.

"Okay. That's probably good. Listen, if I pass out, throw cold water on me. And don't let me throw up on anything expensive."

"You think you will?"

"I might. Like I said, empathic work's tough right now."

"Because of—"

"Yes," she said, "and we aren't going to talk about it."

Luna, sitting next to Rachel, rose to all fours, moved closer to Jaguar and plunked down at her side, resting her chin on Jaguar's foot. Jaguar looked down at her, noticing the warmth and solidity of her physical presence. Maybe, she thought, it would help. She turned her focus inward, and went to work.

When Meris got out on the track and started her warm-up lap, Jaguar was aware of every small muscle move in her hands, her back, her neck. But she was also aware of a voice inside her, chiding her. *You lift too soon. Brake too soon. Keep a smooth line and save the tires. Get more speed in that curve.*

Alicia's voice, instructing Meris, and Meris, contrary, not wanting to listen. Wanting to drive her own way. And yet, what Alicia said was correct and Meris knew it.

On her second lap, she did as Alicia instructed with less resistance. She wanted to earn it on her own, not steal it from her teammate. A silly, counterproductive notion, but Jaguar understood. Meris was as fiercely independent as Alicia, as herself. Only Alex had been able to teach her that it was okay to accept help, to work as a team. Alex, who might be anywhere. Alex, who might be alive or dead.

As his name crossed her mind she felt the image of him, stuck between places as Meris was, as she was. A painful constriction moved through her chest. She breathed it out, and moved her focus back to Meris, listening, staying open so what she heard would absorb into her own skin, her own muscles.

But it remained a struggle. She kept slipping out of herself, falling into a distant place where the sky was blue and the earth the color of gold. She smelled sagebrush under a hot sun, felt the throbbing of grief run through her.

Dammit, not now. Let me work. Let me finish this.

Ten laps. That was all she needed, and then if she could get in the car right away, if it didn't rain, if she didn't pass out from trying too much without the resources to support it. If, if if. Luna shifted her chin and Jaguar was once again aware of this creature pressing her into the ground, keeping her feet where they needed to be. She focused, letting new knowledge burn itself into her neurons.

When Meris pulled into pit lane, Jaguar raised her head, let the room come back into focus. Luna sat up and lapped at her hand, and she petted her absentmindedly. She turned to see Rachel staring at her.

"You okay?" she asked. "Need a bucket, or a cold towel or anything?"

"I'm good," Jaguar said. She flexed and clenched her hands, let feeling return to her. "My neck's a little sore, but I think that's from the drive."

"Huh," Rachel said. "Maybe Luna helped."

"Maybe she did," Jaguar agreed.

Meris entered the garage and looked from Rachel to Jaguar. "Well?" she asked.

"That worked fine," Jaguar said. She pushed herself to standing. "Now it's my turn."

"Oh, God," Meris said with feeling.

Jaguar suited up, using a race suit from the pit crew, and realizing she'd have to get one of her own if this was going to continue. She got in the car, allowed everything she'd absorbed to guide her hands and feet as she made her way around the track. She drove as in a dream, letting go of herself in order to feel what Alicia felt, what Meris felt, as they pushed their grounded rocket around curves, through tunnels, across the straight.

Her speed wasn't anywhere near what she wanted, but she'd gotten enough to understand how to use the car, and she was holding her line, the information she'd gleaned working its way into her body.

She made it back to the garage with the car in one piece, to Meris's great relief. That was all she could hope for her first time out.

With any luck, her skills would improve in time to do what she needed, whatever that might be.

CHAPTER SIXTEEN

Detective Thei called her early the next morning, asking for a report.

"I've got nothing," she told him. "You?"

"We're still waiting for lab reports from the ME. Once we have that, we'll know how, and that should lead us toward who."

"Usually it does," she agreed.

"If you're free for lunch, I'd like to meet with you and discuss some of the findings from the camera footage."

"Not today," she said. "I'm driving."

A long pause followed. "Pardon me?" he asked.

"Meris Grant is teaching me how to drive a Ferrari F1 car," she clarified.

"But—why?"

"As soon as I know that, I'll tell you," she said."

"Are you—do you have experience racing?"

"Not until this week."

"Then, driving an F1 car—that seems rather unsafe, Dr. Addams."

She laughed. "Welcome to my world. If you want, we can meet for dinner and talk about the camera footage then. And listen, you can call me Jaguar."

"May I? Then, Jaguar, I will treat you to La Serre. It is the best French restaurant in this city."

Her name sounded strange in his mild accent, softer and fuller, but not unpleasant. She agreed to the meeting, and when she signed off, she went to Rachel's room, got her and Luna, and proceeded to the track.

They were making their way to the river, about to cross the street when Luna put herself firmly in front of Jaguar and stood there, staring up at her.

"May I pass?" Jaguar asked, and put a hand on the dog's head. She pressed against Jaguar's leg and started to pant anxiously.

"Really," Jaguar said. "Let's go forward. It's that way." She pointed. Luna stood adamantly where she was. Jaguar moved to step around her, and Luna yelped and grabbed her by the pant leg. Startled, she stepped back. As she did, a car zoomed past, close enough to the curb that she knew if she'd taken another step, it would have hit her.

She looked to the car, trying to catch the license, but something heavy fell over her, something she'd never felt before.

It had no mass, but felt as if the weight of a mile of ocean rested on her. There was no substance, but it pressed her down harder than a mountain falling at her back. Surrounded by the sensation of compression, her vision faded, her legs grew weak beneath her. "Hecate," she said. "Not now."

She fell to her knees, heard Rachel's small cry of fear. Then she was bent forward, dry heaves wracking her body. She was vaguely aware of Luna's cool, wet nose pressing against her face, pushing at it again and again. She felt a hand on her shoulder. The weight of grief ran over her like a river, and she waited for it to pass.

Gradually the world righted itself and she saw Rachel next to her, a hand on her shoulder, Luna on her other side, nuzzling her ear. She leaned back on her heels, took in breath and let it out slowly, waited for her body to balance itself. She looked from Luna to Rachel.

"Okay," she said. "I'm good now." She tried to stand and failed. Rachel caught her arm, pulled her back to kneeling.

"What happened?" she asked.

"Nothing," Jaguar said. "I just—I lost track of my legs for a second."

"Lost track of your legs?"

"They went numb, okay? They're coming back now."

"Jesus Christ," Rachel muttered, rolling her eyes.

"It's *okay*. That car that almost ran me over—did you get the license plate?"

"No. I was watching you fall down."

"Xipe totec flay them. Did you hear anything?" She couldn't separate the strands between her own issues and what had happened, didn't know if what she felt was a result of her own condition right now, or something to do with Alicia. Any kind of confirmation in one direction or the other would be helpful, but she didn't get it.

"Hear anything? I heard a car. Lots of cars," Rachel said. "And I heard you making noises."

"Nothing else?"

"Really not. I was busy. Why?"

"I'm not sure. I'll figure it out later. We have to get to the track. We have work to do."

She pushed herself up successfully this time. Rachel stood with her. "Are you sure you're okay?" she demanded.

"I'm fine, Rachel. It was—the empathic thing. Listen, while I'm driving, I need you to do something for me. Detective Thei. I want you to track any involvement with Ron Schulman. Any at all, including if they peed in the same bathroom ten years ago."

"Oh. Really?"

"Really. I don't know if you'll find anything. I can't quite get a handle on him. But we should check, since I think someone just tried to kill me. Or Luna. Or both."

"What?"

"You heard me," Jaguar said. The light changed, and she grabbed Luna's leash and walked ahead fast. Rachel had all she could do to keep up.

* * * *

The driving went well that day, Jaguar increasing her time by a full second, and losing her reflex to brake in the tunnel. Meris shook her head at it, not believing it was possible. "It's some kind of voodoo thing, isn't it?" she asked Rachel.

"No. Planetoid Teachers have to keep in top shape, and they've got great reflexes. They go through driver training for high speed chases, all kinds of situations. And Jaguar's got quite a few tricks up her sleeve besides her glass knife."

"Her what?" Meris demanded.

"Never mind," Rachel said.

Everything she said was true, but when Jaguar brought the car in she looked absolutely played out. "Done for the day, almost," she said. She pointed to Luna, who lay by Rachel's side. "Take care of her tonight, okay?"

"What're you doing?" Rachel asked.

"Dinner with Detective Thei," she said, "at what he says is the best French restaurant in town."

Rachel frowned. "Dinner? Like, a date?"

Jaguar put her hands on her hips. "What?" she demanded.

"Nothing," Rachel said. "Just—nothing."

"I should hope not," Jaguar replied, and made her exit.

* * * *

The restaurant was as lovely as Detective Thei promised, softly lit with candles all around, and the kind of service that made itself ubiquitous and invisible. Jaguar enjoyed her escargot, her germiny l'oseil, and her duck breast in cherry port sauce.

While they ate and drank good wine, they spoke of nothing more consequential than the weather in Montreal compared to Planetoid weather. Jaguar asked where the best jazz joints were, and Detective Thei told her, then suggested she should go to Notre Dame cathedral for high mass, where the singing was the kind that lifted you up over the earth.

Jaguar recognized that he was handsome, and smart, and shared many good qualities with Alex. She also recognized that he'd arranged this dinner not just for business, but because he was attracted to her. She wondered at herself, that she didn't return the feeling. Unlike her to pass up such an opportunity when she was on her own, as she surely was now. She could chalk it up to grief, but that emotion sometimes inspired a yearning for comfort, which she certainly could get with him. And yet, here she was, her heart beating normally, her only concern how soon she could get back to her hotel room and climb into bed. That, she thought, was not a good sign for her personal life, though it might be a good thing for the investigation. Long ago, Alex had advised her not to eat her meat where she bought her bread.

Whether Detective Thei read her signals or was just not inclined to push, as soon as she'd disposed of her duck and ordered desert—three layered chocolate terrine—he shifted gears, going back to business.

"I've drawn up a list of possible ways to melt a heart," he told her as she brought a forkful of cake to her mouth.

"I take it you're not speaking metaphorically," she noted.

He smiled. "No. That is a different area of pursuit. For this, I mean Alicia's heart."

"Rachel's looking into that, too," she noted. "Let me see your list, and I'll compare them, let you know if hers has anything else on it."

He reached into the pocket of his jacket, pulled out a piece of paper and handed it to her. She lifted it with one hand and read, as she continued with her cake. "Nanoworms," she said. "That's a good one. But I thought the UN had them all destroyed."

"They said as much. There's still such a thing as terrorism."

"Sure," she said. "But Alicia's death wasn't about that."

"Of course not," he agreed. "However, if someone wanted to make it look that way, they would use this."

"And who, in our cast of characters, would have access?" she asked.

"Well, Meris Grant has a brother who works for the Pentagon," he said.

She put her fork down, stared at him. "That's interesting," she said.

"I thought so as well," he noted. "I am looking into it."

"Let me know what you find." She kept reading the list. "How about this one—Talaraze nerve gas?"

He shook his head. "It cannot be directed so closely. It would have melted other hearts as well. Specifically, anyone within a thousand yard range of its dispersal."

"Then no," she said. She put the paper down. "You're focusing on Meris, aren't you?"

He shrugged lightly. "She is one of a few people who profit by Alicia's death, and profit is the primary cause of murder."

Jaguar felt a pang of sorrow for Rachel, who would hurt the most if Detective Thei was correct about the nanoworms, then discarded it. What mattered above all else was solving the problem. Rachel would understand that. Nor would she want to continue messing with a woman who killed her teammate. Still, Jaguar doubted her culpability.

"She was surprised when she learned Alicia was dead. And dismayed," Jaguar said.

"You saw her?"

"My assistant did, and I trust her."

"Then perhaps she meant only to stop her from winning, and did not know her actions would kill her."

"That's possible. What about Didier? He wants her seat."

"I have considered him. I continue to do so. He has motive and opportunity, but not means. I do not think he is as bright as he would like to believe."

"That's for sure," she agreed. "Listen, there's something you need to know. When we were on our way to the track, a car tried to run me over. At least, I think it did."

His fork clattered against his plate and he raised a face that showed fear to her.

"Don't worry. I'm fine. Luna got me out of the way. It was a new looking black sedan, but I didn't get the license."

"Well, it's understandable. For safety's sake, let us theorize it was an attempt," he said. "What time did it occur?"

"About eleven fifteen. Can you check on Meris's whereabouts for then? And Didier's?"

"Yes. Of course," he said. "Your investigation—perhaps it troubles someone. In one sense that is good. In another—I do not want you to face unnecessary danger."

She shook her head. "If it was a grab, it's also possible they were after Luna," she said.

"The dog again. It is—growing strange."

Jaguar smiled. "Growing? I think it started that way, and it won't get less so. I just wish I could get at what Luna knows."

She was watching his reactions closely, and was surprised to see a microexpression she knew as satisfaction cross his face. But then, quickly, he knit his forehead into a frown, making her uncertain if she was reading it right.

"But she is a dog," he said. "Surely you can't…talk to them?"

"Surely I can, usually," she answered. "And given a few more days, I will. Right now, it's a little tricky…" she let the sentence trail to silence. He filled in the rest.

"You are having difficulty with your gifts. Perhaps because of what happened with Springer Todd."

She was a bit spooked that he'd parsed his way through all that persiflage to get to such a conclusion. She avoided the error of denying it. "What makes you go there?" she asked.

"I know it was an important case to you, in many ways. And I have already guessed that it is still causing you personal trouble, and interferes with what we face now."

She noted the plural noun, noted the way he kept his gaze sharply on her. "You think so? I'll give that some thought," she said, staying cool. "I do know Luna witnessed something, and someone believes I might be capable of getting that information from her. So they went after her. Or me. Or both. There's few people who fit that bill, and one of them already tried to get the dog away from me."

"You mean Didier?"

"No. I mean Ron Schulman, through Larry Engle. He's selling out to Schulman, and they are literally thick as thieves right now."

A small twitch at his jaw. Anger? Anxiety? She couldn't tell.

"You must leave that terrain to me," he said. "I am best placed to manage the politics around it."

"Sure," she said. "As long as you don't ignore it."

"You know I will not."

She wasn't sure she believed him, but she moved on. "Can you tell me if you heard anything unusual in the camera footage we sent you?"

"Heard?" he asked, and she saw all his interest perking up at the word.

"This is right. Heard."

He leaned away from her, and his eyes moved from left to right as he considered. "No," he said at last. "But you did?"

"Not sure," she said. "Nor do I trust myself to read it all correctly right now."

"You are cautious," he said. "That is unusual for you, but I'm glad of it. I will listen again, and let you know."

"I appreciate that," she said, meaning it. She'd been hungry for someone she could talk to, someone who understood and believed her.

"You're welcome," he said. "And now, would you do something for me?"

"If I can, I will."

"Say my name."

She blinked at him. "Detective Thei?" she asked.

He touched the back of her hand. "No. If I am to call you Jaguar, you must use my first name. Say it."

She smoothed her face. "Francois," she said, speaking the soft syllables.

He drew in breath, and his eyes sparked with pleasure. "Thank you," he said quietly. "Your voice gives music to the name." He moved his hand away from hers. "Now, when we speak, you can use it. I prefer that you do so."

When they left the restaurant, she allowed his kiss on her cheek, but she did not return it. Her heart was too far away to beat in passion at the touch of a handsome man.

* * * *

Rachel and Meris, left to their own devices, found food and a few ways to amuse themselves until Rachel said she had to go back to her hotel room. She had work to do.

By the time she got to work on looking for connections between Detective Thei and Ron Schulman, between Meris and Schulman, it was after nine. She found nothing except for a brief interview Detective Thei did with Schulman, in connection with Alicia's threatening emails. She was able to dig up the recording in old records, long since closed, and she heard nothing on it except what you'd expect.

However, she did find out that he had troubles of his own, in his deeper past. His father was murdered by his mother. That would raise a red flag for Jaguar, who paid close attention to the traumas people carried through their lives. For her part she wasn't sure if it had any significance. It happened during the Killing Times, when everyone was killing anyone, sometimes for no reason at all. Still, she put the information in the file, along with everything else.

For Meris, she found camera footage that put her in the GM garage last year, but it showed her talking to Alicia rather than Schulman. There was no audio on it, so she didn't know what they were talking about, but she supposed it had to do with Alicia bringing her on to the Ferrari team. At least, she sincerely hoped that was the case. With due diligence, she looked as hard as she could for any other connection, and was relieved to find none beyond the lunch they'd had, which she would continue to assume was an attempt to win her to GM.

When she was done, to soothe herself before she went to sleep, she made her daily check on Alex.

The horse ranch he'd gone to showed a photo of him dealing with a difficult horse. The time stamp was a few weeks old, but she knew they didn't change their website photos very often, so she was content that it indicated he was still there. He wasn't smiling, but he looked focused. It made her think of him and Jaguar, and it gave her more hope. At least it meant he was working, which was good. He was someone who could be saved by work, if the work was good.

A part of her wanted to call him. He was the only one she trusted to deal with Jaguar's most difficult aspects. She chewed on her lip and thought about it for a long time, and then decided to give it a few more days. After all, how bad could it get?

She closed up her computer, and got herself ready for sleep, changing into her pajamas, checking to see if anything good was on TV tonight. After all, she'd come here for vacation, and should be able to get at least an hour or two of down time.

She was just settled in to a cooking show, Luna sleeping on the floor at her side, when she heard a knock on her door. Groaning, she rose and went to the door, looked through the peephole. On the other side she saw nothing.

"Who is it?" she asked.

"Message from Doctor Addams," the voice said.

From within the room she heard a low growl, and looked over to the bed to see Luna standing now, at attention.

"It's okay," she told her. "Just more work." She opened the door, and in less than a second, realized that was a big mistake.

Hands wrapped around her throat, and she was shoved back into the room. She struggled against them, staring at a face masked with a stocking. Behind her, Luna began to bark wildly and then lunged, latching onto the arm that held her.

Her assailant yelped and released her, and she screamed as loud as she could, the way Jaguar always told her. Don't yell help, she'd instructed. People don't really want to help. Yell fire. Then they'll move.

"Fire!" she screeched. "Fire! Fire!"

Then, darkness, and an absence of sound.

She woke to the sensation of someone slapping a wet washcloth against her face, and opened her eyes to see Luna licking furiously at her face, Jaguar and a hotel security guard bent over her.

"Hey," Jaguar said. "You with us?"

Rachel sat up, patted Luna. "I think so," she said, not quite sure herself.

"Need a medic, miss?" The security guard asked.

"Don't know. What do you think? Did he shoot me?" Rachel asked.

"No," Jaguar said. "No blood. What happened?"

"I'm not sure. I think he just—you know, throttled me. Then he left."

The security stood. "I'll get the police," he said.

Jaguar grabbed his arm. "We are the police," she said, and showed him her Planetoid ID. She waited until his face showed the proper awe and appreciation, then nodded at him. "We're on a case. I can take it from here. You need confirmation from my boss?"

"No," he said. "I'm good. Just—I'd rather not have the guests disturbed."

"We'll do our best," she agreed. He left, and Jaguar helped Rachel to her feet, got her back into her room and sat her on the bed. "Sit, stay," she said, and went to the room phone, called in an order for whiskey and soda, then turned up the heat in the room.

"Jaguar, it's warm out," Rachel protested.

"Shock," Jaguar answered. She went to the bed and sat next to Rachel, touched her pulse, put the back of her hand to her cheek, gave a grunt of satisfaction. "Tell me what happened," she said.

Rachel shook her head. "Someone came to the door. Said they were here from you. Luna—she was growling, but I didn't pay attention. I should have, right?"

"Always trust the dog," Jaguar noted. "They smell everything. What happened next?"

"I opened the door, and he grabbed me by the throat, pushed me in the room. I couldn't—I couldn't do anything about it, but Luna attacked him and he backed off. Then I remembered what you said about screaming fire, so I did."

Jaguar considered her own hands, raised a pinched face to Rachel. "I shooed the guard away because he seemed like an impertinent asshole, but *do* you need a doctor?"

"No. I'm okay. Really."

Another knock on the door, and Rachel jumped, gave a small yelp.

"Sure you are," Jaguar said, and moved to the door, looked through the peephole, and opened it. A waiter offered a tray, which she took and brought into the room. "Maybe this'll help," she said, and poured a stiff glass of whiskey for Rachel, then one for herself.

When it was down, Jaguar ran her eyes over her friend. "You said he. You think it was a man?"

"I—I think so. Now that you ask, I'm not sure. He had a stocking over his face. Or she did. Whoever it was, they were strong."

"Drivers have to be. Male or female. Think about it, Rachel. Was there something that made you think it was a man?"

Rachel squeezed her eyes shut, then shook her head. "I don't know. Just someone strong. They muscled me right back in the room. If it wasn't for Luna…" She let the sentence trail to silence. Not something she wanted to think about.

"Do you mind if I take a look?" Jaguar asked.

Rachel knew what she meant. She waved a hand. "Go ahead."

Jaguar put two fingers lightly to Rachel's forehead, but in short order gave a small gasp and pulled away.

"What?" Rachel asked. "Something bad?"

Jaguar shook her head. "Nothing. I can't—just nothing. Hell. You know what? I'm getting Scott here."

"Jaguar, you don't have to. Not for me."

"Are you nuts? Of course I do. And it's not just you if that makes you feel any better. Luna's also in danger."

"What?"

"I'll lay any odds you want that whoever did this wanted to take the dog," she said.

"But—why?"

"Because she *saw* something, and they think I can get it out of her."

"Well, can't you?"

Jaguar, her cellcom already open, glowered. "Let's not talk about that." She punched in numbers, and got a sleepy looking Junius on the other end.

"It's 5 am here," he said.

"It's about midnight here," she replied.

"Yeah. Do you ever call during regular hours?" he asked.

"I called you twice during your work hours," she said. "I need Scott. Pronto. Can you do it?"

"Yeah," he said. "On the way."

"Don't you want to know why?"

"I want sleep," he said drowsily. "Sleep, sleep, sleep."

"When will he be here?"

"I'll set it up now. You figure out the timing." He signed off, and so did she.

She stretched, looked around. "Nice room," she said. "I'll take the bed near the door."

"Are you staying?"

"Bet your ass," she said.

"You don't have to," Rachel started, but Jaguar cut in.

"I'm sticking like glue," she answered, and that was that.

* * * *

While Rachel slept, Jaguar considered her options. She had to call Detective Thei and report the most recent incidents, and she should check on Didier, see what he'd been up to this evening. And there was one more person she had to see. Time to start calling the shots, instead of waiting for them to graze her flesh. But she couldn't do any of this until Scott arrived, so she continued with what she was used to doing. She waited.

Over the next few hours Rachel dozed, waking occasionally with a gasp, then seeing Jaguar or Luna watching her, and subsiding back into sleep. When she woke for real the room was lighter and Jaguar sat on the couch, turning the pages of a magazine.

"Anything good?" Rachel asked.

"Some really fine shoes," she noted. "Not much else."

"Oh, hey. I meant to tell you, I made that list for you. Of things that can melt people? It's on my notepad, along with some stuff about Meris and Detective Thei."

Jaguar went to the desk, opened the file and looked it over. The first thing she saw was about Detective Thei. "His *mother* killed his father?" was the first thing she said.

"I figured you'd pick up on that."

"It does make me go hmm," she agreed. "He mentioned that his father was murdered for being an empath, but he didn't say his mother did the killing. More hmm."

She put that information aside, and moved on to the list of ways to melt a heart. After a while, she picked her head up, stared past Rachel. "Sound," she said.

"What?" Rachel asked.

Jaguar turned to her. "You didn't hear anything during Alicia's crash, did you? From the video?"

"You asked me then, and I told you I didn't."

"But I did," she murmured. "And Detective Thei didn't. Nor was this on his list."

"You got something?" Rachel asked.

"Maybe. Let me worry about it. Get some more sleep if you can."

As Rachel subsided back into a doze Jaguar tossed the list aside and went back to her magazine, though her eyes rested on the page merely as a place to put them. She trailed her own errant thoughts until a knock on the door interrupted them, and woke Rachel. Jaguar stood and peered out the peephole, opening the door to admit Scott.

"Good to see you," she said. "Come in."

He entered, nodded courteously at Rachel. She wiggled her fingers at him in return. Jaguar grabbed her room key from the bureau.

"Now that you're here, your job is to make sure nobody, and I mean nobody, gets to Rachel or Luna," she told him. "I've got an errand, but it shouldn't take long."

As she moved to the door, Scott stepped in front of her. "Your destination, ma'am?" he asked politely.

She grinned. "Two five five Rue St. Paul."

"Purpose?"

"Rip a new one for an old acquaintance."

"Jaguar, no," Rachel said imperatively.

Scott glanced at her, then brought his gaze back to Jaguar. He stared at her a moment, then spoke. "Would that be Ron Schulman?"

Of course he'd know Ron was in town. Know that his presence was what brought her here, and kept her here. He was a young man who did his homework. "It would," she said.

"Oh, God," Rachel said. "Scott, go with her."

"Nope," Jaguar said. "Your job is here, and you accepted it."

Scott made a move toward her but she raised a hand, held his eyes with hers, and he stood very still, listening.

"Got it?" she asked.

"Yes, ma'am," he said.

She lowered her hand, turned away from him and left the room.

CHAPTER SEVENTEEN

The narrow, cobbled streets of Rue St. Paul were busy with tourists, all shops open. She made her way down them, not stopping to look in any windows until she got to her destination, a square brick building, unassuming and anonymous. She stood at the glass door, saw the door-man on the other side, lifted a shoulder and let it fall. Everything she was about to do was something she'd been taught not to do. But because she'd been taught well, that meant she knew exactly how to carry it out.

She smiled at the man, gestured to the door, her demeanor suggesting an invitation to be friendly. His stern look dissipated and he smiled, opened the door a crack.

"Looking for someone?" he asked politely.

"Ron Schulman," she replied.

"Not available," he replied.

"Sorry," she said quietly, and put a hand on his shoulder, entered him empathically and found the room she was looking for. Then, in a swift move that hurt her more than it hurt him, she suggested he would be glad to let her enter the building. He swung the door open wide, stepped away, and she breezed past him, heading to the elevator.

She rode to the top floor—of course it was the top floor—exited and stood in a lobby. There were two doors. One was glass and showed a receptionist seated at a desk, taking calls. The other was oak, finely carved. She chose that one, put her hand on the elaborate hook knobs, shaped like dragon heads. Locked.

"Okay," she said, and focused, another painful moment of work she was not quite up to. Usually, locks were easy for her, but this was old fashioned, and working it gave her an immediate headache. But she felt it give, lifted the handle, and entered the room, closing the door behind her.

She stood inside a finely appointed office. A large mahogany desk, a good persian rug on the wood floors. There were no windows, but he wouldn't want windows, and the expensive lighting mimicked sunlight well enough that he didn't need them.

Ron Schulman sat at the desk, looking unchanged from the last time she'd seen him. His personally tailored grey suit was well pressed, his short cropped grey hair thick as it had been, his angular face carrying no new wrinkles. He was fit and trim, which made him look younger than his sixty some years.

He was on his telecom, speaking in clipped tones, and he kept talking, but he turned his bright blue eyes her way. "The contract stands," he said. "Tell them they're fools if they think they can get out of it."

She moved to his desk, leaned over and pressed a key on his computer, ending the call.

He leaned back in his chair, stared up at her.

"It sounded like you were done," she noted.

"I was," he agreed.

She got in a chair and leaned back, lounging. "How's it hanging, Ron?" she asked. "Probably a little lower since you got your daughter killed, but I hear there's good meds for that."

He folded his hands on his desk. "I'm not sure how you got in, but there's a security detail nearby, ready to walk you out."

"If you didn't want me here, they'd already be in the room," she said. "So I'm guessing you wouldn't mind having a word or two with me."

"What do you imagine I'd want to talk to you about?"

"The weather? Politics and religion? Or how about sports? Racing, for instance. I hear a really fine driver bought it this weekend."

"Yes," he said. "A tragic accident."

"You're good with tragedy. Also good with sound. And infrasound killed Alicia."

He shifted in his seat. "That's what the ME says?" he asked.

"Not yet. Right now it's what I say. I know how, and that means I know who."

"Whoever it is, I hope they catch them."

"Of course you do, because you had someone else do your dirty work for you—as usual. Now that we've covered the amenities, tell me how you plan to get rid of me."

"Dr. Addams, I don't engage in violence," he said.

"Did I say anything about violence? I did not. Must be on your mind. Maybe I just meant get me off the investigation, or get me the hell out of Montreal. Ron, tell me honestly, am I the only woman who can make you blink?"

He showed a brief scowl, and buried it in cordial laughter. "I'll admit you're a real pain, but I have lawyers to manage things like harassment. It's not something I'd worry about personally."

"Your lawyers don't hire out for assassination, do they?"

"That's just your paranoia speaking. The same paranoia you expressed after you got my grandson killed."

"Oh, Ron," she said. "Is that supposed to hurt me? Sorry, but it doesn't even pinch. So you're saying if I die, it'll be mischance rather than murder. Like Alicia. But you know how many assholes tried and failed with me. You want to join the list?"

He glanced down at his hands. She chuckled softly. "Two blinks in one day. I'm doing just fine."

He lifted his face to her. "How's Alex these days?" he asked. "Or isn't he with you on this assignment?"

She knew the name would come up, and she thought she'd prepared herself for it, but she hadn't expected dizziness to wash through her, hadn't expected the room to spin. She pressed her lips together, breathed in deeply, hoping she didn't look as bad as she felt.

He regarded her with satisfaction. "Dr. Addams, you're not well. Something serious?"

The dizziness passed, the room righted itself, and she pushed on. "I'm not as sick as you. Then again, sick is normal for you, isn't it? Unless you think it's normal for a father to try and sire a child on his own daughter."

"Really," he said, "if you persist in this kind of talk, I'll have to have you removed."

"No you won't," she said. "I'm not staying that long. I just came to let you know a few things."

"Go ahead," he invited.

"It's simple, really. I know you arranged to have Alicia killed, and I'm here to get you for it," she said.

Ron lifted a hand, held it palm up for a moment, then let it drop to the desk. "That's the kind of slander my lawyers deal with," he said. "Anything else?"

"One more thing. If you go after me or Luna or any of my other friends again you won't live to regret it."

"Do you mean Alex? I haven't gone after him. Though really, it would be a kindness to put him out of his misery, don't you think?"

She fought off a rising nausea, only because her anger was stronger. "Try it," she said. "You might get me, but you won't get him because he's covered."

"Don't bluff me," he said.

She reached over, put a hand on his wrist, and opened just enough to let him stand witness to her position, and what it meant. He was a telepath rather than an empath, lacking skill for the task, but he paid attention to this because it touched his interests. She had to work hard not to disturb forces she wanted kept in place, and she'd pay for it later with her own pain, but it was worth it, because one more time, Ron Schulman blinked.

Everything she'd shown him was beyond his measure. He couldn't account for it, couldn't manage it, couldn't field it.

She pulled her hand away. "Fair warning," she said softly. "You won a skirmish. Now it's game time." She stood, straightened herself, and left the room.

When she was gone, Ron stared at his wrist, rubbed it hard. "Fuck you," he muttered. "I always win."

Then he shook it off, and got on with his day.

CHAPTER EIGHTEEN

Home Planet, New Mexico

Alex spent the next few days with Maya, or working around the place at Jake's instruction. He weeded, picked beans, held tools for Johnny while he fixed the tractor, fed chickens and gathered eggs for One Bird. The sun and the scent of sage seeped into him as he worked. Under its influence the darkness surrounding him began to lift, leaving him with the sensation of light poured into him, which he found disturbing.

He tried to call back the darkness, reluctant to relinquish his comfortable shroud. In spite of his will, it continued to dissipate. It wasn't who he was. It was just something that happened to him.

One afternoon, Jake found him while he was helping a family repair part of their adobe home. "Go with Johnny," he said. "He's gonna dig manure over at Sam White's and needs some help."

"Sure," Alex said. Digging shit was about what he felt up to. He lifted himself into Johnny's beat up old pickup and they rattled down the bumpy road.

They weren't far down when they hit washboard, which rattled the car vigorously as Johnny worked to control the skittery wheels. They raised dust, driving in a cloud of it, and that explained why neither of them saw the doe until it was too late. Or maybe it was that she leapt at the truck, flinging herself at them as if she meant to die.

"Holy shit," Johnny said, and tried to veer away, but it was way too late. The deer crashed against the grill with a heavy thud. Johnny braked, threw the truck in park, and sat still.

"That's not good," he noted.

"Let's go see," Alex suggested.

They got out of the truck and Alex knelt by the doe, whose eyes were wide with the terror of impending death. He thought of his son. He'd seen nothing like this in his eyes. Springer had no fear, only a wild release, an even wilder triumph Alex still didn't understand. As he'd done with his son, he bent to the doe, and breathed in her last breath.

Right behind him, Johnny muttered something in Hopi, words Alex didn't understand though he sensed approval. The doe kicked her legs out, stretched her neck back, and ceased breathing. Alex stayed where he was, silent, aware of yet another death he'd caused. Johnny knelt and smoothed his hands over the doe's flank.

"She's pregnant," he said quietly. "She's got a fawn in her, still alive. I felt it kick."

"You got a knife?" Alex asked.

"Yeah. Why?"

"Give it to me."

Johnny went to the truck and came back with a good size Bowie knife. Alex took it, hefted it, considered what he was about to do. He leaned over the belly of the doe, found a good spot to begin and pushed the knife into her flesh, slit her belly open.

"You know anything about deer anatomy?" he asked Johnny.

"Can't be that different than horses. Look. There's the uterus. Just keep going.

Alex put his hand on the slick surface of it, felt the motion within it, and made another slit. He dropped the knife, submerged his hands in blood and groped around until he found something hard and long, maybe a leg. He grabbed it and pulled.

The creature poured out like water in a wake of blood. A fawn, male, perfectly still. Alex pressed it against his chest. "Cut the cord," he said to Johnny, who did so.

Alex held his burden close, leaned down and breathed onto its face, willing it to live. The fawn kicked, its eyes open in the same terror his mother had just shown. Life and death, the change points, always terrifying. But unlike his mother, he clamored to his feet and stood, shivering. His chest heaved in and out, and the two men breathed with him, welcoming him to this strange and difficult world. Alex felt the first moment of pure satisfaction he'd had in a long time.

Johnny slapped him hard on the back. "Good work, man," he said. "Now what the hell do we do?"

"Let's bring him back to the village. Maybe Jake'll have an idea."

"He usually does. Help me put the doe in the truck. I don't like leaving her here."

By the time they got the dead body of the doe into the back of the truck and the fawn into the front they were both well covered with slime and blood. They drove carefully to the village and parked near Jake and One Bird's house. Both of them, with Maya in tow, showed up as soon as Alex was out of the truck.

Maya oohed and aahed over the fawn, and One Bird beamed at her, then turned her shining eyes to Alex and Johnny. "Good men," she said.

"Yeah," Johnny said. "Now what?"

"We need a doe whose fawn didn't live. She'll take in this one," One Bird said.

Maya closed her eyes, opened them again. "There's one near the arroyo. A doe had twins, and one died. She'll take him."

Jake scowled at her. "You aren't supposed to travel."

"I didn't," she said, petulant as Jaguar could ever be. "I just *saw* it."

Alex touched her shoulder. "We'll bring him there. I'll go with you."

Jake turned an angry face his way. "No. You got something else to do." He turned to One Bird. "Leave the doe here. You take the fawn."

"Sure," she said. "Johnny, you drive us." She moved to Maya, and the three of them herded the fawn forward, dragging the body of the doe out of the truck, leaving Alex alone with Jake.

"So," Alex said when they'd gone. "What am I doing?"

Jake eyed him. "Take her to the mesas. The place you and Jaguar went. Gut her there."

Alex frowned. "That's a long way up to carry her."

"You look pretty strong."

"If you want the meat, shouldn't I take care of her here?"

"It's not for me," Jake said. "It's for Old Man Coyote. That, and an offering from you."

Alex sensed something beyond his discipline. Coyote was Springer's animal guide. "Okay," he said. "Sage? Tobacco?"

"No," Jake answered. "She gave you a life. You have to give her something just as precious."

"I've got nothing on me."

"You got something in you. Your son's death. And it's time to let it go or move on. The deer says so."

Alex stiffened. Jake was telling him to release the last connection he had with his son's spirit, because a doe had thrown itself at the truck he was riding in. In any other worldview, that would be a non sequitur, but Alex understood, and a shiver of apprehension moved through him.

He faced the old man squarely. "What if I can't?"

"You know the answer to that," Jake said. His face was held closely in pain and in hope, that cruel mistress.

Alex, the Adept, knew when time had caught up with him. He dragged the doe to Jake's truck, threw it in the back and drove away.

* * * *

Carrying the dead carcass of a doe up a mesa was a slow, messy, and laborious task. He'd found a tarp to wrap her in, but she was slippery with blood, and he had to stop and adjust his burden repeatedly. Then he had to stop and drink water. Then he had to adjust it all again. By the time he crested the flat surface of the top, the sun was a bowl of red at the rim of the horizon, the sky in the east already dark and star studded. He didn't have much light left.

He put the doe down on the sandy surface of the mesa, unwrapped it from the tarp and and ran a hand over her back. She was a creature of grace and strength whose spirit ran in his blood as his son's did. He thought of his own animal guide, the wolf, who also ate this flesh. He got out a knife, and began his work.

He slit her belly open above the uterus, plunged his hands into the still warm interior and pulled out entrails, stomach, organs, and scattered them around, ignoring the sharp and brittle stench. Let Old Man Coyote and all his little brothers feast tonight. They'd find their way to this. Carefully, he removed the skin, cleaned the meat from the bones and tossed it after the guts and organs.When he was done her bones were revealed and he admired the shape of the skull, the graceful make of the creature in skeletal form.

"A beautiful one came into my hands," he murmured. At first he wasn't sure where the phrase came from, then he remembered it was a chant Jaguar taught him, said at the birth of a child. The thought made him wince. He moved away from the beautiful bones.

He found sagebrush nearby and pulled off a long stem, got a lighter from his pocket and lit it, sent fragrant smoke over the flesh and bones, chanting a blessing for cleansing and release he'd also learned from Jaguar. When he was done, he poured water from his bottle on the burning sage, dropped the crumbly remains over the remains of the doe.

He looked around. The sun was gone, the sky a deep indigo fading to black. The moon was rising, a thin crescent of light. In the distance, he heard howling.

"Old man Coyote," he said. "This is for you, and your little ones."

At his words, they went still. They were waiting on his choice. If he chose one way, they'd feast on deer. If he chose another, they'd also feast on him. And Jake was right. Either way, what he kept of his son would leave him. He could no longer hold onto him. He peered out into the infinite night. Cool air brushed against his face.

On this mesa he'd held Jaguar's body as the greatest blessing he'd ever known. Here, he'd taken her knife in his chest to save her. What more could a man ask for in one lifetime? What more could a man do? His work was finished, as far as he could tell.

He walked across the flat surface, not deciding, just moving. One step after another he went until he stood at the rim of the mesa, the rim of his life. He took a deep breath and prepared to move on. When he lifted his foot, he hit a wall.

He stared down at his feet, tried again and still couldn't move. Something warm and demanding as fire blocked his way. He stopped, straightened his back and lifted his head. What he saw stole his breath, stopped any action he might take. The Nahauk stood between him and death, visible for the first time.

She was made only of light, and that light a piercing energy. She was familiar as old dreams and new as epiphany. Something he'd never seen before and something he knew existed from the beginning of time. Pure as new water, fierce and wild as fire, and complete as the fullness of the moon, she poured herself over him unstinting, a washing of light that left him skinless in the howling wind. There was nothing but her. Nothing mattered beyond or before her.

This is the face of love, he thought, and she's looking at me.

Where are you going? she asked, without judgment, only seeking information.

"There," he answered, gesturing beyond the mesa, toward the infinite blue.

She turned her attention that way, then back to him. *I go with you,* she said.

"No," he said. Nothing this beautiful could leave the world because of him.

My choice. You make yours.

And he understood. That's what love did. He'd made the same decision for Jaguar, in a different hour. But he'd chosen that end with full knowledge, and he wasn't doing so now. The Nahauk asked him only to consider all he moved toward, and why. Asked him to understand all he left behind, all he would drag with him.

He hesitated, afraid of making any move for the wrong reasons. The Nahauk explored him, concerned only for his well-being, wanting only to help. She was thoughtful, seeking the right direction.

What do you want? she asked.

The question was a slice out of his heart. What he wanted, he couldn't have. To undo the past. Make his son live again, be with Jaguar, their life and work an ocean of wonder, thick with passion and joy. But even this creature couldn't make that so.

"I want to do what's right," he whispered hoarsely.

The Nahauk breathed against his skin.

You must do what love requires, she said. *Only that. Nothing more.*

The phrase swept through him like an act of God. He must do what love required. Only that. Only that? He raised his face to the face of love and called it.

This way, he told her. *I'm going this way.*

He jerked himself away from the edge of the mesa and strode toward the carcass of the doe. He stood staring down at it. This, he thought, is going to hurt like hell.

He knelt by her skull, pressed his lips against the cool bones that still carried flesh and blood, preparing to release the burden of his son and the continued penance that went with carrying him, as if that served either of them well. But it wouldn't, because it didn't move them toward love. Only relinquishment would. He let breath leave him like heavily burdened water.

Past error and future possibility drifted away. Pain opened in his chest. The world grew dim and spun around him in an ecstasy of stars and darkness and grief. He fell back on his haunches, raised his knees, put his elbows on them and buried his face in his hands.

"Aah, God," he moaned, and felt the wetness of his face. He was crying. When did that start? Sobs wracked his chest and he let them. There was no reason to still them. He wept as he hadn't since he was a boy and his first dog died, hit by a car while chasing a ball he'd thrown into the street. That ancient guilt pounded him, joined by the pain he'd felt when Springer's mother rejected him because he was an empath, the more excruciating pain of Springer's death, the unbearable pain of turning away from Jaguar.

Grief roared over him like a reckless tsunami, dragging him out to deep oceans where he could no longer tell water from sky. He realized how hard he'd been running only now that he was still. The spirits of the mesa—coyote, wind and stone—drank his pain as if they'd waited only for his raging tears to sustain them. He felt their satisfaction, and surrendered to it.

It was only grief, after all. He'd had an immeasurable loss, and he grieved it. Why had he fought it so hard? Old pain, new pain, coursed through and out of him. The smell of rank flesh and recently burned sage entered him. The sky grew thick with stars that spun in the music of a wild universe, well beyond his ken.

He was lifted into their dance and he grew silent, emptied of tears and noise, carried through light and dark, rounding out the edges of time and stars and heart until he returned to who he was, his own body, his own soul, alone.

CHAPTER NINETEEN

Home Planet, Montreal

When Jaguar left Ron's office, she went in search of Detective Thei. At the cop shop, they told her he wasn't on shift for another two hours. "I need to talk to him now," she said. "Where's he live?"

"We do not give that information," a secretary told her, keeping her English precise.

"But you know, don't you?" Jaguar asked.

The woman's face moved in conflict, and Jaguar did a quick dip into her thoughts, easily pulling out what she needed to know. "Never mind," she said. "I understand."

She left the cop shop and made her way down the block, cut across Rue St. Jacques, where she took a left and looked for the number she wanted. She scanned the names on the mailboxes, found Thei, and pushed the buzzer for his apartment.

Soon, his voice spoke to her. "Qui est?" it asked.

"Jaguar," she said.

A momentary pause, and then, "Entrez." The buzzer sounded, she opened the door, and ascended to his apartment, on the fourth floor.

He was waiting for her at the door, dressed in sweats and a t-shirt. "I am sorry," he said, as he ushered her in. "I run before I go to work. I have not yet changed."

"No problem," she said, going inside, hearing the door close behind her. He smelled of fresh air and sweat, reminding her of times she'd shown up to find Alex just back from his daily run. The thought gave her a jolt, particularly after her conversation with Ron. Unexpectedly, she was caught in a reeling of stars cupped in a velvet dark sky, and she smelled the scent of the mesa lands, her nostrils filled with recently shed blood, newly cut flesh. She stood still, recovering herself.

"Jaguar," Detective Thei said. "Again?"

She was aware that she was once more white as a ghost. "Sorry," she said. "Can I use your bathroom?"

"Down the hall, to the left."

She stumbled toward it, closed the door hard behind her and ran water, hoping to cover the sound if she retched. She put her hand under the water and breathed in and out slowly, making herself look at everything in the room. Toothbrush, toothpaste, lemon scented soap, purple towels, a hairbrush. She put her hand to the brush, felt its wooden handle solid and smooth beneath her hand. The room stopped buzzing, her vision, her stomach, and her legs stayed steady. She took a few more deep breaths and opened the door, going back into the living room.

When she did, Detective Thei wasn't in evidence, and she heard kitchen sounds nearby. Sounds, and scent. Coffee? Bacon? Could it be bacon?

She stayed where she was, and he appeared, bearing a tray holding a plate of scrambled eggs, bacon and toast, and a cup of coffee. He put the tray on the coffee table in front of the couch. "Sit," he said. "Eat."

She did so. He sat in a chair across from her, watching silently. When she'd had a few forkfuls of eggs, some toast and a slice of bacon, he seemed satisfied.

"Thank you," she said. "I appreciate your patience with my—my oddities."

"Oddities? That is not the word I would choose. What is it you do that steals your strength?" he asked. "Was I right in thinking it has to do with Springer Todd?"

She lifted the coffee cup, took a sip. "Not something I can talk about," she said.

"But if it's part of this case, you must talk," he said. "We have an agreement, yes?"

"We do," she agreed. "What's going on with me is—it's unrelated."

"No. It has to do with Springer Todd, and that has to do with Ron Schulman," he insisted. "Springer was killed by your Supervisor, who left soon after. And he was a man you—you felt strongly for."

She lifted a hand as if to ward off a blow. "Don't," she said sharply. He was silent, regarding her with compassion. She wasn't up to fielding compassion right now. It would crumble her. She straightened her spine. "It's not something I talk about," she said.

"It is six months since that case, yes?" he asked. "How long will you mourn him?"

She didn't ask if he meant Alex or Springer. She thought she already knew. "As long as it takes to finish the job," she said.

"The job? Getting revenge on Ron Schulman for your loss? If that's what you are here for…"

"It's not revenge," she said. "Believe me, if we find out Schulman's connected to Alicia's death, I'll dance on his indictment papers. But right now, I only want to know who killed Alicia."

He crossed his arms at his chest and studied her. "But you carry that case like a cross. And not just for your supervisor. For the prisoner as well. Why? The young man—he killed many innocent people, and then his own mother."

"It's more complicated than that," she said. "The killing spree was staged by someone else. Killing his mother—more of the same."

Detective Thei's brow knitted down. "You know this, or would like to believe it?"

"I know," she said. "There's nothing I can do about it, so yes, it troubles me. But I'm only here to deal with Alicia's death. I don't want her killer to get away with it. Do you?"

He let his arms drop to his side, held out a hand, appealing to her. "You know I don't. But if you are sick and cannot work, who will help me?"

She shrugged. "I suppose you've got a point."

"You suppose correctly. Isn't it folly to continue doing what brings you harm, and interferes with your work? Perhaps you should leave off mourning and go forward with your life, in easier ways. Wouldn't anyone who cares about you want that?"

She folded her hands in her lap and stared down at them. He was offering her something. Himself as a lover? Yes. But even more, he offered respite, telling her to let go of her bitter waiting and search for justice in a case that might never be resolved. Saying she should let go of her empathic gifts and live. Simply live, and live simply. The notion was tempting. How long had it been since she felt the pleasure of her body? Any pleasure at all? Anything beyond emptiness alternating with the heaviness of sorrow. But the weight of the dead, the weight of the living, was heavier than her sorrow.

"I have to finish this," she whispered, more to herself than to him, though he heard.

He put a hand on hers. "Alicia said the same to me, and now, she is dead," he answered.

She lifted her head, saw the anger contained in the muscles of his jaw. His hand on hers was soft and warm, an encompassing comfort from someone who understood sorrow from raw experience. She couldn't accept it, nor could she reassure him of her safety, if that's what he was worried about. In fact, she could only make it worse for him, and she did so.

She pulled her hand away from his and spoke briskly. "I understand the risks better than you do," she told him, and filled him in on the incident with Rachel.

"You should have called me immediately," he scolded when she was done. "It is dangerous to keep such information hidden."

"Is that what Alicia did?" she asked. "Didn't let you know her danger had increased?"

"Did she say as much to you?"

"No. I—inferred it."

"Yes. Of course. You have skills."

"So did she," Jaguar said. "Makes me wonder why you chose her, given how you feel about the empathic arts. Unless, maybe it's a hobby of yours, fixing empath women. Something to do with your father's death, perhaps. But no—the woman who killed him wasn't an empath, was she?"

"Don't insult me," he replied crisply. "My mother killed him, as I'm sure you well know. And that has nothing to do with what Alicia and I shared."

"Then tell me what you did share."

He shook his head, a small movement, then brought his gaze to hers. "I will, only because you may have something to learn from it, about holding on, and letting go."

He leaned back, looked away, as if viewing a different time and place. "Last year, during the race, she came to us with the threatening emails. I spent a great deal of time interviewing her. She was so beautiful, and so alone. It seemed she wanted someone she could trust, and so we had dinner." He lifted a hand, let it fall. "We were congenial. Good together. We proceeded from there."

"Was it still going on this year?"

"We saw each other when we could. The pleasure we had together was not enough to compel either of us to leave off our lives, but we continued to enjoy what was possible. Do you see what I mean, Jaguar? She was beautiful and passionate, and I was honored that she chose to spend some of her days with me. It did not need to be more than that."

"And you're suggesting I should learn to do the same."

"I suggest your health might improve if you did so. But no matter what you choose, I will not have you disregard your own safety as Alicia did. You'll have police protection from here on in."

"Not necessary," she said. "I called in security from the Planetoid."

"What security?"

"The best. Believe me when I say we're even better at it than you are. We have to be. As for the rest, I'm doing what I must." She stood, gave him a smile. "I'd better be on my way," she said. "Thank you again for your hospitality."

She moved to the door, but he was also on his feet, and standing in front of her. Then his hand was on her shoulder. She startled, raised her head to stare at him.

"Jaguar, must you waste your days in grief, when there is so much pleasure waiting for you beyond it?" he asked quietly.

She didn't try for empathic contact. She didn't have to. The flash in his forest shaded eyes, the grip of his hand, told her all she needed to know. "Aren't you grieving for Alicia at all?" she asked.

"What we had, it was complete," he said. "I'm saddened because she should have had the fullness of her life, but I do not waste my heart in pain."

She was cool as a winter morning when she answered. "If you can say that, you've never known love. There's no waste in matters of the heart, Detective Thei. I mean, Francois."

A flash of sorrow crossed his eyes, and he released her. She made her way past him, and out the door.

She was not far from his apartment when she realized two things. First, she'd never told him about her meeting with Ron Schulman that morning. Second, she'd taken his hairbrush, and she had no idea why.

* * * *

Rachel answered the door immediately when Jaguar knocked, and she entered the hotel room to find Scott standing at her side, his hand on his weapon.

"Glad one of you stays alert," she said. "Rachel, you're supposed to be careful."

"I knew it was you," she said. "I know your knock. What happened?"

"Nothing," she said.

"Jaguar," Rachel protested.

"Nothing happened," she repeated, and rubbed at her forehead. The headache was only getting worse. She'd done too much, and she'd pay for it.

"Then why did you go?" Rachel demanded.

"To goad him," she answered.

Rachel gestured toward Scott. "You see? It's what I said. All this time, she's been doing that. She let it out that we were Planetoid, made sure everyone knew it, just to lure him here. And now she's trying to get him to kill her."

"Ma'am?" Scott asked. "Is that what you're doing?"

Jaguar lowered her hand from her head, felt a spike in pain. She turned in the small space, went into the bathroom. "Do you have aspirin?" she demanded. "I need aspirin."

She found nothing on the sink, and whirled back toward the door, only to find herself face to face with Scott, who regarded her with careful eyes.

"Dr. Addams," he said quietly. "It would be helpful if you let me know your plans."

She threw her hands up in the air, then dropped them to her side. He was a former SEAL, the world expert on teamwork. And he was right. A team member should know all aspects of a program. None of them could get the job done alone.

"Yes, I came her hoping to lure him my way. And yes, I told him I'm after him for Alicia's death. Do I want him to try and kill me? Only if it works. If not, events will occur. At least, I hope they will, because this is the best shot I've got at him."

Scott took this in, gave a short nod. "Yes, ma'am," he said.

She stood and tilted her head at him. "Scott, do you by any chance speak French?"

"French, Mandarin, Urdu and Farsi. What do you need?"

"I should've guessed. How would you translate this phrase—agneau sacrifice."

He worked his face around this. "Ma'am, I'm not sure about that pronunciation."

"I haven't got the nose for French. Let's try it this way." She lifted a hand and made telepathic contact, letting him hear what she'd heard that first time she'd seen Didier and Detective Thei talking. *Agneau sacrifice. Donner du fil e retrordre.*

Scott chewed on his lip a moment. "In English idiom, I think it means I'll give you away. Sacrifice you. Throw you under the bus. Twist the threads my way."

"Huh," Jaguar said. "That's interesting."

"What?" Rachel demanded. "What's interesting about it?"

"I'll let you know after I think about it," she said. "Right now I'm going to the track to drive. I'll pick up aspirin on the way."

"Ma'am," Scott said politely. "I'll be going with you."

Of course he would. Now that he knew, he'd be on her as much as the job allowed.

"Rachel, bring the dog. We'll all go together," she said.

* * * *

The aspirin helped, and by the time they got to the track she was ready to drive. Scott kept himself in the background just outside the paddock, a skill he was particularly good at, while she geared up in her own race suit, recently purchased at what she considered an exorbitant price. Before she got in the car, she turned to Meris.

"Tell me about Alicia and Francois," she said.

Meris blinked at her, surprised. "What?" she asked.

"Alicia and Detective Thei. They had a thing, right? Last year? Was it still going on?"

Meris shifted, looked uncomfortable."How would I know?"

"Because you don't miss much. So tell me."

"They had a thing," she admitted. "I think it was all fine, but that night we had dinner with you, he showed up and she wasn't happy to see him. She told me it was over."

"Say more," Jaguar requested.

She cast a worried glance at Rachel. "Not much more to say. I mean, with our life, the way we travel, it's impossible to keep a relationship going unless the other person's willing to pick up and leave. He wasn't. And even if he was, she wouldn't keep him."

"Why not?"

"She said Luna didn't like him. That mattered to her."

Jaguar hissed in breath between her teeth. Rachel jerked around and looked to her.

"What?" she asked.

"Nothing," Jaguar said. "I need to drive."

She got in the car and tore out of the paddock. She no longer needed to keep empathic contact with Meris while she drove, but the events of the day had disturbed her equilibrium. Though her eyes saw the track, in her mind she stood under a starry sky, heard the howling of coyotes, a mournful sound, and one she didn't need right now.

"No," she insisted. "Goddammit let me *work*." But it wouldn't let go.

The coyotes kept howling and grief entered her, with the promise of permanent residence. Ahead of her she saw the cement at the Wall of Champions and wondered what it would feel like to make a unity of concrete and flesh. Why not? Alex was gone, Springer was dead, and Schulman always won. She could do nothing to change it, or to let it go.

See who you are. Be what you see. She'd done all that, and perhaps what she was had run its course. The Wall of Champions loomed ahead, a good way to make an exit.

Then, suddenly and inexorably, her mind was filled with another image: Luna, sitting upright and panting happily. Luna, looking to her for direction in an awful mess. And next to her was a young girl, eyes bright and alert. Maya, who put a hand on the dog's head. No words occurred, but Jaguar heard the message loud and clear. She had work to do, and others depending on her to finish it.

A shiver ran through her, and she pulled herself back into focus. "Oh fucking 'kay," she said. "I'll fucking drive until I get there, god *fucking* dammit."

She let go of effort, of will. Let go of despair and outcomes that existed in some dim future. In one sense following the advice Francois gave her, she put herself in the pleasure of the moment. She stayed strictly in the present, released all attempts to get it right, and followed her skin. Everything in it felt like Alicia's regal voice, telling her how to work the gears, when to lift, when to push. She paid attention.

Her body took over the task at hand, and she moved around the track at top speed, with ultimate grace. One lap, two laps, three, and then Meris's voice speaking to her over the radio, excited as if she was driving herself. "You got it," she said. "You *got* it."

"You bet your ass I do," Jaguar said. "And it feels pretty damn good."

CHAPTER TWENTY

New Mexico, Home Planet

Alex returned from the Mesa to find Jake and One Bird still awake, waiting for him. When he entered the house their relief was apparent.

"I'm back," he said, stating the obvious.

One Bird nodded. "Sit down. Eat something."

"No," he said. "I need to sleep."

"You still sleeping outside?" Jake asked.

Alex nodded. "But if you're willing, I'll sweat again tomorrow."

"How come?" Jake asked.

"I'm still a few answers short."

"What's the question?"

He debated how to phrase it. He knew one thing, but not another. He couldn't just walk off a cliff, but he wasn't sure if he needed to kill Ron Schulman, which would be the death of him in a different way. He made his answer honest.

"There's more than one way to die," he said. "I don't know if I've still got one of them to face."

"Yeah," Jake said. "Okay. Tomorrow. Get some rest."

* * * *

Alex slept like a baby rock thrown into an ocean, with nothing but silence all around him. When he woke, he found One Bird and spent the morning working the garden with her. Late in the afternoon he went to the place where the sweat lodge was set up and found Jake waiting for him, the fire already built, the stones already in the lodge.

Jake tossed a nod at the lodge and Alex entered the darkened space, listening for the spirits who might join him here. Jake joined him, and they honored the east, which held no terror for him now. But when they turned to the south, Alex felt a burning, a searing heat of fire. It smelled of Jaguar. Tasted only of Jaguar.

He held up a hand to push it away, then remembered that whatever was available, he'd have to accept it. He dropped his hand to his side and listened to what the spirits had to say. Almost immediately he was sorry he'd done so.

All his time with Jaguar recurred to him in a sweeping flash. The first time he'd seen her, only nineteen and seeking work on the Planetoids. Her lucid eyes taking him in, the vision he'd pursued his whole life. And their years of working together, when he'd held sharp longing for her at bay, the times she'd come to his aid and the times he'd gone to hers, the moment they met as lovers, and what they'd shared beyond that—all of it came back to him directly, without mediation. Undistilled desire, pure as lightning struck mint. Pure as Jaguar.

He'd forgotten how much he'd felt then. Forgotten how hard he'd worked to block it. And in remembering, he realized he felt that way still.

"Okay," he muttered. "I know. Now what?"

In response, another kind of warmth filled the space. The Nahuak, watching him, warm as the sage fed stones, warm as the heat that led him toward Jaguar, always toward Jaguar. He blinked through darkness, looking for the light he'd seen on the mesa. The face of love, feeding him. But he saw none of that.

Instead he saw sunlight streaming into the living room of an apartment he knew well. Bunches of sage and mint hung from the ceiling. A clay bowl with a red feather sat on the windowsill. Jaguar's apartment. And instead of the Nahauk, he saw a creature made of flesh as well as light.

Jaguar.

She stood at the wall in her living room, carving the image of a winged creature into it with her glass knife. When she was done, she turned her sea deep eyes his way.

I wait for you, she said.

"No," he gasped. "Not you."

Not her. Not now. He wasn't ready for it. He still had a decision to make, and he couldn't make it if he saw her. He rolled toward the door, his only goal to get away from her, from all she made him feel. He scrambled out of the lodge and lay on the ground on his back, staring up at wide sky, breathing hard. He'd been wrong when he thought he'd already felt the worst.

As he lay there, steam rising from his skin, Jake emerged from behind the deerskin door and hunkered down close by. "Tell me," he said, though Alex had no doubt he'd already perceived it. He just wanted Alex to say the words, to taste them in his mouth.

"I saw her," he said. "She was here. But she can't be. I blocked her."

"Her," Jake said. "You mean Jaguar?"

"Of course," Alex said, still unable to speak her name.

"You sure?"

"You think I'd mistake her for someone else?"

"Well, what the hell is she up to?"

"I was hoping you'd tell me."

Jake sat down hard on the ground and ran a finger through the dusty soil. Then he looked at Alex, his dark eyes sharp and bright as stars. "You been dreaming?" he asked.

An unexpected question. "No," he said. "But when I go to sleep there's a presence."

"Not a dream?"

"Definitely not," he said. "I saw her on the mesa, with the deer. She calls herself Nahuak. The Nahuak."

Jake jerked his head up. "Nahuak?"

"Yes. It's from One Bird, isn't it?"

Jake uttered a long string of Zuni words, giving voice to what Alex suspected were some really interesting profanities.

"What is it?" he asked.

"She's waiting," Jake said.

His response made no sense. Alex sought to clarify. "One Bird?" he asked.

"Jaguar," Jake said fiercely. "Goddammit to hell. She's *waiting*."

Alex remembered what she'd said before he left, words spoken imperatively. "She said she'd wait for me," he mentioned. "What's it got to do with the Nahauk?"

"It *is* her," Jake said. "The Nahauk is Jaguar. I'll kill her myself, if she's still alive."

"Jake, you better explain, because I don't have a clue what you mean."

He put his finger to the sandy soil and drew circles in it. "Nahuak—it's Mertec. It means—well, if you say it right it means heart of the jaguar going into the night and carrying all toward day."

"Sure it does. But what is it?"

"It's a part of yourself you send out to stay with someone when they're grieving, to keep them safe. Something she knows how to do. She taught us how to do it."

Waiting. When she said it, he'd taken it at literal value, but he wasn't surprised to learn it had an empathic meaning. Against his will he found he was interested. Her gifts went beyond his known field, and he'd always enjoyed learning from her. Apparently that remained true.

He thought of the times he'd watched over her empathically, protecting her, his energy near hers. This was more substantial, but also more disconnected. Nor did it feel like her chant shape, which appeared as the biggest cat he knew. The Nahuak held the complexity of human folly and human compassion.

"It's not a chant shape," Jake said in answer to his unspoken thoughts. "More like what Maya does when she travels. We've used it here, but only when it's necessary—when the grief is the kind that shatters the soul. The Nahuak helps someone remember what an unbroken soul feels like. Reminds them it's possible, and helps them heal."

"So it's just for big grief."

"Yeah. And we do it in a group. Take turns. It's draining. Hard work, to live with your heart somewhere else."

"Her heart?" he asked.

"Her sacred center. She ever say the phrase *Ze Adakal*?"

A term that meant eye of the soul. Another way of saying I love you, in Mertec. "I know it," he said.

"It's that part of her. She sent it to stay with you, when the rest of her couldn't."

Alex sat up, swore with feeling. What was the point in running when truth pursued you like the Furies? Like—like Jaguar? "She knows where I am? What I'm doing?"

"*She* doesn't know a damn thing. Her Nahuak is here. She's wherever she is, just doing what she does, half in and half out."

"Can you show me?"

Jake lifted a hand and touched Alex's forehead, letting him feel what it was like for a piece of someone's essential energy to stay with another person, guarding their most shadowed places, subtly moving them away from harm, soothing where they could, and just being there when they could do nothing else.

Alex perceived the strength it took to maintain such a position. To continue living your life while your soul focused all its intent on the well being of another. He remembered the Nahuak on the mesa, the face of love, shining on him. This was the heart of Jaguar, composed of love in its most primal and unrelenting form.

When Jake broke contact, Alex blinked up at him. "She's doing that? For me?"

"It's no more than what you did for her when you took out the Greenkeeper."

"That was different. That was—to save her."

"What the hell do you think this is?"

"I don't need saving."

"Christ," Jake muttered. "You two deserve each other," he said.

"Jake—"

"—Look, when you partner the warrior, the warrior partners you. With Jaguar, that's forever. You oughta know that by now."

Alex did. Some people thought of her as fickle, unreliable, but he'd never met a more stalwart loyalist in his life. Now she was keeping him alive against his own worst judgement, just as he'd once done for her. But if the soul had gone out of her, who was she now? Did it hollow her out, make her cold and bitter with anger, as she'd been when he first met her?

"What does it do to her?" he asked.

"Who the hell knows? Nobody was ever stupid enough to try it alone before."

"Fuck," Alex said, with feeling.

"I said she was crazy, didn't I?"

"Why didn't you help her?"

"You think she told us?"

"But you suspected something," Alex said. "That's why you called me."

"Maya dreamt about you taking a dive off a building. Probably a dream the Nahuak sent. We were worried about *you*. That's why I called."

There it was. Another connection. More people who cared about him. A part of him resented it. He wanted to own his pain alone, as Jaguar did. But of course, he never let her do that for long. He would, as she had, give her just enough time to dig her hole, then jump in before she got herself killed in it. He wondered if they'd always be pots calling kettles black.

Thinking this made him realize he was more like her than he cared to admit. Still considering killing himself to expunge the evil Ron Schulman put in the world, great as any evil the Greenkeeper might create. And just as he'd accepted his own death to save her, the Nahuak would accept his choice, if he made it in full knowledge. Was that what love required? And what would it mean to the Nahuak? To Jaguar?

"Jake, how long does the Nahuak stay?"

"Usually the person it's waiting on releases it when they're better. There's a ritual."

Of course there was. "What if the person doesn't get better? I mean, what if something happened to me?"

"You mean if you decide to die," Jake clarified.

Alex nodded. They only spoke the truth here. "What happens to the Nahuak—and to Jaguar?"

Jake narrowed his eyes. "Why're you asking that?"

"She said she'd stay with me. By my side. Always."

He spit into the sand. "Hell. I wouldn't put it past her."

This was Jaguar. All bets were off. Did that mean he couldn't kill Schulman? What the hell did love require of him, in these complicated circumstances?

To answer that question, he had to discern if killing Ron was about ego and anger, or his responsibilities to his son. He also had to figure out a way to keep Jaguar alive, regardless. And he needed to do all that quickly, for her sake as well as his own.

He ran a hand through his hair and wiped the damp from his face. "I'll be sleeping inside tonight," he said.

"In Jaguar's room?"

He nodded.

"Still can't say her name?"

"Nope."

"And what the hell does that tell you?" Jake asked.

Alex had no answer. Jake sniffed. "Let's go," he said. "It's time for supper anyway."

* * * *

They went back to the house, where One Bird and Maya had food waiting. Throughout the meal Alex was tense, anticipating what it would mean to sleep in the room where he'd slept with Jaguar. All those cues of scent and sight, the angles of moonlight pouring through the narrow window. He wasn't sure he was up to it.

During the meal he focused on Maya's chatter, paying attention to her needs, joking with her. But her eyes remained solemn and sad. She knew he was faking it. Knew he was still hanging on to the possibility of death.

Before she left, she turned solemn eyes his way. "I don't think you're supposed to kill him," she said.

He frowned at her. "Kill who?" he asked.

She lifted her shoulders up, let them fall. "I'm not sure. A man. A very bad man. You're thinking about killing him, but I don't think you're supposed to."

She was honest with him. He'd be honest with her. "Maybe you just think that because you don't want me to die," he said.

"Maybe," she said. "But that's important, too. I mean, if killing him means you'll die, and you aren't supposed to, you should know that, right?"

Her eyes held all the hope of a child who believed her wishes could influence outcomes. He had to speak to that without lying to her. Had to somehow let her off the hook. "Maya, what I choose has nothing to do with you. You get that, right?"

"But it should," she said. "Shouldn't it?"

She was right, and he knew it. What the children wanted was all that mattered, now and forever. "I'll do my best," was all he could say.

She huffed out breath and walked away, her eyes still sad.

When she was gone, One Bird turned her equally perceptive glance his way. "You want coffee, or are you ready for sleep?"

"Sleep," he said. "Or whatever's hanging around in her room."

* * * *

Alex took the step down into the room that was always and perpetually Jaguar's, where the window let in the exact angle of light he remembered from other times spent here. He sat on the bed, adjusting himself to the sense of her presence. He was expert at reading a scene, picking up on the residual presence of anyone or anything that hung around, and she was all around him. The memory of sleeping with her, the sweetness of that time, lingered here. He pushed himself away from it.

As soon as he did, the warmth of the Nahuak moved against his back. This time he felt her connection to Jaguar, an inarticulate part of her, composed of realities beyond words. He was torn between bliss at knowing this, and irritation that it should show itself now, when he most needed to be on his own.

"I know who you are," he said. "I appreciate what you've done, but you have to leave."

I go with you, she said quietly.

Not what he wanted to hear. "You can't stay with me if I die," he said.

By your side, she said.

"No," he said. "It could kill her, too."

We know, she whispered back. *Her choice.*

Whatever part of Jaguar this was, it was insistent as water. And Alex, patient to his own core, knew that water always won. But he resented the responsibility he was being asked to assume. Resented how it forced him to consider the consequences of his actions to others.

"I left her because I didn't want my choice to affect her," he noted reasonably.

He felt confusion emanating from the Nahuak. *How?* she asked.

He had no answer, so he took a defensive stance. "Why would she do this?" he demanded.

She promised.

"I asked nothing of her."

She promised your son, The Nahuak said patiently. *To stay with you. By your side.*

That was the last thing he expected to hear. "She promised Spring-er?" he asked.

Yes. That was what love required, the Nahuak answered.

His flesh shifted around his bones, giving space enough for this light to enter him. Jaguar would risk her life not only for him, but also for his son. She was wild enough to choose that, just as he was. He always thought he'd loved her even though she wasn't safe. In truth, he loved her because he was as unsafe as she was. He didn't know whether to call that joy or agony, grief or praise. Too much to feel. Not nearly enough to know.

"I can't," he said. "Let me sleep."

He rolled over on his side, and the Nahuak retreated, but she did not leave the room.

CHAPTER TWENTY-ONE

Montreal, Home Planet

Rachel went to sleep that night with a sense of being blanketed by protection, knowing Scott was just outside her door, near enough to both her and Jaguar to intervene in case of any more trouble. She would have slept through, but she was woken at around 3 am when Luna started whining and scratching at the door. Trust the dog, she thought, and dressed hastily, got Luna on a leash and opened the door. As soon as she left her room she saw Scott, waiting down the hall. He joined her.

"I have no idea what's going on," she told him.

"Yes, ma'am," he said, and followed as Luna pulled relentlessly until they stood in front of Jaguar's room. Once there, she sat at attention, staring at the door. Rachel listened, and heard noises emanating from within. Noises that sounded like great distress.

She knocked on the door. "Jaguar?" she asked.

No response, but she heard a moaning, deep and low. "Jaguar, answer me or I'm getting a doctor," she said.

No answer, and Luna kept whining. She turned to Scott. "Get the door open. I'm calling security."

Scott worked on the door while she used her cellcom to dial the front desk and speak curtly to someone, saying she needed help at room 310. As soon as she signed off Scott got the door open and went inside, Rachel and Luna right behind him.

Jaguar was in bed, the covers twisted around her. Rachel moved to her, and saw her forehead was beaded with sweat, her breathing rough and shallow. Shel put a finger to her wrist. Her pulse was rapid and weak.

"Miss?" a voice asked. "You need help?"

The security guard, answering their call. Rachel turned to him. "I'm not sure. She's—not well."

The guard stepped into the room. He was young and blonde and, she thought, not very secure. "Drugs?" he asked, looking scared.

"No. She has a—a condition. Just give me a minute," Rachel said. She looked to Scott. "You read anything?" she asked him.

"Just stress," he said, uncertain himself. "Talk to her," he suggested.

Rachel leaned over her, touched her head softly. It was hot, her face flushed.

"Jaguar, it's me, Rachel," she said quietly. "What do you need?"

Jaguar's eyes opened, wide and wild. She looked at Rachel, breathing hard, as if she'd been running. "It's too big," she said, struggling to fit words between breaths. "I can't field it." Then, a deep moan of pain. "I have to finish this. *Please,* just let me finish. It's almost over."

Rachel turned to the guard. "Get a doctor," she told him.

He moved to the door, but Jaguar suddenly sat up, held a hand out. "No," she snapped. "I can do this. Just a little while more."

The security guard hovered between action and stillness, then looked to Rachel, who held up a hand. "Wait," she said quietly. Then, she put a hand on Jaguar's arm. "What's almost over? Is it something I can help you with?"

A shudder ran through Jaguar. Her eyes came into focus and she stared down at Rachel's hand, up at her face. Then she saw the other people in the room.

"Scott?" she asked. "Is that you?"

"Yes, ma'am," he said.

Jaguar blinked at Rachel, then saw the man hovering behind her. "Who the hell are you?" she asked.

"Hotel security," he said. "You need a doctor?"

"Not unless you got a witch doctor," Jaguar noted mildly. "You can go. I'm okay. Just a bad dream."

He hesitated. "You're sure?"

"I am," Jaguar said, sounding like herself again. "Sorry to bother you."

He cast a look at Rachel, who nodded in confirmation, and he left. When he was gone, Rachel turned to Scott. "Thanks," she told him."Would you mind giving us the room? I have to yell at her, and she'll take it better if we're alone."

He eyed both women, gave one quick nod and made his exit, though Rachel knew he wouldn't go far. She brought her attention back to Jaguar.

"Start talking," she said. "And make it good."

"Really, Rachel. Like I told the man. A bad dream. You can go back to sleep."

"Fuck that," Rachel said adamantly. "I want the truth, and I want it now. It's fucked. Not talking about him. Not letting us talk about him, and you keep getting sick. You better tell me what's really going on or I swear I'll say his name."

"Rachel, don't."

"Stop me," she said, and glared. She opened her mouth as if to speak, and Jaguar held a hand up to stop her.

"Okay," she said. "Just—don't."

Rachel's eyes showed large and dark. Jaguar lowered her hand, composed her face. "When you say his name, it—it connects him to me. Disrupts what I'm doing. And he needs what I'm doing."

"It's something empathic?"

"Yeah," Jaguar said.

"To help him?"

"To keep him alive."

"Oh. It's that bad?"

"Imagine the worst, then make it worse than that." Jaguar ran a hand over her face. "What I'd give for a shot of tequila," she said.

"That," Rachel said, "can be arranged." She stood, left the room and returned with a bottle and some glasses, lime and salt. "I had some stashed, thinking we might want it," she said. She arranged the shots, and they each threw one down, and then another. When they'd let it settle Rachel waved a hand at Jaguar.

"Your turn," she said. "What, exactly, are you doing?"

"It's hard to explain," Jaguar said.

"You're good with hard stuff. Go ahead."

"You're not going away, are you?"

"Not even," Rachel said.

"I'm waiting," Jaguar said.

"And I said I'm not leaving."

Jaguar grinned. "That's not what I'm waiting for. Or on. However you want to put it."

"Okay. Now I'm lost."

"Me, too. Well, just part of me. It's—it's like this," she said, and explained.

As she spoke, Rachel remembered the carving in Jaguar's wall, the chant she sang, and the feathers, a new one every day. When she was done, Rachel chewed on her lip.

"You get it?" Jaguar asked.

"Kind of. That thing you drew on your wall. It's you. Or part of you?"

"A Nahuak. A part of me I sent out to him."

"To wait. But it's more than waiting, isn't it?"

Jaguar nodded. "Mertec is a heavily imaged language. Waiting means to serve the heart of the universe, to enfold with the warmth of sunlight, to carry on great wings, to part the self in service to another. You want more? Because there's more."

"I'm good. But that means, all this time you've been doing…all that?"

"Yeah," Jaguar agreed. "All this time."

The events of the last six months fell into place. Since Alex left, a large part of Jaguar was simply not present. Quite literally, the heart had gone out of her. Rachel understood the concept, but couldn't begin to imagine what it felt like. Maybe like any waiting for some important conclusion, maxxed out.

"Does it hurt?" she asked.

"No. Not really. It's just—hard work. Makes the empathic stuff tricky, tires me out."

"Can't you get help? From Jake and One Bird?"

"If they helped, he'd know. And if he knew, you think he'd let us?"

No, Rachel thought. Of course he wouldn't. He'd just put up his personal shields or whatever it was he did to disappear. "I get that, but it's making you sick."

"It's not that bad," Jaguar said.

"Wow," Rachel said. "Either you're really good at lying to yourself, or you've got some definition of not that bad I don't know about. Jaguar, it's awful, and it's getting worse."

"Not as awful as having a knife stuck in your chest, or facing a Telekine, or waking up in a room full of animated dead men, or a death walk, or anything else he's done for me."

"Okay," Rachel said quietly. She understood, and there was no point in arguing.

"Rachel, you have to trust me on this," she said. "I got this far, so I'll just keep going. I don't think it'll last much longer."

"You said that. It's almost over. I didn't like the sounds of it."

"One way or another, it's a good thing."

"Jaguar—"

"Dammit, Rachel, I have to see this through. And you are *not* to tell anyone else about it. Do you understand? Not anyone. Not that I'm waiting, not that I threw up, not about the Nahuak. Not under any circumstances. Promise."

Rachel opened her mouth and shut it hard.

"Do it," Jaguar growled.

Rachel sighed. "I promise. I won't tell anyone you're waiting, or that you threw up or your legs went numb or any of that. And I won't mention the Nahuak. Okay? Okay?"

"Yeah," Jaguar said. "Okay. Give me the rest of that tequila. In fact, we may want to think about getting some more."

CHAPTER TWENTY-TWO

Home Planet, New Mexico

Alex spent the day doing chores for Jake and One Bird, sitting with Maya and listening as she talked about her friends, her life here. When the sun set he went to the sweat lodge, ready for one more.

Jake was already there, standing by the fire, which was going strong. "You're doing this one alone," he said, and handed the pitchfork to him.

Alex put his hand on it, felt the wood beneath his skin. Jake scanned him, top to bottom, and left.

Alex dug the rocks from the fire and brought them into the lodge. He tossed the pitchfork outside and closed the door. He put sage on the rocks, poured water over them. Now he was in the dark, and the dark was absolute.

He honored the spirits of the east, and quickly felt them closing in around him, as the Nahuak stood sentinel, watching, always watching. He sat in the quiet dark, studying the contours of his heart. He had a choice before him, and he knew all its moving parts. He waited only for answers to emerge within him.

Then, in the darkness, the Nahuak's shape took on different contours. She became a coyote, lean and scruffy, who sat on the other side of the lodge, staring at him. He stared back. The coyote shimmered and reshaped itself until he was Springer, grinning at him, his orange eyes pinging like laser fire. Alex felt his heart beat rapidly, and tears welled in his eyes. Springer lifted a hand, offering his life, all he'd been and done in his short time on the planet.

For you, Springer said. *If you want it.*

"You bet I do," Alex answered.

Springer gave him all he'd known and done, from the confusion of his childhood, to the ecstasy of his singing, and the wrenching of his spirit through the malfeasance of others who wanted him only as a commodity. He shared each moment he stood before an audience and knew bliss of the ultimate kind, all bitterness purged from him through that joy. And he offered his death, which he'd chased like wind, knowing he couldn't achieve what he wanted without it.

"Why?" Alex asked. "Why did you do it?"

At this, small laughter. *Had to happen. You'll see why*, he said. *I'm just saying you did the right thing.*

As Jaguar tried to tell him, he'd done what his son wanted. Two Adepts, each fighting for the future they perceived. Then, in a moment of intuitive action, the father relinquished his vision, and leaped forward to help the son achieve the one he wanted.

And he'd done it because he was, like his son, wild. If Springer was coyote, his father was the wolf howling at the naked moon, ready to take a knife for the one he loved, ready to snap a neck, his hands filled with death. Every accusation he'd ever thrown at Jaguar applied to him as well. He was as wild as she was, wild as his son. He raised a hand in acknowledgement, and mirroring him, Springer did the same.

And now, at last, Alex saw where the genetic dice had rolled from father to son.

"You have my hands," he whispered.

Yes, Springer said. *Your hands, and more.*

His father's hands, and the wildness of his father's soul. He looked at his son, and saw himself.

They sat in the dark, seeing each other, like looking in a mirror gone slightly askew. Springer brushed his ghostly fingers against Alex's face. Alex lifted a hand to his strange eyes and blessed them. Their sparking fire reflected the fire in his own eyes, as if his son had somehow given him the best part of himself, the part that brought him to Jaguar.

Springer nodded. *Your gift to me.*

And yours to me, Alex answered.

He'd thought to ask for forgiveness, but it wasn't required. His son had lived a complex lifetime too quickly, but very fully. Grief and anger blew away like yesterday's storm. All was calm, shining with the painful light of truth, and the face of love.

Alex's hand clenched and released. He wanted to do something, wanted, in some way, to earn this blessing. But the lesson came home to him again and again. Love was an energy that took no account of debit and credit.

"What's next?" he asked.

Do what love requires, came the unhesitating response.

Springer lifted a hand one more time to brush against his father's face, and then he moved away. His form was absorbed in the smoking of the stones at the center of the lodge. Somewhere far away, a lone coyote howled.

The space was emptied of all except Alex, and the dim warmth of the Nahuak, distant and aloof, leaving him in the silence of himself.

* * * *

He didn't speak with Jake or One Bird after the sweat. He went directly to his room, to Jaguar's room, lay on her bed and slept until day became night and night became day again. Though warmth crowded his back, no voices disturbed his rest.

When he got up in the morning, One Bird was in the kitchen, making breakfast. She turned from the griddle where eggs and bacon were frying, pancakes going golden nearby. She looked him up and down.

"You slept good," she said.

He nodded. "And I'm hungry," he said with surprise. Of course he'd kept eating all this time, but he hadn't remembered real hunger, or the way the smell of bacon could inspire it, since before Springer came to Planetoid Three.

"I thought you would be," One Bird said. "Sit down. It'll be ready in a minute."

As she tended her griddle, she asked, "You know what's next?"

He hesitated. There was a great deal he wasn't certain about. "I think so," he said.

"You'd better name it," she suggested. "Make it real in the room."

He gave it some thought. The words were important, and needed to be spoken and witnessed with absolute clarity. Though he was by no means a monotheist, he remembered a biblical passage: It is in your mouth and in your heart, that you should know it. Therefore, choose life, that you shall live.

"I'm—I'm choosing my life," he said. "I choose to live."

As he said it, he felt something that had eluded him since Springer's death. His hand tingled. Adept space.

It had tried to find him before this, but he'd stopped it any way he could. Now he thought of what Jaguar said before she entered the minds of her prisoners. See who you are. Be what you see. He was an Adept. He had to live that, for good or ill. Once again, he entered the web of time and timelessness. With full willingness, he attended to it.

What he saw made no immediate sense. Jaguar, driving fast, focused only on the driving. Yet, under her focus he sensed a river of tears held in abeyance. If he touched her hands, they'd be cold. And at her side, a dog. A black dog.

The image dissolved and Alex frowned. "A dog?" he asked.

He turned his wondering face to One Bird, who smiled. "That's good," she said. "Very good."

And she tended to her griddle, where pancakes were ready to be flipped.

CHAPTER TWENTY-THREE

Home Planet, Montreal

The next day, Rachel made an executive decision. She'd avoided bothering Alex, wanting to let him get through his grief in his own way, but with Jaguar going out on the edge of her own cliff, she needed to talk to him. He might not come back, but maybe he could offer some advice. At least she'd give it a shot.

She called the horse ranch. When a handsome man in a cowboy hat answered, she took a breath and dove in. "Hi," she said. "I'm Rachel Shofet, from Planetoid Three, and I need to talk to Alex Dzarny. Could you find him for me?"

The man scrubbed at the side of his nose, pushed his hat back on his head. "Love to oblige you, miss, but he's not here right now."

"Oh. Well, I can call later. When will he be back?"

"Not sure, miss," the cowboy said politely.

"This is an emergency," she said, "I really need to talk to him. Can you give him a message, ask him to call me right away?"

"Fraid I can't," he said.

"Why the hell not?" she demanded.

"Not sure where he went."

Something wasn't right. Her program hadn't notified her of any cash card use or vehicle rental indicating he'd left. "When is he coming back?" she asked.

"Not sure *if* he's coming back," the cowboy replied.

Rachel, persistent as a truffle hunting pig, tried another angle. "So *why* did he go?"

The man shrugged. "He said it was a family thing."

"His family's mostly dead," Rachel noted. She tapped a finger against her desk. "I understand you don't want to give away any secrets, but he's in trouble, and I can help him. Do you know who he is? What he does?"

"Not much, but I saw pretty quick he had a lot going on."

"I'll tell you some of that," she said, and she did, filling him in on what Alex did on the Planetoids, telling him about his son, and his decision to leave. She let him take all this in, and then asked, "So, can you tell me anything that'll help me find him?"

The cowboy surveyed her, taking stock of her personal rather than her professional credentials. He seemed satisfied with what he saw. "I'll tell you this. Right before he left he got this call and it seemed important."

"Oh. Who called?"

"An old guy, from New Mexico."

New Mexico. An old guy. Rachel thought of Jaguar's mentors. "Someone named Jake?" she asked.

"That's right," the cowboy confirmed. "Does it help?"

"It helps," she said. "Thanks. A lot."

"Glad to be of service," he said, and signed off.

Rachel didn't waste time castigating herself for losing track of Alex. Instead, she found and punched in the number for Jake and One Bird's telecom. Either they'd help her find him, or they'd help her with Jaguar. Not that she was going to tell them about the Nahuak, or Jaguar throwing up or anything. She'd just wait for them to figure it out. It shouldn't take them too long. When her telecom indicated her call was answered she was ready to speak with anyone except the person she saw on her screen.

Alex appeared, looking as surprised as she was.

She gasped hard. Her mouth opened, closed. No words emerged. Alex, recovering first, helped her out.

"How'd you find me?" he asked.

She blinked back tears. "Oh, Alex," she said. "Didn't you know I'd be tracking you?"

He rubbed at his forehead. "I disabled all my technology when I left," he noted. "Didn't use my cash card or flash my ID."

"Like I need that?" she said. "There's surveillance cameras everywhere in New Manhattan, and I know how to run a face recognition program. Then, I guess it was kind of weird, but I found a good clear shot of you talking to the guy who gave you the brochure for the ranch."

"Weird," he said, not at all surprised.

"It was, right? So I called the ranch, and a guy told me you left after you talked to someone in New Mexico. Jake, he said. Even if they didn't know where you were, they might tell me how to help Jaguar. But I didn't expect *you* to answer. And I'm so damn glad to see you."

That was surprisingly sweet to him. Knowing he wasn't dismissed, unforgiven. "Then we're even," he said. "I don't know why I picked up, and I'm just as damn glad to see you." And he was. Glad to see her wide brown eyes, shedding kindness and tears over the miles between them.

"You're okay?" she asked. "You're not—not—"

"I'm better than I was," he said, understanding what she was trying to ask. But his mind quickly covered ground and got to a place he didn't like. "What you said about helping Jaguar," he said. "Is she in trouble?"

The first time he'd said her name out loud, and it didn't hurt. In fact, it felt good. Like an anchor holding his soul steady in a storm.

"She is," Rachel said. "We're in Montreal, and there's this race car driver who got killed. Paul set us up for a prelim on it."

He thought of his times in the sweat lodge, driving and crashing, and his moment in Adept space. Jaguar, driving fast. "Paul did that?" he asked. "Why?"

Rachel chewed at her lip. "It's—you know, an assignment he gave her."

That didn't explain anything. Rachel was being cagey, an unusual phenomena. He'd test it. "It's a prelim," he noted. "She can handle it."

Her eyes widened. "Of course she can," she said, her voice rising in pitch. "It's not *just* that. There's this dog, and—and other stuff." She took in breath, tried for casual and missed by a mile. "I just thought maybe you could—I don't know, take a trip here and check it out."

He frowned. Rachel wasn't just being cagey. She was lying, badly. He needed more information before he decided how to proceed, and he'd like it to have some truth in it. Besides, he'd imagined himself conducting a dignified return to the land of the living. He'd let Jaguar know before he got back, give both of them a chance to prepare. He didn't like the idea of leaping into a cryptic maelstrom.

"Tell me more," he suggested.

"I can't." She closed her lips tightly, as if to keep certain words from escaping.

He knew both Rachel and Jaguar well enough to read between these lines. "She made you promise not to talk?"

Rachel almost nodded, then stopped herself. "Of course not," she said, trying hard to sound like she meant it. "I just—I can't say."

"Rachel, I know about the Nahuak."

She shook her head with determination. "I absolutely can't talk about that."

Well, he thought. At least she knew about it. "What *can* you say? For instance, can you tell me how she is in other ways? Just—in general?"

"My opinion, with no specific instances or examples?"

"Sure," he agreed. "Whatever works."

"She's a wreck," Rachel said bluntly. "Shredded and soldiering on."

Alex was surprised. Before he knew about the Nahuak, he was pretty sure she was pissed off at him. Even when he understood what she was doing, he imagined her in her coolest aspect, her most detached self.

Jaguar without a heart, cursing him soundly for a fool. In his worst moments he saw her laughing self, carelessly naked in bed with some other man. He never got specific with which man. She had her choice of the field.

"Shredded?" he asked.

Rachel rolled her eyes. "Well, yeah. If you know about the—that word I can't say—what did you expect?"

"Bad temper, mostly."

"Really, Alex. Sometimes you're such a—a man."

"Then use small words. This shredded thing—what are the symptoms?"

Rachel's face worked around this. "No symptoms. I mean, it's not like she's passing out or anything. Not like she keeps getting sick and can't sing, and can't do her empath thing. Not like her legs haven't been going numb or anything. In fact, she's fine. She keeps telling me she's *fine*."

He felt his shoulders tighten. Sick? Can't sing? Can't do empathic work? He made a gesture, asking for more. Rachel shook her head. She'd gone to the limits of her promise and could go no more. He made a quick dip into her thoughts, and saw an image carved on the wall of Jaguar's living room. A winged creature, spreading warmth at his back. The Nahauk. And something else. Jaguar, with her hair shorn.

"She cut her hair?" he demanded.

"That's not fair. You can't just pick it from my brain."

"Rachel, she cut her hair?" he repeated.

She sighed. "Really short. It's growing back, but she wants to cut it again."

He didn't need more. She was Mertec. Cutting her hair was a sign of the most profound grief. All his fears and fantasies of her were wrong. Instead, she was a wreck. He should have known. Her fiercely guarded independence made it seem as if she could subsist on air alone, but he'd met her unclothed soul, and it was made primarily of love, savage and unremitting. He stared down at his hands, remembering how they moved over the skin of her back, over her face. A shudder ran through him.

"Okay," he said quietly. "I'll think of something to do."

"You really should be here," she insisted, looking more than a little panicked.

Jaguar needed him. Nothing else mattered in the whole damn universe. But he'd never dealt with a Nahuak before. He didn't want to make things worse for her.

"Rachel, it's complicated. I should talk to Jake and One Bird first. And I need at least a minute to consider," he said, trying to curb his own panic. "Listen, see if you can get Scott up there. He'll look after her."

"He's here already. She made him come to guard the dog."

The dog again. He didn't even ask. If nothing else, it confirmed that his Adept capacities were working. "That's good," he said. "I'll figure out what to do on my end, and let you know."

She backed off, but didn't look happy about it. She gave him her hotel room number, Jaguar's hotel room, all important contact information. Then she signed off. When she was gone he stared at the blank screen. It was complicated. He needed a minute.

All his time here moved through him, with the Nahuak at his back, the scent of sage and stones around and within him. What he'd seen on the mesa, and what the ghost of his son said to him. Adept space tingled in his hand and he felt the face of love shining on his, all of it pure Jaguar.

What wouldn't a man do to feel that again? What wouldn't a man do if that was offered to him freely? But he was not someone who leaped before he looked. He should consult with Jake and One Bird, should consider all the options. A minute passed.

He opened his cellcom and punched in some numbers. When a familiar face appeared on the screen he talked.

"Paul," he said. "Good to see you. I hear Jaguar's got some trouble in Montreal. Anything you can tell me about it before I go there?"

"Jesus Christ," Paul said. "It's about damn time." And he proceeded to talk.

* * * *

Alex was in his room packing when Maya appeared in the doorway, took in the scene before her.

"You're leaving," she said.

He zipped his bag shut and turned to her. "I am," he confirmed.

She smiled. "When you see her, tell her I'm *excelling* in my math classes. She'll want to know that."

He tilted his head at her. "When I see who, Maya?"

"Jaguar, of course," she said. "Tell her to come visit after you leave Montreal. And she should bring me a dog. A black dog."

"Why black?" he asked.

"It's something I dreamt. She'll understand."

"Okay," he said. Then, in case she needed to hear it, "Maya, you don't have to worry about me anymore."

"Oh," she said. "I *know* that. Just tell her about the dog, okay? I really want one, but it has to be the right one."

"I will," he said. "I promise."

He left the house, his intent to go directly to his airrunner, but he spotted One Bird walking toward him, her basket of herbs on her arm. He waited until she stopped in front of him, put her basket down.

"I'm going to Jaguar," he said.

She nodded. She'd figured that out. "She's done enough waiting. So have you."

He looked around, grateful for the time he'd spent here, grateful for the land, and for Jake and One Bird and Maya. Though he'd lost a son, he'd found a family, in the truest sense of that word.

"Thank you," he said. "For everything you've done. You and Jake."

She did something she'd never done before. She spoke into him. *You are necessary,* she said. *We would go far for you.*

He stood still, allowing himself to feel it fully. One Bird spoke out loud.

"The Nahuak," she said. "You have to take care of that. It won't go back to Jaguar until you send it."

"Okay. Tell me how."

One Bird recited in a language that sounded like Jaguar's. As she did, the words translated into meaning in his mind. What he would say. What she would reply. The final dismissal of the Nahuak. He took a minute to absorb it. It seemed too easy.

"That's it? Nothing else?"

"Nothing else. She'll see the truth in you."

"Thanks," he said. "I'll do that first thing. Do you know where Jake is?"

She waved to the east. "Out in the corn fields. I'll tell him you left. You're probably in a hurry to see her."

He looked at the wide sky, at the land. "I am," he said. "After all this time, I am."

"That's as it should be." She put a hand to the side of his face, said words in her own language he couldn't understand, but he caught the feel of them.

A blessing. A gesture of love, mingled with considerable relief.

CHAPTER TWENTY-FOUR

Montreal, Home Planet

Jaguar had another day of waiting for lab reports and getting none, another lunch with Detective Thei, who continued his patient courtship of her, as courteous as Alex could ever be, and another afternoon of driving.

She was aware that the week was winding down, and she couldn't keep the teams at the track much longer, but she also knew there was nothing she could do beyond what she was already doing. After her driving session, she took Luna back to her room, thinking she might be up to another try at empathic contact. But when they were both inside, fatigue folded over her like a heavy blanket, and she knew she'd get nowhere. Instead, she ran a bath, put in lavender salts she'd purchased at the spa, and lowered herself into the steaming water, leaned her head back and breathed in. This, she thought, was what she needed. A way back into her body, or as much of it as she still owned.

Waiting was an out of body experience, a letting go of self. And it had repercussions for her neural system, for her empathic work. Right now her heart was held together with paper clips and bad glue. The larger part of her was simply not available, and the rest of her was battling with the disjunction. But she had to carry on. She'd made a commitment to this, and she would see it through, if she could. If it didn't rip her apart, neuron by neuron.

She sipped at a glass of whiskey she'd put on the side of the tub, considering what she knew about Alicia's death. It didn't get her much of anywhere. Maybe in the morning, when she was rested, she'd have another try at Luna. While she thought this, Luna came padding over to the tub, as if she'd heard her name called. She stopped and stared at the froth of bubbles surrounding Jaguar, tilting her head at them, her ears perking up inquisitively, sticking out like the wings of an airplane.

"Not edible," Jaguar said.

Luna wasn't convinced. She licked at the air around them. Jaguar lifted a handful of bubbles to her and she and lapped at them once, then sighed a doggy sigh, reminding Jaguar of one of the primary differences between cats and dogs. Cats didn't sigh. They never felt the need.

But dogs did. Usually they sighed when they wanted something they weren't getting. Jaguar knew what it was. Dogs needed to explode their energy into the world physically, joyously, and Luna hadn't gotten much of that lately. Neither had she, for that matter. Her body ached for action, for something other than waiting.

She also sighed, and as she did, her cellcom buzzed. She reached for it, just on the side of the tub, and when she answered, saw Didier's face on her small screen.

His gaze moved over her, noted the amount of skin visible, and the bubbles on her shoulders. "Am I interrupting?" he asked politely.

She laughed. "Bath night," she said. "Sorry."

"No need to apologize," he said. "The view is quite splendid. I called to see if all was well with you."

"Well as it's been since I got here," she replied.

"Jaguar," he said, "would you like company?"

"No, Didier. I would not," she replied.

He didn't hide his disappointment, but neither did he press. "As you wish. Always and exactly as you wish," he said, and signed off.

Jaguar closed her cellcom, put it on the side of the tub. Luna sniffed at it, then thumped her tail gently, with hope. "You're right," Jaguar said. "We need to move."

She got out of the tub, dried off and got into pajamas, went to the radio in her room and tuned it to something Latin and hot. Luna stood, her tail waving with more hope, more enthusiasm. Jaguar snapped her fingers at her. "Let's dance," she said.

She put herself into rhythmic motion, hips swaying, feet moving to the beat of a samba. Luna, quickly getting in the mood, tapped her feet against the floor and followed.

"That's it, moon doggie," Jaguar encouraged. "Dance with me."

Luna yipped and circled Jaguar in concert with her mood. Jaguar moved high and then low, going into a ritual dance she'd learned at 13 Streams, a dance of completion, a dance of all things coming around to their natural conclusion. Luna stayed with her, waiting for her commands, and Jaguar found joy in the communion between animal and human. When the song ended, she collapsed on the bed and Luna, panting at the side, regarded her with doggie joy and licked at her face.

Jaguar felt a shift, a change close at hand. She explored it, but couldn't tell if it was good or bad. Just a tingling in the air. She gave it up and lay back on her pillow. "Okay," she said to Luna. "You can come up."

Luna hauled herself onto the bed, got herself situated. She rested her head on her paws, looking at Jaguar with careful eyes.

"I think you're my Nahuak," Jaguar said, and smoothed the rough fur on her back.

As she did, she was surprised by a rush of energy. She stopped her hand. She hadn't made empathic contact. Luna sniffed the air as if something new had entered the room.

Then, a voice, speaking through Luna, female, and young.

Jaguar? it asked.

Maya? Is that you?

Yes. I saw him.

Saw who?

Alex. I saw him.

Jaguar took this in. Maya wouldn't say that if it wasn't true. *Tell me,* she requested.

An incursion of static followed, and then Maya spoke again. *I'm sorry. I'm not very good at this. And I'm not allowed to travel yet.*

The voice faded, and the energy dispersed. Jaguar frowned down at Luna, who shook her head and scratched at an ear as if she'd dug a little girl out of her brain.

"Well then," Jaguar said. "That was…something."

Something. Something good? Impossible to tell. Where had Maya seen Alex? She was good at leaving her body, but Jake and One Bird had forbidden her to do so until she was older. Maya obeyed them, in her own way, but she'd needed to get in touch with Jaguar and had found a way, through Luna.

Jaguar grinned. Maya was a girl after her own heart, already skilled at getting around rules. And she was connected to Luna in some way Jaguar didn't understand. But what did she know about Alex?

There was no answer. She considered calling Jake to ask directly, then decided against it. It might disrupt the Nahuak, the worst thing she could do. Her job was only to wait. She had to keep at it, for as long as she could keep it up.

Luna nuzzled her hand. Jaguar lay down and tried for sleep.

CHAPTER TWENTY-FIVE

Rachel only pretended to be surprised when Alex showed up at her hotel room that night. She made some noises about it, and he dismissed them, moved on.

"Paul got me on with Lotus as an alternate test driver, which means not much at all, but it puts me where I need to be," he said. "I'm Dan Legacy, retired Interpol, gentleman driver. I'll be in touch with you and with Jaguar, but you don't know me."

"Okay. But—can you actually drive these cars?"

"I'll be driving an Aero for the time being," he said. "Now tell me what Jaguar's up to."

"She's learning how to drive an F1 car," Rachel said, "though God only knows why. Oh, and someone tried to kill me, or Luna. Or maybe both. And Schulman's here. Also, there's a video you probably should see."

She explained all she could, showed him the video of Jaguar going bonkers on Larry, which made him laugh wickedly.

"Did she know about Schulman before she came here?" he asked.

"You bet," Rachel said. "She wanted to get to him, though it was supposed to be a spa vacation."

That meant she had as much of a plan as she ever did. Jaguar was an opportunistic hunter. Her clairvoyance made her very good at it. Events will occur, he'd heard her say more than once. Or at least, she hoped they would.

He considered, and Rachel could see all the information working its way through the web of his knowledge, which included present and future. When he was done, he nodded. "Okay. I'll see you tomorrow, probably. Don't tell Jaguar a damn thing. And remember, you don't know me."

"Sure," she said. "Fine. Um—she might be upset."

"Like I'm not used to that? I'll manage. And thanks, Rachel."

He put a hand on her shoulder. She reached over and grabbed it. "It's good to have you back," she said.

* * * *

Jaguar brought Luna to the racing paddock the next day. She was scheduled to review telemetrics from her last drive, but she didn't feel much like it. She was twitchy. Something was happening, and since she was clairvoyant rather than Adept, she assumed it was happening now. Close to her in both space and time.

When she got to the paddock, Meris and Rachel were seated in front of the computer, Rachel taking notes and Meris commenting as graphs moved over the screen. Jaguar stood behind them, tapping a foot impatiently. If she could squeak some wheels it would at least give her the illusion of control. And she had a feeling she should be on the track, though she didn't know why. Something waiting for her there. Something.

After twenty minutes of discussing the fine points of gear shifting and braking, which she didn't give a rat's ass about, she spoke. "Put me in the car," she said.

"We're working here," Meris commented.

"Go ahead. Knock yourselves out."

"You need to pay attention," Meris said. Rachel looked up, but stayed quiet.

"I'm here to drive," Jaguar replied.

Meris shook her head. "Not the Ferrari. The engineers are working on it."

"Then I'll take the Berlinetta. Keys," she said, holding her hand out.

Meris looked to Rachel. Jaguar made a noise.

"Look, as soon as I leave you can talk about me behind my back. Just give me the fucking keys and let me drive."

"You make Alicia seem like a peach to deal with," Meris pointed out.

Jaguar snapped her fingers. Meris got the keys and gave them to her.

* * * *

She drove, enjoying the feel of a free track on a sunny day, a moment of peace, so rare these days. The Berlinetta was easy to handle, and had all the power she wanted. It felt good to drive fast, to move on the edge of recklessness and control it. Hit the apex. Don't lift. Listen to the engine. Keep track of your backside. Only the present needs mattered. She didn't enjoy it for long before another driver appeared in her mirror, driving a car she didn't recognize.

"Rat fuck," she muttered. "Now what?"

The track was cleared for Lotus, McLaren, Ferrari and GM, but this car was none of those. Maybe it was a test driver, taking advantage of the down time to drive his own car. If so, they'd ignore her and she could just drive on.

No such luck. The car came up fast and made a move to pass. She pushed against her racing line but he went around her when they hit Parabolica. She worried his back end, but he blocked, staying in front. She cursed silently, then did a quick empathic survey of the driver. She felt maleness, focused and intent. Not Didier. He was neither focused or intent. She tried to move deeper into his thoughts, and to her surprise, he held her off. He was blocking her in more ways than one.

"I don't think so," she said, and began racing rather than driving, looking for a way around him, readying herself for trouble. It could be one of Schulman's minions, staging yet another car accident for his boss.

In her earpiece she heard Meris, sounding frantic. "Who the hell is that?" she asked.

"How would I know?" Jaguar answered.

"Come in. Now."

"Nope," Jaguar said.

"Listen, you can't—"

Then, in the background, Jaguar heard a voice cutting in. Rachel.

"Don't worry," she said to Meris with perfect assurance. "She can take him."

"You bet I can," Jaguar murmured back, and worked the throttle.

The other car stayed ahead, continuing to block, moving back and forth in front of her. That told her his car was slower, and he was bullying her to stay behind.

"Oh yeah?" she said. "We'll see about that." She stayed on his back, and when they reached the straight she pushed the throttle.

"Come on, you bucket of bolts," she told her million dollar car. "You've got a thousand horses under your hood. *Take* this asshole."

He drifted out slightly. She saw the opening and grabbed it, passing him on the inside, tapping him just hard enough to make sure he felt it before she got ahead. She hit the throttle and roared away. In her mirrors she saw him wobble, then spin. When he righted himself he was rapidly diminishing in her mirrors. She took the rest of the track easily, and roared into pit lane well ahead of him.

She squeaked the wheels going in to the garage, braked hard and came to a stop. She got out of the car, still full of adrenalin, to find Meris standing and glaring at her.

"What?" she asked as she pulled off her gloves.

Her focus was all on Meris, so she didn't notice when Rachel's eyes went wide, as a tall, dark-haired man with broad shoulders appeared in the entrance behind her. He stayed where he was, staring at her back with a still and focused gaze, swinging his helmet slowly back and forth in his hand.

Meris glanced at him, then away. She had other things on her mind. She examined the Berlinetta closely, saw it was unharmed, then looked to Jaguar.

"You want to race, you have to follow the rules," she said. "You'd get a penalty for what you just did. Two penalties. You bumped him, intentionally. And you were driving over speed in pit lane."

Jaguar pulled off her helmet, put it on the hood of the car, and shook out her hair. "Maybe," she said. "But at least the son of a bitch didn't catch me."

"That's what you think, Dr. Addams," the man at the entrance said.

She went still, her entire posture registering surprise. From where he stood, the man who watched her could see her spine trembling. She composed herself and spoke subvocally.

Alex, she said, a carefully neutral statement.

That's right, he replied.

She shifted her stance enough to indicate she'd gotten herself under control.

I'm working, she said. Testy, now. Petulant.

I know. So am I.

She let this sink in, and when no more was forthcoming, she turned to face him.

"Long time and all that," she said.

He stayed where he was and appraised her. Her shorter hair made her look younger, and though the racing suit fit her well, she was thinner than the last time he'd seen her, her face drawn, dark circles under her darkened eyes. In spite of that, she looked like every memory of happiness he'd ever had. While all his molecules thrummed with joy, he worked hard to return her deliberately cool gaze.

"All that and then some," he replied.

Before either of them could say anything else, Luna stretched, rose, clipped over to Alex and licked at his hand. He put his helmet down on the ground and patted her. She sniffed with enthusiasm at his pant legs, then sat at his side, gazing up at him with confidence. Jaguar made a sound he couldn't interpret. He looked to the dog.

"Hello," he murmured. "Dream dog?"

"That's Luna," Meris said. "She's okay."

"Sure she is." He moved forward, put his hand out to Meris. "I'm Dan Legacy. Consulting with Lotus."

She took his hand and shook it. "Meris Grant. Good to meet you." She tilted her head at her companions. "This is Didier, our test driver, and Rachel, who's helping out."

"Hi there," Rachel said, struggling to keep her face on straight. She turned quickly to Meris. "Isn't it past time for lunch? I could use some food."

"Now?" Meris asked.

Rachel rose and clutched imperatively at Meris's elbow. "I think we should," she said.

"Sure," Meris said, sounding a little confused. "I guess so."

"Didier," Rachel said brightly. "You should come with us."

"In a moment," he said. "You go ahead."

Rachel sought for a reason to compel him and found none. She offered Alex a brief apologetic smile and moved out, Meris with her.

Didier remained implacably present. He stepped toward Alex, put a hand out. "It's a pleasure to meet you," he said.

Alex noted how perfectly handsome he was, and how well he knew it. But like most drivers he was a small man, and Alex towered over him, a thought he relished. He took Didier's hand and shook it, perhaps a little too hard.

"The same, I'm sure," he said.

"That Aero—it's yours?"

"It is. I took it out to learn the track. I didn't expect to have company."

"But you know Jaguar?" he asked. He moved to her side, put a hand on her shoulder. She ignored him, keeping her gaze on Alex's face. He directed a flash of anger at Didier, and quickly subsumed it into courtesy.

"We met some time ago. In Paris." He smiled at Jaguar, professionally. "Sixty-eight, wasn't it?"

"Sixty-nine," she replied. He felt her quick dip into his thoughts, and her even quicker retreat. When she emerged she knew what his cover was and what he wanted her to say. Whatever her feelings were about him, her attachment to the job came first.

She spoke to Didier. "He was with Interpol then, consulting on a Planetoid case."

"Interpol?" Didier said. "Then I'd better be careful."

"No need," Alex said. "I've turned to more lucrative pursuits. But our engineer told me a Dr. Addams was here, and I had to see if it was the one I knew." Then, to her. "I thought you were on the Planetoids."

"I am. Just troubling the waters here."

"Always do what you're best at."

"It looked like she was troubling your waters on the track, Mr. Legacy." Didier laughed, showing his very white teeth.

Alex didn't like the smoothness of his talk or his visage, but he made an effort and spoke politely. "She always was a challenge. And I always liked that about her." Again he turned to Jaguar. "I'm glad to find you. I need to consult with you about some left over business. From the old days."

She didn't answer, and he continued, addressing Didier. "I keep in touch with some of my friends at Interpol, and one of them posed a question I think Dr. Addams can answer."

"Oh? About what?" Didier asked.

"I'm sure you'll understand if I can't give particulars." Then, to Jaguar. "Can we take some time to talk? I'd rather get it done quickly. A good friend is waiting on me."

The smallest flicker of her eyes told him she understood. Didier's hand moved on her shoulder. "But we're booked for today," he said. "We're going to a Cirque du Soleil matinee, then having dinner at Estoril. They have the best sardines, and she likes sardines." He lifted his hand to touch her face lightly.

"She likes lobster better," Alex said, his voice low and, he realized, pretty rough.

Jaguar bit at her lip, Alex assumed to keep from laughing at them both. "Business before pleasure," she said to Didier. "You go ahead to the show. I'll catch up with you."

Didier removed his hand from her shoulder and sniffed, not pleased at this response. Jaguar kept her gaze on Alex. Her eyes were dark and deep, an ocean filled with debris.

"One more time around the track?" Alex asked her. "We'll figure it out after that."

She gave him her most dangerous smile. "Okey-dokey. If you think you're up to it."

"Absolutely," he said.

She got in her car and made it to the track ahead of him, but he was close behind. He let her stay ahead until they got to a corner. When she took it a little too wide, as he knew she would, he pushed into the gap and went around her on the inside, moving ahead. As he did he contacted her subvocally.

Where'd you learn to drive? he asked.

Same as you. Teacher training. And Meris showed me a few things.

Not Didier?

She's the better driver. Alicia taught her.

He hoped she could feel his immense satisfaction at this response. *We have business to complete. Come to my hotel room. 604.*

What hotel?

Same as yours, he said.

How the hell do you know where I'm staying?

He only smiled. As if he wouldn't know. As if he'd stay anywhere else.

He sensed the jagged emotions of her response. When they reached the straight where she had the advantage, he saw her on his tail, driving into his mirrors. She crowded his back, her moves rough but determined as she pulled around on the outside, pushing him toward the grass.

Pushing back would take them both out. He chose to survive, drifting to the green. The victory he wanted had nothing to do with racing. She roared away, leaving him to breathe in her dust.

He sat back in his car, and for the first time in a very long time, he laughed like he meant it.

CHAPTER TWENTY-SIX

Alex made it back to his hotel room before Jaguar arrived. He was standing at the window looking out when she entered without benefit of key, as she always did. She could break a lock without taking breath. He heard the door open and close, and he turned to face her, his blood coursing through his veins in oceanic waves.

She still wore her racing suit, and her eyes still carried their burden of darkness. Where are you going, they asked. He would answer her now. He spoke subvocally, saying the words One Bird taught him, officially releasing her from her charge.

Your light led me through shadow. I can walk again, and all my steps will honor you.

She closed her eyes, opened them again and scanned him, seeing for herself that he was done with death. She responded, as One Bird said she would.

You owe me nothing. The work was honey on my tongue.

And now, he replied, *it's complete.*

She shuddered, the ritual words flowing through her. He felt the shift, easy as One Bird said it would be. The Nahuak's job was done. All her considerable energy was returned to her. He let her adjust, let all the empathic dust settle. When the air around them was clear he continued to face her, entirely open, ready for whatever she had to offer, ready to give whatever she needed next.

She ran a hand through her hair. "That's that," she said. "So am I done here?"

He almost laughed, but then saw she meant it. She was giving him an easy out. Everything she'd done was only to save his life, and she'd leave without argument if he asked her to go. That knowledge pierced him more deeply than her knife.

"No," he said. "Not by a long shot."

She tensed, but her gaze remained at absolute zero of neutral. "Okay," she said. "Talk."

The next step was entirely his call, and he could dare that road. There was no road he wouldn't dare for her. He held a hand out, palm up and empty. "Jaguar, can you still love a man like me?" he asked quietly.

For a moment, her expression remained a lesson in the unfathomable. Then it twisted into something combining fury and sorrow in equal measure. She tried to speak and failed. With a growl of frustration she strode over to him and hit him hard on the chest. He looked down at her fist, up at her face. She hit him again, and again.

He'd seen her rip the heart out of a man with that hand. He hoped she was just blowing off steam, but if not, it would be a good day to die. He stayed still and took it until she stopped, her fist coming to rest where her knife had pierced his flesh. The scar he still bore tingled under her touch. She spoke through a throat tight with tears, and tears ran down her face.

"A man like you," she said savagely. "With that scar. Yes, I can love you. Yes. Yes. *Yes.* You *get* that?"

I can dare myself, the Nahuak said, and the Nahuak was Jaguar, who loved rarely but fully, without reserve. Jaguar, who waited for him.

He leaned down and put his mouth to her skin, drinking her tears. She pulled in a sob and he curved his hand at the back of her neck, keeping her face arched to his.

"I get it," he whispered. "And I'll keep it."

He kissed her, giving her all his joy at seeing her again, larger than any pain he'd ever felt, and she wrapped herself around him. His hands couldn't find enough of her at once, and her mouth was wild with wanting. As she tugged at his shirt he tore at the zipper of her suit, pulling with such fervor it split in his hand.

That'll cost you, she laughed.

Worth any price, he replied. *Any price at all.*

Further talk would wait. Their bodies spoke beyond words, telling all stories that needed to be told.

CHAPTER TWENTY-SEVEN

Didier was already upset when he walked into Estoril, because Jaguar never showed for the Cirque du Soliel matinee. And he'd had a hard week, dealing with business he thought would be simple, and now was just another mess. Alicia was dead, though she shouldn't be, he was being questioned by police and Planetoid workers, and he'd yet to get his deal from Ferrari. And the man who showed up to claim Jaguar—who was he? Someone from Interpol. Though he said he was retired, his presence made Didier nervous. He'd already gotten in too far over his head.

He was even more upset when he saw Ron Schulman at the restaurant, seated at a table with a young, red haired woman, both of them involved with paella and glasses of wine. Mr. Schulman, he'd read in the gossip columns, liked his women young and red-haired. Not that it mattered what his pleasure was. Let him take it where he liked, as they all did. But his recent interactions with Mr. Schulman had been inconclusive, and he had no idea where he stood in this man's thoughts.

He didn't know what he should do, under the circumstances, but Ron looked up, lifted a hand and gestured him over. Didier went to his table and sat across from him.

Ron gestured at the woman. "This is Darlene, who's about to use the ladies room."

Darlene pouted briefly, then stood and went. Ron kept his eye on Didier.

"It's good to see you, Mr. Schulman," Didier said.

"Sure," he said. "You meeting someone?"

"Yes," he said. "Jaguar said…well, she had something come up, but she said she'd find me here."

"Dr. Addams? What came up for her?" he asked.

Didier blinked, not sure why he wanted to know, but certain he wanted to stay on this man's good side. "An old friend," he said. "Someone from Interpol. They had to talk. They should be done by now."

A brief smile moved across Ron's face. "She won't show," he said.

"But—how can you know that?"

"I know things. It's what I do. I also know she's after your seat."

Didier shook his head. "Impossible. She only started driving a few days ago."

"You underestimate her. She's after your seat, and she might get it, because Meris and Ferrari want an all woman team. It's good for their PR profile."

Didier pressed his lips together, said something profane in his native tongue.

"All that," Ron agreed. "So what'll you do about it?"

"I—I do not know," Didier declared. "I have never heard of anything like this."

Ron glanced away, toward Darlene who was returning to the table. "Maybe I can help," he said. He reached in his pocket, pulled out a card. "Give me a call, and we'll talk about it more. For now, you should leave."

"But she may still show up," he said.

"I told you. She won't. She's otherwise involved. Tomorrow, call her friend Rachel and ask about it. Tonight, you're on your own. But don't worry. We'll take care of it."

Didier took the card, turned it over in his hand. "You are sure?"

Darlene approached, oozing a pleasure that Didier would not get tonight. Ron smiled at her, then at Didier. "You know what happened to Alicia?"

Didier shifted from one foot to another. "It was not intended," he said. "Not at all."

"Not by you," Ron said. "And that doesn't matter. All you need to know is that I'm sure I can deal with Dr. Addams, and take care of you." He waved Darlene toward him, offered a slow smile. "I always win," he said.

CHAPTER TWENTY-EIGHT

The sun was down and the moon was up by the time Jaguar shifted in Alex's arms and raised herself up on one elbow. There were still questions to be asked and answered.

"Dan Legacy," she said. "Where'd that come from?"

"He's retired Interpol. He owed me one, and he said I could borrow his name."

"Okay," she said. "But how'd you find out about the Nahuak?"

"She spoke to me. Told me what she was."

"That's not supposed to happen."

"Jaguar, what am I?"

"It's still not supposed to happen."

"Maybe Jake's sweat lodge had something to do with it. Or maybe it was just being in New Mexico, the Land of Enchantment."

She furrowed her brow. "Sweat lodge? Jake?" she asked.

Of course she didn't know where he'd been, what he'd done. The Nahuak was separate from her, not there to spy, but only to keep him safe. "I'll show you," he said.

He took her hand in his and pressed it against his heart, opening empathically as fully as possible, letting her explore the last six months of his life. She walked through it all with the swiftness of dreaming and the meticulous care that was part of the empath's skill. She left nothing untouched, from his time in Manhattan to the horse ranch in Wyoming, and the healing of Jake and One Bird. She saw each moment he debated whether to kill or die, saw his attempts not to feel his grief and rage. He held back nothing of his errors, his self-loathing and despair. Nothing of the wild soul he'd found in himself.

She took it in without judgment, asking no questions and offering no comment. Here and there she paused and considered more deeply— when he almost walked off a cliff, when Jake called. She watched as the Nahuak folded over him at night, heard the conversations between them. She moved with him through each sweat, through his butchering of the deer and what happened on the mesa. Saw him speak to his son. Finally, she witnessed his conversation with Rachel, and his decision to return to his life.

When she was done, she moved out of him smooth as a sigh and continued silent. This was who he was, and she would know it. That was all. She lay back on her pillow and gazed up at the ceiling.

He waited, letting her process what she'd learned. He considered his next words carefully. Any apology he offered would be an insult to her courage, any explanation an insult to her intellect, which had figured it out long since. And he knew forward was her favorite direction. He would move that way.

He kissed her forehead lightly. "I had a few things to learn, but that's done now. I don't have to learn it again."

"You might have to learn other shit," she noted.

"If I do, I'll learn it with you," he said. "Whatever's in me, bad or good, it belongs to both of us now, if you want it. That's one of the two most important things I found out."

She took this in. Tasted the truth of it. "What's the other?" she asked.

"That I'm no less wild than the woman I want in my bed," he said. "And I wouldn't have it any other way."

She closed her eyes, rested the back of her hand against them. "Okay," she said, though she sounded tentative, uncertain.

She was still hurting. He'd left her, and he was the one person she counted on to stay. The store of trust they'd built was almost depleted and it had to be restocked. That would take time, and truth, and tenderness. He'd make sure she had all three in ample measure.

"Your turn," he said. "Tell me about you. The Nahuak. All that."

She shifted away from him. "Not just yet," she said.

He sensed the possibility of pain. Had she found her pleasure elsewhere in his absence? And how could he fault her for it? "Jaguar, if there was someone else," he began, but she cut him off.

"No other men," she said. "No other beds."

His relief was great, and he didn't try to hide it. "Not that I have any right, but I'm glad. You know, don't you, that there was no one else for me?"

"I was wondering," she admitted with a rueful smile.

"No more wondering," he said. "But why can't you show me?"

"I was there a long time and it wasn't much fun. I like it better here." She turned her sea green eyes to his dark ones, raised a hand, moved her fingers slowly over his face.

"Okay," he said gently. "Not tonight. But sooner or later, I'll ask again."

She sighed. "Just—not now."

He stroked her arm, wondering where he might go next that would help rather than hurt her. Back to work, he thought. She was always comfortable there. "What are your thoughts on this situation, Dr. Addams?" he asked.

She shifted her position and her mood, all business now. "My first thought—Maya's gotten pretty skilled. Her dreams about you. She was connected to the Nahuak."

"She was," Alex said. Maya deserved recompense for what she'd done, once again saving their lives. "She wants a black dog. We'll have to find her one."

Jaguar sat up, stared down at him. "She told you that?"

"Very insistently. Is that one I saw today available?"

"In fact, she is," Jaguar said.

He rolled onto his side, raised up on an elbow and faced her. "Luna?"

"She was Alicia Senna's dog. And she likes you."

"Of course she does. I like dogs. They're kindhearted."

"Apparently you never saw them rip apart a bunny carcass. What they are is hungry. All the time. And this one knows a thing or two."

"What does she have to say?"

She smiled. "You're the only man I know who'd assume I already tried empathic contact with a dog, and succeeded."

"I suppose that's why you're here naked with me," he said.

"One reason. There's others. Anyway, Luna's carrying a lot. I tried to get at it, but you know dogs. They live in the now. And it's kind of tough to do deep work in a Nahuak."

He'd forgotten how good she was at understatement. Tough. For any other empath, no matter how practiced, any contact at all would be impossible. "Maybe it'll be easier now. And I'm here. I'll help."

"Maybe. What are you doing here, anyway? I mean, besides finding me. How'd you get an Aero? I didn't even know you could drive the things."

"I have an inherent interest in risk and speed, Jaguar. You should know that."

"Yeah, but how'd you get in on it?"

"Paul set it up. I called him, to find out what was going on. The Aero's rented from a company he has connections with."

Her face showed relief. "You're going back to work?"

"I already am. That's why I'm here. And Paul's pretty damn glad about it."

"Of course he is, the pluperfect idiot. So you know the whole story?"

"I know what Paul told me, and Rachel filled me in some. I'm guessing you've got a few ideas kicking around you haven't mentioned to her yet."

"Maybe," she said. "But I can't confirm them until I have a talk with Luna. She's with Rachel. I'll call and get her over here." She rolled away from him as if to rise, but he caught her arm and stopped her.

"Tomorrow," he said.

She stayed where she was, her back to him. "What're we doing tonight?"

"Ordering in, something expensive. Then maybe a long hot bath."

She swung around and rested on an elbow, facing him. "Anything else on your agenda, Supervisor?"

"Making up for lost time. Lots of that. And TLC for you. As much as you'll put up with. Then you're getting some sleep. A real sleep, with no waiting."

She regarded him with eyes full of mischief. "But I have a date. Didier will be very disappointed if I don't show. I should at least call him."

His hold on her arm tightened. "No you shouldn't," he growled.

She grinned. "Jealous?"

"Absolutely and without exception."

"Huh. And you don't even know about Francois," she said.

"Who?"

"You've got no cause to complain. You're the one who left me alone to fend off handsome men with French accents."

"Right. But we're still staying here. And I brought handcuffs, in case you had any objections."

She raised an eyebrow. "Start that kind of fun and I doubt either of us will get much sleep."

"But what we have will be exceptionally good."

She laughed and rolled over onto him. He gathered her in, contemplating the benefits of both his position, and hers.

CHAPTER TWENTY-NINE

Alex woke just at dawn, emerging into consciousness from a dream of walking high arid lands, with a well-known and well-loved companion. The scent of sagebrush was all around, and hot sun streamed across his back. The dream was so rich he was surprised to find himself in a hotel bed, with Jaguar next to him. Not only next to him, but stroking his face, her sea green eyes filled with turbulence.

"What is it?" he asked.

"I didn't know if you'd come back," she whispered. Her eyes held all her pain at the prospect. Six months and a universe of hurt.

He touched the ends of her hair, silk beneath his fingertips. "Is that why you cut it?"

"No. I couldn't declare you dead. It was for Springer."

He continued stroking her hair. She'd had her own untended grief. She had loved his son, too. Had yearned for a better end to his story. He reached down and put a hand to her face, called her lucid eyes to his and spoke subvocally.

Rocks would melt and seas burn before I'd leave you again.

She kept her gaze on his face and spoke out loud. "You might have to take that back," she said.

"Why would I?" he asked, speaking aloud in his turn.

"Because I won't give you another son."

That, he thought. She'd relinquished childbearing to keep her most powerful empathic gift of Sunwatcher. In a bad moment he'd thrown that at her, but in truth he couldn't bear it if she was anything other than her complete self.

"You chose that with good reason," he said. "I'm not about to kick back about it."

A long pause followed, and then she said, "Wrong order."

Her words made no sense. "What?" he asked.

"I probably would've been a Sunwatcher anyway, but I took it on after I knew there'd be no children. What happened in the Killing Times left me injured. Permanently."

He took a moment to consider. She'd known this for a long time, and had let him believe otherwise. Because she wanted him to accept her on her own terms? Because she felt her own grief?

"Why didn't you tell me?" he asked gently.

"It didn't matter before. Now you have a right to know. It's not something I can change my mind about. I can't have children."

The complexity of it twined around his heart with threads that only bound him closer to her. What she made of her life it was a lesson in turning poison into medicine. And she was here, with him. Beyond despair and hope, she remained. He grasped her hand and began kissing the tips of her fingers.

"Then neither will I," he said, between kisses.

He heard her intake of breath, just short of a sob. He continued kissing her fingers. When he'd gotten through one hand and moved on to the next, she regained her composure and spoke.

"Starting early, aren't you?" she asked.

"Early and often," he replied. "That's my motto when I'm making up for lost time."

She offered him the palm of her hand. "You missed a spot," she said.

Dawn rose outside the window as they explored all missing places, and neither one worried about the necessity of sleep.

CHAPTER THIRTY

It was early afternoon when they heard a soft knock on the door. Alex muttered something that sounded like 'go away,' and retreated back into sleep. Jaguar put a hand on his shoulder and spoke into him.

It's your room. Better answer it.

He groaned, rolled over. "Be right there," he called.

He rose, grabbed his bathrobe and wrapped himself in it, went to the door and looked through the peephole. Jaguar heard a muffled voice on the other side, unrecognizable. She slid under the covers, back into a languid contentment better than sleep. Alex opened the door and Rachel entered, holding a leash that connected her to Luna, who thumped her tail with enthusiasm.

"G'Morning," he mumbled.

"Afternoon, actually," she replied. "A helluva day to sleep in. Didier's all pissed off because Jaguar didn't show for dinner, and Scott's frantic because she's not in her room."

As she spoke, Luna yipped and tore the leash away from her grasp, raced into the room and leaped onto the bed, where she wiggled and licked relentlessly.

"Because I'm here," Jaguar called as she tried to dodge the onslaught. She sat up, gathering the covers over her. Luna plunked down next to her and panted happily.

Rachel blinked. "Holy shit," she said. She beamed at Jaguar, then turned her beam to Alex. "This is good," she said brightly. "I like this."

"So do we," Alex admitted.

"Wow. Well, I'm better now. I'll leave you two alone. And I'll let Scott know. Luna, come here," she called.

"No," Alex and Jaguar both said at once. Alex turned and looked to Jaguar. She lifted a hand, undulated her fingers to call both humans toward her.

"We need to talk to that dog," she said to Rachel. Then, "Alex, could you get me some clothes?"

CHAPTER THIRTY-ONE

Jaguar and Alex, Rachel and Luna, considered the items in plastic bags on the small table in Alex's hotel room. Jaguar had gotten dressed and taken them out for perusal, intending to use them in what came next. Rachel had gone down the hall to let Scott know all was well, and when she returned Jaguar looked to her.

"You can stay or go, as you choose, but you'll have to be quiet."

Rachel drew thumb and index finger across her lips, zipping them, and took a seat in the chair near the window. Alex and Jaguar knelt by Luna, who lifted her head, beat her tail against the floor. She sensed a good game, about to begin.

"Sure you're up to it?" Alex asked Jaguar. "It's just yesterday you stopping waiting."

"I'm good, Alex. The change is immediate, and there's no lingering effects," she said. "Let's do tandem contact. I'll be primary, and you take secondary. Okay with you?"

He nodded, and Jaguar placed a hand on Luna's head, spoke softly in her native tongue until Luna sighed a deep doggie sigh, put her head down and relaxed.

Alex put a hand on Jaguar's shoulder—probably not necessary, given their long history of working together, but it had been a while since they dealt with an animal, or since they'd tried this kind of contact, where everything would flow from Luna to Jaguar, and from there to him.

Jaguar groped for one of the bags, opened it and got her hand inside, pulled out the glove inside and held it near Luna's nose. The dog snuffled at it, and as she did, images emerged, moving from her to Jaguar.

A hand, reaching down. The permeating scent of something sweet, an overriding sense of satisfaction. *Good dog*, a female voice said. *Good dog, Luna.*

Then, the scent changed to something dark and smokey, but the same hand reached, the same words were spoken. *Good dog. Good dog, Luna.* Alex heard Jaguar chuckle, and he grinned. They both released from contact, and smiled at each other.

"Donuts," Alex said.

"And smoked meats," Jaguar replied.

"Is that some kind of code?" Rachel demanded.

They looked to her. "Aren't you supposed to be quiet?" Jaguar said.

"Sure. As soon as you tell me what the hell you're talking about. Is it—Did Meris…" She let the sentence die, and moved her hand in a gesture of inquiry.

"Meris," Alex said, "liked to sneak treats to Luna. Donuts."

"And smoked meat," Jaguar added.

"Oh. Then she's okay?"

Jaguar waved a hand across the room. "She may pass go, and collect 200 dollars."

Rachel fanned herself. "I'm pretty damn glad about that," she said.

"Me, too," Jaguar agreed. "Next item."

Alex handed her Didier's racing sock, and Jaguar put it to Luna's nose. She sniffed, and began a low growl. No smoked meats, and no donuts from that source. She didn't like Didier. Didier didn't like her.

Then, images appeared. Didier, moving about the garage, seen in motion as a dog sees, his colors muted, his motion broken in time. He approached Alicia, and Luna stood, leaned against Alicia's knee, not letting him near. Alicia's laughter, and Luna leaning in more, feeling human flesh against her flank, liking it.

Another image—Didier leaning over Alicia's Ferrari, his hand moving over it. Alicia entering the scene, snapping out angry words at him. Luna barking, falling back at Alicia's command. She spoke to Didier, and though Luna didn't translate words, the intent was clear: Alicia taking the pack leader position, warning off a threatening presence. Luna stood at attention, but wouldn't attack unless told to do so. Jaguar eased herself out of contact, looked to Alex. Simultaneously, they reached down and began soothing Luna, who was tense, ready to defend her humans, living and dead.

"It's okay, girl," Alex said. "You're fine."

Luna looked from him to Jaguar, who leaned over and breathed near her mouth, letting her catch the scent of approval and reassurance. "Treats for you," she murmured.

She stood, went to the remnants of their breakfast, and brought crusts of danish over to her. Luna sniffed them, thumped her tail, and accepted the gift.

Alex stood, ran a hand over his face. "I'm not sure that told us anything useful," he said. "At least, nothing we didn't know already. Didier wants a seat. Luna doesn't like him. Neither did Alicia."

"Let's try one more thing," Jaguar said.

"What?"

"You'll see."

She reached into the third bag, pulled out a clump of hair.

Rachel leaned forward. "What's that? I didn't get it for you."

"Nope," Jaguar said. "And if you don't mind, you can continue that zipped lip position."

Rachel receded. Alex raised an eyebrow at Jaguar. "Are you going to tell me?"

"Not yet," she said. She put her hand on Luna's head. Alex put his hand on Jaguar's shoulder. She brought the clump of hair to Luna's nose and let her snuffle.

The response was immediate, and unpleasant. Broken images appeared of a lean, dark-haired man holding Alicia by the shoulders, shaking her. Alicia, pushing him away. Images of that same man standing with Didier while Luna watched, tense and growling. They bent over a computer together. Didier laughed. The other man's face remained grim. Then, a sense of dread, and the presence of death in the room, and Luna bared her teeth, ready to attack.

Sitting next to Jaguar, Luna lifted her head, and howled. The room filled with sound beyond bearing, the sound of infinite terror, the sound of a dog howling.

"Holy hell," Rachel said, and rose from her seat, pressing her hands against her ears, moving to Alex and Jaguar, to Luna, who was howling. Jaguar leaned over Luna, holding her secure against fear, against death. Alex moved in with her and did the same. Rachel remained standing, hovering over them, waiting for instructions. Luna subsided into whimpering, and everyone breathed again.

"What the hell was that?" Rachel asked.

"Alicia's death," Jaguar replied. She leaned back on her haunches. "You okay?"

"Um, sure. What should I do?"

"Nothing yet." She turned to Alex. "You heard it?"

"I felt it," he said. "Something I never felt before."

Jaguar nodded. "Sound, used to kill."

"Fuck," Alex said. "Infrasound."

Rachel gave a small gasp. Alex and Jaguar turned to her.

"He had an algorithm," Rachel said.

"What?" Jaguar demanded.

"When I was in the paddock during qualifying I saw a program on Didier's computer. I asked him about it, and he said it was his investment program, but it wasn't. It had to do with—with herz values and volume. Jaguar, I *saw* it, and I didn't know what it was."

"You sure?" Jaguar asked.

"Well, yeah. But what does it mean?"

"It's how Alicia died," Jaguar said. "Infrasound, creating cellular cavitation and meltdown. Easy enough to put it through her earbuds, and whoever did it knew how to aim it specifically toward her heart." She looked to Alex. "The Pentagon experimented with it, didn't they?"

"Yes, but they called it off. Too nasty even for them."

"But the ME hasn't mentioned it," Rachel said.

"She won't," Jaguar said. "I'm not even sure if lab testing will identify it. But it was on that list you gave me, and I kept almost hearing it." She looked to Alex. "We both know the only man who understands it well enough to set this up."

"Schulman," Alex said grimly. "Bands work with it, at a low level. The kids at Springer's concert—they felt an ominous presence. One of the special effects of infrasound, used in the right way. But it won't help us nail him. As usual, he had someone else do his dirty work. We can't connect him."

He moved to the window, and stood looking out. His hands clenched and unclenched. Jaguar watched his back.

Rachel thought they needed a moment. "Um—how about if I take Luna for a walk? I think she needs it. So do I."

Jaguar kept her gaze on Alex. "Sure," she said. "But not alone."

"Scott's down the hall."

Alex gave a curt nod. "Come back here when you're done."

"See you in a bit," Rachel said. She grabbed Luna's leash and made her exit.

Alex waited to hear the door close, then ran a hand through his hair. "Jaguar, who is that man?" he asked. "The one Luna showed us."

"The other guy who wanted to bed me," she said.

He shifted his posture, scowled. "Someone *else*?" he demanded.

She laughed softly. "That'll teach you not to leave town."

His scowl softened. He lifted a shoulder and let it fall. "Tell me about him."

"Detective Francois Thei. He's a Montreal cop who had an affair with Alicia," she said. "A cop with issues about empaths. I'll show you."

She moved to him, touched his face and let him see her experience with Detective Thei—his vexed relationship with the empathic arts, his reaction to their conversation about communicating with Luna, the way he'd courted her.

"Shit," he said when she was through. "Is there any man who doesn't fall in love with you or try to kill you? Or both?"

"There's Paul Dinardo. He tried to kill me, but he certainly didn't fall in love," she offered, and that pulled a laugh from him.

"Okay," he said. "So Didier and Francois worked together on this."

"Looks that way, but I'm guessing Didier wasn't in on the full picture. He only wanted to make Alicia lose. He's not a killer by nature—not enough anger in him. Detective Thei is another story. But I'll bet he's covered, too. He works for Schulman."

"Then maybe we should focus on Didier. The algorithm was on his notebook."

"Didier. And to think I almost let him see my breasts. Maybe we can squeeze a confession out of him. I could twist his nuts 'til he squeals like a pig."

"No, Jaguar," he said. "Coerced confessions aren't admissible either. What was that about your breasts?"

"Not important. Maybe I could twist his nuts anyway? Just for fun?"

"If you like," he said. "After we figure out how to work this. You *didn't* let him see your breasts, did you?"

She rolled her eyes at him. "Sometimes," she said, "you're such a man."

"Rachel said the same thing. But my sense is you like me that way."

"For the most part." She touched his shoulder lightly. "You okay?"

"Just figuring out what's next," he said. "We can connect Didier to Schulman, but only loosely, and he probably didn't know what he was doing. We can connect Didier to Detective Thei, but only through empathic contact, which isn't admissible. And we can't connect Detective Thei to Schulman, though I'll bet he knew exactly what he was doing and why."

"Ron's good at keeping points of separation between him and his kill. But I have an idea."

Her ideas were usually high risk, with lots of *ex tempore* moves. He eyed her suspiciously. "What?" he asked.

She ran a finger down her nose, tapped her lips, then spoke. "Three men went after Alicia. She couldn't outrun them, and she was one of the fastest humans on the planet. Now I'm guessing they'd all love to have a shot at me—especially Ron. So maybe instead of running, we should present them with a still target."

"No," he said.

"I didn't think you'd like it much, but it's all I've got."

"Get something else. I won't have you putting yourself on the line for this. Not again."

"Now that's interesting. Just a few hours ago there was a man in my bed who told me whatever he had to learn next, he'd learn with me. I wonder who that was."

For a moment, he hated her, and her damn memory, and her damnable capacity to toss out truth as if it was popcorn. Then, he laughed. "You're a real pain in the ass," he noted.

"Rachel said the same thing," she replied, "but you seem to like me that way."

"On some days, I do," he admitted. He ran a hand through is hair. "Jaguar, you've done more than enough already, and this is my job to complete."

"That's what my lover says. But what about the Adept?"

Alex stared down at his hands, thought of the visions he'd seen in the sweat lodge. He was driving fast, crashing deliberately into another car. She was driving fast, too.

No. Not just that. There was more.

She was racing hard and he was driving to her, watching as she smashed her own car into the side of a wall. Then, she was in a hospital bed, and he had his hands around Ron Schulman's throat, rage running through the room like a bull with its horns down.

He drew in breath. The images faded into grey. All the moving parts of what he'd seen fell into place to create a complicated and risky plan that might or might not work. But she'd bear the brunt of that risk. He shook himself back into normal time, and stared up at her. She remained silent. She was so good at that.

"You're right. I don't like it," he said.

He felt her brief empathic contact, light as cobwebs, there and gone. "Just because you know it's the only way," she said. "Tell me what you saw, Spider Magus."

He closed his eyes, opened them again. "I saw you racing with Didier. There was a crash. You crashed. Then there was a hospital room, and you, in a bed, not moving."

"Huh," she said. "That's pretty much what I had in mind."

"What?" he demanded. "Killing yourself? You took considerable risk to pull me back from the edge of the cliff I've been standing on for the last six months. You think I'll let you trip over it now?"

"I have no intention of killing myself," she said. "I want to end this, and live to gloat about it."

"What if you can't? What if all you can do is pin Didier down?"

She glowered at him. "Did Schulman hurt you? Did he kill someone I love and get away with it? I won't walk away with just Didier's head. Who could I show it to? Where's the honor in that?"

"Fuck honor," Alex said. "He won't steal another drop of blood from anyone I love."

"Then why did I cut my hair?"

They stood glaring at each other, and each glare contained the heat of love without measure. They'd held this stance in the past, and they both knew what it signified. Her passion knew no bounds, and she thought of his son as her own. He would do anything to protect her, and he held his responsibilities as all his own. She'd cut her hair for Springer, a promise kept. But he had a promise to keep as well.

"I told Springer I'd do something about Schulman. I drive the car," he said.

"Won't work," she replied. "We don't have the time it'd take you to learn to drive. Besides, Ron wants to kill me before he kills you. It's part of making you suffer as much as possible."

He wanted to fight her, but he couldn't. She was right. He turned his hands into fists, looking for other ground.

She put a hand on his arm, spoke gently. "Don't you get it, Alex? Springer was an Adept, too. He knew his death would lead us exactly here. And he expected us both to finish what he started. He gave his life for that. We can't deny him the results of his sacrifice. At least, I can't."

Everything she said was true, and everything in him rebelled against it. "I've got a lot more experience than Springer, and I still think odds are high this won't work," he said.

"That's because you're a wolf, not a cat," she said demurely. "Cats hunt by sitting still and waiting for rats to come to them, and the rats do just that. You know why? They've got tiny parasites in their brains that makes them forget to be afraid of cats."

He knew about that. Rodents who carried a protozoan parasite named Toxoplasma gondii in their brains lost their aversion to cat scents, and, in fact, often ran right to them. This served the parasite well, because it could only continue its life cycle inside the intestines of the cat. Thus, a one celled creature buried in the brain of the rodent drove it toward its own demise.

"Are you saying Schulman's a rat?" he asked.

"You bet," she said. "Rat, and rat fucked. With parasites in his brain that make him arrogant as hell. Alex, the smartest thing we can do is create a situation where one or more of these guys sees me as an easy target. They'll come after me anyway, and at least this way we can establish the terms."

Her voice was cool as still water, fed by the deepest spring. She had no fear about this. He took her hand and kissed it. She was wild. So was he. And his son trusted her to do her part. He would have to trust that as well. They would try one more time, the two of them, acting together for a young man they'd both loved.

"I'll be on you every step," he said. "You don't do a millisecond of this on your own."

"Sure," she replied.

"Let's work out the details" he said, and they did.

When they were done, he pulled her close, moved his mouth against the side of her neck.

"You didn't let Didier see your breasts, did you?" he asked.

"Would I waste them on him?" she replied.

* * * *

Rachel left Luna with Scott, and was happily ensconced in bed with Meris after a few hours of pleasure, when she reached up and touched her face.

"I'm glad it wasn't you," she said.

Meris startled, frowned at her. "What isn't me?"

"Nothing," she said.

"No. Really. What?"

"Nothing—just…" She tried to think like Jaguar, who was a horrible liar, but the master of evasion. "Well," she said. "You're here, and I'm just visiting. So I'm glad we're not, like, thinking of a future or anything. That kind of thing."

"That doesn't make any sense," Meris said.

"Neither does what we're doing," Rachel said.

"Right. Well, seize the day. And the night. And whatever else you can get away with."

And so they did.

CHAPTER THIRTY-TWO

Jaguar called Didier, and arranged to meet him for dinner at Menara, a Moroccan restaurant in Old Montreal. She wore her best gold silk pantsuit, and under the soft lighting of the room, she glimmered like the beginnings of fire. He was already at their table, lounging on the low couch that served as seating here, and he stood, looked her up and down and smiled.

"I'm not sure if you are Joan of Arc, or a soothing angel," he said.

"Neither, I hope," she said. "Joan met a bad end, and my understanding is that angels don't get much fun." She sat, and so did he.

"The bisteeya here is particularly good," he mentioned as he looked over the menu. "I'd recommend that, and the lamb."

"I may defer the lamb," she said. "I have to watch what I eat if I'm going to race."

He paused in his perusal, lifted his head to look at her. "Are you?" he asked.

She shrugged. "Looks like it. Meris is amenable."

"Of course she is. She knows you can't beat her."

She heard the jagged edge of anger in his voice. "No she doesn't," she said.

He lifted a hand, placed it on hers. "But I do."

She squeezed his hand. "Have you seen my times? They're better than yours."

The small muscles around his mouth went tight and then quickly relaxed. "Darling one," he said, "You're beautiful, intelligent, strong, and there are many things you do well, but you don't need to pretend you can go beyond your limits in a field where you have no experience. Unless, perhaps, that man—Dan Legacy—encouraged you in folly?"

"Don't tell me you're jealous," she cooed at him.

"Of course not."

"But you are. I'm just not sure what you're jealous about. Dan, or the fact that I'm stealing your Ferrari ride. Every driver's dream, isn't it?"

He removed his hand from hers and leaned in toward her. "Jaguar, you can't," he said, meaning it. "You'll—you'll hurt yourself."

She leaned away from him. "I'd hate to do that. Tell you what, I'll race you for it."

He pushed himself back against the couch. "What?" he asked.

"I'll race you," she repeated. "If you win, I'll slink back to the Planetoid and you can have the seat."

His finger tapped against the table. "You mean that, don't you?"

"Sure. How else will I know if I'm good enough?"

"Where, and with what cars?"

"On the track, with the Ferraris, of course."

He shook his head. "The stewards will never let you."

"You forget who's backing me."

"Ah. You'll play the Planetoid card?"

"You bet. I'll say it's a crime re-enactment, and you're helping. That is, if you're not too chicken shit to try."

He lifted a hand, let it drop on the table. "My only fear is making you feel bad about yourself, something that should never happen."

"Better men than you have tried and failed," she reassured him. "We'll do fifteen laps, and winner takes all. How's that?"

"That is fine. Jaguar, no matter who wins, I want you to know I still admire and respect you. And I'll continue to court you. I think you'd be a very interesting lover."

She leaned over, put her face next to his neck and flicked a tongue against his ear. "No matter who wins, there's one thing I want *you* to know."

"Yes, my love?"

"You'll never get to see my breasts."

He remained silent, not sure she'd actually said that. She helped him figure it out.

"See you on the track, little boy," she said. She pressed her hands against the table, rose and left the restaurant.

* * * *

When she returned to Alex's hotel room, he was awake and waiting for her.

"How's Didier?" he asked as soon as she entered.

"Small and inconsequential," she said. "Any way you look at him."

"Hmmph. You set it up?"

"Good to go," she said. "You?"

"Ready. I'll be on your back the whole way, Dr. Addams."

She grinned. "Maybe we should practice that, Supervisor."

Precious, he thought. There was not a woman like her in the universe, and he'd been lucky enough to find her.

"Allow me to demonstrate," he replied, and moved to her.

CHAPTER THIRTY-THREE

Alex put his call in to Paul the next day, making the necessary arrangements for what would happen after the race. As he explained, he saw beads of sweat breaking out on Paul's high forehead.

"That sounds damn crazy, so I'm guessing it was her idea," Paul said, "You sure you want to go along with it?"

"You want me to remind you how we got here?" Alex asked in his turn.

Paul showed a handkerchief, which he wiped across his face. "I guess not," he said.

"You're smarter than you look. Can we count on you?"

"Yeah," he said. "I'll be there."

When he signed off from Paul, he turned to Jaguar. "Your turn," he said.

Jaguar nodded, and opened her cellcom, dialed Detective Thei's number. When his face appeared on screen, she showed him a tense aspect. "Francois, I have to tell you a few things I learned. Also an idea about how to conclude this mess."

He showed concern and interest. "Go ahead," he told her.

She explained enough to make him understand—that they suspected infrasound killed Alicia, had evidence that Didier was involved, but not proof enough to arrest him. That she'd use his ambition for a Ferrari seat to make him act again, and then they'd grab him.

He listened without comment, then made her go back over a few key points. "How do you know it was infrasound? The ME has said nothing about that."

"They need molecular exam, spectography, infusion, the whole works to parse it out," she told him. "But I know what happened, and I know Didier's involved because my assistant saw a program on his computer, which he's since wiped out."

Detective Thei's face showed more concern. "There is no other way to do this?"

"None I can think of. And I want to do it. For Alicia."

"Yes. For Alicia. But I'll be there," he said. "No arguments on that."

"Sure," she said. "But just you, and you stay in the paddock, with Rachel and Meris. I don't want him to suspect anything."

"Yes, of course. But when it is done, and we have him, then you need to take some time off. Stay here, and truly relax. Let me show you better ways of living your life."

"Maybe I will," she said, and signed off.

She turned to Alex, who had arranged himself discreetly on her couch, out of view. "Well?" she asked. "What do you think?"

He was silent a moment, then said, "I think I'd like to make his face resemble paper pulp."

"Metaphorically, I think you already have," Jaguar replied.

They continued making arrangements, talking with Rachel and Meris, who would both be present, running telemetry, witnesses ensuring there was no unfair technical advantage on either side. Rachel was nervous as hell, Meris even more so.

"It'll be fine," Jaguar told them both, and both women groaned and threw their hands up at the same time. Jaguar chuckled, and Rachel showed a smile, mirrored by Meris.

"Well," Rachel told Meris, "she does have a very high accuracy rate."

"One hundred percent," Jaguar confirmed. "And Alex'll be there. You know he won't let it go wrong."

"Where?" Rachel asked. "Where will he be?"

"In his Aero, at the end of pit lane and ready to move."

"He'll be, like, in touch with you?"

"Constantly," Jaguar said.

"Good," Meris said. "That's good."

* * * *

The race was set for just after dawn, and Didier and Jaguar met in the garage, shook hands, and got in their cars. They made their way to the start-finish line, and waited for the signal to start. Meris, Rachel, and Detective Thei stayed in the paddock, reading telemetry. Detective Thei kept his car pointed toward the track, ready to go if Jaguar needed him.

Silver light poured over the track, over their eyes. The red lights went off one by one, and both cars took off at speed, staying next to each other around the first turn. She had fifteen laps to get it right, and she'd do so, as soon as she figured out what that meant.

As they'd planned, she let him take the lead during the first three laps, and then took him on the inside as they went through the tunnel in lap four. By lap five she was two seconds ahead and holding back, letting him catch up.

Then, communication from Alex, who was reading them both. *Fine driving*, he said.

I'm better than he is, she replied. *What's he using to get me?*

Laser fire weapon. When he gets close enough, he'll go for your tires.

Is that what we want? she asked.

He listened in to Didier, then took a chance and listened to Detective Thei, where he learned something he didn't like, a lot. Something in his mind beyond the crash.

No, he said to Jaguar. *When he blows your tires Detective Thei hits you with infrasound.*

Can't, she said. *No earbuds.*

Alex worried this for one second only, then understood. *The telemetry*, he told her. *He's connected through that. Jaguar, he can get to you.*

What's my move? she asked, cool and calm and still racing.

Didier was coming up behind her fast, putting on all the speed he could. She couldn't let him stay behind her for long. Alex calculated quickly, saw the one place on the track that might interrupt infrasound. One place only, and only one thing for her to do, though he had no idea how she'd do it.

Get in the tunnel, he said. *And get behind Didier.*

He felt her considering while Didier drew closer. *Only one way to do both*, she said, and showed him what she had in mind.

Theoretically, her car had enough downforce to drive across the tunnel's ceiling, and come down at Didier's back. In reality, that capacity had never been tested. Shit, he thought. Really? She'd try that?

Of course she would. And he had to make sure it worked. His heart thumped hard in his chest, and he moved his Aero onto the track, glad that pit lane emerged close to the tunnel. He screeched out at speed, going the wrong way, staying in touch with her. Didier was less than a second behind her now.

Move your ass, Dr. Addams, he said, and then she was at the midpoint in the tunnel and he was at the entrance, close enough to see her.

As he watched, she drove her car up the side of the tunnel wall, onto the ceiling, then dove down in back of Didier's car, which did a donut and headed toward her. Alex hit his throttle and came up fast, smacking him in the rear, sending him reeling. Jaguar spun out and smashed into the far side of the tunnel, flipped once, then landed right side up, while Didier's car pummeled itself against the tunnel wall.

All moving objects came to rest. All motion and all sound ceased. Alex sat in his car, breathing hard. Don't move yet, he told himself. Find out what's happening. He made empathic contact with Didier and found him out cold, but still alive. He started to make contact with Jaguar, then thought better of it. He got out of his car, went to hers.

As he approached, he saw that her hands were off the wheel. That meant either she remembered to take them off to avoid having her wrists broken, or she was unconscious. Or dead.

"Jaguar," he said out loud.

She turned to him, got her helmet off and showed him a grin. "Pretty good driving, Supervisor," she said.

Elation was a drug that filled him, top to bottom. "Ditto, Dr. Addams," he replied.

She moved her head toward the car behind her. "How's Didier?"

"Down, but not dead."

"Don't look so sad about that. Go take care of him."

"You're okay?"

"Fine, Alex."

She meant it. He leaned down and kissed her quickly, then went to Didier's car, observing how meaningless he looked, slumped in the seat, hands loose at his side. Alex pulled his helmet off, tapped his cheek a few times. When his eyes opened, Alex grabbed him by the throat and shook him hard. "What the hell did you do to her, you son of a bitch. For Ron? I'll kill him. Tell him I'll kill him."

Didier's eyes went wide with terror. "I—I don't know what you're talking about," he stuttered.

Alex pulled back a fist, swung, and hit him hard enough to knock him out again. He rubbed at his knuckles, nurturing a distinct sense of satisfaction, then walked back to Jaguar. He looked down at her, and rubbed his knuckles some more. "What was that about your breasts?"

When she started to laugh and didn't look like stopping any time soon, he shook his head at her.

"Dr. Addams, if you remember the script, you're seriously injured. Near death, in fact. You really should stop laughing before the ambulance gets here."

* * * *

Detective Thei was on the scene immediately after, to find an unconscious Jaguar and a distraught Alex on scene, just as the paramedics pulled in. He didn't recognize that one of the men in attendance happened to be a former Navy SEAL. Alex also gave no sign of recognition, but showed himself to be lost in a kind of madness, continuing to yell wildly about his son, and Ron Schulman.

Soon after, to Detective Thei's surprise, a Planetoid board governor showed up and put hands on Alex, pulling him away from the scene and putting him in a car.

"Sorry," he said. "This guy, he's a little off. Had some bad things happen to him. We'll take care of it."

"It is difficult, the work you do," Detective Thei said sympathetically.

"Yeah," he agreed. "I'm Paul Dinardo. Governor for zone 12. And you're Detective Thei, right? Montreal police? How's the lady?"

Detective Thei looked to the ambulance. "Alive, I think."

"She'll pull through?"

"I do not know," he said sadly. "The medical men look worried."

"Yeah. Okay. Lemme take care of this guy. I'll be in touch to see how she's doing."

"Certainly," Detective Thei said.

Didier, once he recovered from Alex's fist, walked away from his wreck and refused medical attention. "I can walk," he insisted. "And I don't need the hospital."

He was allowed to leave the scene. Nobody really cared.

When Paul got in the car, Alex lifted his head. "How'd it go? he asked.

Paul straightened his tie. "I took acting lessons in college. They came in handy."

"Sure," Alex said, but he looked nervous. "We have to spread it around that I'm nuts, and she's paralyzed, can't talk, all that. Also that the Planetoid has abandoned her. You know that, right?"

"You only told me three or four times. You sure you don't want another guy or two at her door?"

"Scott's there, and he won't be alone. If we add more they'll get suspicious."

"Yeah," Paul said. "If you're sure."

"Paul," Alex said. "You sound like you actually give a rat's ass what happens to her."

"I'm used to her," he said. "If she goes, who the hell knows what other crazy woman you'll find."

"No other," he said. "I don't think there's another like her anywhere."

CHAPTER THIRTY-FOUR

Jaguar lay in her hospital bed, hooked up to a variety of monitors that beeped and hummed in response to the signals of her body. This, she thought, was the hardest part of the plan. Waiting. She'd had way too much of that already.

An orderly came in and checked her monitors, touched her shoulder lightly. She sent her thoughts to him, seeking connection.

Anything yet? she asked him subvocally.

No, ma'am, came the response. Scott, there as watchdog again. He played an orderly as well as he'd once played a prison guard. She found her task of playing a paralyzed woman not so easy.

We don't know if he'll show tonight, she said.

No, ma'am, he said again, and left the room.

We don't know if he'll show at all. We could be wasting our time.

Another voice spoke into the impatient gloom of her thoughts. *He'll show,* it said. Alex, somewhere outside her view but nearby, ready to pounce at a moment's notice.

Before I go insane? she asked him.

Yes, the voice said with certainty.

When, Spider Magus?

A brief pause. Then, his voice again. *Now,* he said.

She reached out to him, felt what he felt. Now. She stayed still, forced her eyes to stay closed. She heard soft footsteps moving toward her. Felt the near presence of another human. He smelled of expensive cologne and despair. She tried not to tense. He had to believe she was paralyzed. They all knew if he touched her, it would be to kill her.

Then, pressure on her arm. She opened her eyes, and saw the forest shaded eyes of Detective Thei looking down at her. He lifted a hand, and it held a needle. She allowed herself to whimper softly.

"Hush, my love," he said, just as softly. "It will be better this way. You would not want to linger in agony."

She couldn't allow herself to move, though every instinct in her wanted to grab his wrist and twist until he yelped like a little boy. Instead, she made empathic contact with him, spoke into him, knowing he could hear.

Wait, she said. *Tell me first. Was it for Ron?*

He stopped his motion, the needle hovering just above her vein. "For Ron, and for me," he said out loud. He didn't like the empathic arts. He wouldn't use them. "A confluence of events, you might say. Alicia would not give up her gifts, and Mr. Schulman offered me a great deal of money to make sure she didn't continue using them unfairly against the other drivers. I despise all that is unfair."

But—why me? she asked.

"You would not relinquish your gifts any more than she would," he said.

And he never forgave his father for being an empath, for dying because of it, she thought. Never forgave his mother for killing him. But none of that mattered right now. She was not here to rehab him. She just had to make him talk.

Who showed you how? she asked, still speaking subvocally.

"Ron did. He knows the technology, from his music business. Didier helped, for reasons of his own, though he knew nothing of our ultimate goal. He had only ambition, and wanted to make her lose. What I did, that was for principles."

"Principles?" she said out loud. "You lay claim to principles for murdering women, you rat fuck son of a bitch?"

Detective Thei's eyes went wide, and he brought the needle down hard, but not fast enough. Her hand shot up and grabbed his wrist. Scott came up behind him and wrapped an arm around his neck. "Drop it, asshole," he snarled.

Jaguar sat up. "Scott," she said. "I'm shocked."

"Sorry, ma'am," he muttered. "I had to call this one as I see it."

* * * *

Soon enough Scott had Detective Thei cuffed, and Jaguar unhooked herself from her medical equipment. "That went well," she said. "We got the recording?"

"Yes, ma'am," he replied. "You want me to take him away?"

"Absolutely," she said. "There should be a car downstairs, waiting for him. You go ahead. I'll bring the recording equipment. I'll be down as soon as I'm dressed."

"I think you should come with me," Scott said judiciously.

"We got him. I'm fine."

Detective Thei struggled against his bonds, and glared at her. "You," he said. "You are no different than she was. A bitch goddess who makes a mockery of love."

"If you ever get off the Planetoid," she noted, "you should consider taking up a different hobby than trying to flip empaths. Scott, get rid of him, will you?"

Scott pulled him out of the room, and Jaguar was left on her own. She rose from her bed, pulled her clothes out from the drawer in the dresser, took them into the bathroom and dressed. As she did so, she heard movement in her room. "Alex?" she asked. "We got him. I'll be out in a minute. Grab the recorder, okay? It's tucked under the bed."

Good to her word, she emerged from the bathroom fully clothed, to find herself face to face with Ron Schulman who was tucking a small recorder into his pocket.

She pulled herself up tall. "Another asshole," she said. "What are you doing here?"

He smiled. "What no one else can do," he said. "Ending you."

He didn't waste time with more talk. He grabbed her wrist, twisted her around and pulled her close. He lifted a hand toward her chest, and she saw that he held something in it—a small device, black and round. An infrasound delivery system, she supposed. She raised her foot to smash it into his instep, but got no further before she felt him torn away from her.

She whirled around in time to see Alex throw Ron into the wall so hard he made a dent. What Ron held went skittering across the floor.

"You put your hands on her, you putrid prick?" Alex roared. "You dare *touch* her?"

Ron's eyes went big. He was used to negotiating, but there was no talking to the force he faced now. He made a sound like whimpering. Alex grabbed his shirt front and turned him, slammed his face against the wall, grabbed his wrists and put cuffs on them. As he did, Scott appeared in the doorway.

Alex turned his way. "What?" he growled out.

"Just thought you might need me, sir," he said.

"I don't," he said. He turned back to Ron, pulled him around again to face him. "What did you bring? More infrasound?"

"I just—I wanted to see how she was doing." His voice was high with panic, but Jaguar figured he was already working out his escape plans. She was right.

"You're—you're insane," he told Alex. "They told me you're messed up. Let me go. You have no right to hold me."

"In your pocket is a recording of someone naming you as co-conspirator in murder," Jaguar mentioned.

Ron whipped his head toward her. "Detective Thei? Alicia's lover? Who'll believe him?"

Alex shook him once, hard. "Don't even look at her," he said, his voice icy. He nodded to Scott. "Pick that thing up and bag it," he said, indicating the device Ron had tossed away. Scott did so, and Alex twisted Ron's shirtfront until he made a noise.

"You made poor choices today, Ron," he said. "Assuming I'd leave Jaguar alone was the worst. Nobody touches Jaguar. Not on my watch." His free hand clenched and unclenched at his side. He kept his gaze fixed on Ron. Jaguar stood poised for disaster.

"Another poor choice—trying to stop her heart. It's unstoppable, but yours isn't." He twisted Ron's shirt tighter. "There's a place in the cardiac wall that if you hit it hard enough, everything stops. A sudden cessation of function. It leaves no mark. It just kills."

Scott looked to Jaguar, and she made a small gesture with her hand to hold him back. Alex had to choose this. Had to choose what came next.

Ron cast her a terrified glance."Stop him," he pleaded. "Make him stop."

"You're begging *her*?" Alex demanded, his eyes as feral as she'd seen only once before. "That's cheap. Try begging me instead."

"Please," Ron said.

"Please what?" Alex asked.

"Please, don't kill me," he answered.

"What'll you give me?"

"Anything," Ron said. "Money, anything you want."

"Then give us back our son," Alex said.

Ron gasped, his eyes growing even wider. Jaguar caught the plural noun, took a step forward, and stopped. He had to choose what to do. Had to choose this for himself, one way or another. She watched as he raised his free hand, unclenched it, pressed it against Ron's face.

Then it was clear to her what he intended. Something empaths weren't supposed to do, under any circumstances. Something he needed to do, for Springer. For their son. She stayed where she was, but moved her thoughts into his and listened.

Alex paid no attention to her. He was busy, pouring his own experience into Ron like water, giving him everything he'd felt about Springer, his life and his death. Giving him what Springer felt, and why. It was the emotional equivalent of waterboarding, enough feeling here to drown in. When he'd gotten some ways in, Jaguar added her lot to the mix, showing Ron her experience of hearing Springer sing, showing her last empathic contact with him, in his courage, in his death.

When she shared the Nahuak with all its resonant passion, Ron began to shake all over, body and soul groaning under the weight of sorrow they'd forced him to drink. Alex released him and watched him collapse in a heap on the floor. He turned to Scott.

"Mind taking out the trash?" he asked.

"No, sir," Scott said. "My pleasure."

As Scott dragged him away, writhing and weeping, Alex turned to Jaguar. "Handy thing, being an empath," he noted.

"Sometimes it is," she agreed. She touched his elbow. "Call it in," she said.

CHAPTER THIRTY-FIVE

Ron Schulman made his confession in the interview room where Detective Thei once had dominion, though right now both Francois and Didier were sitting in similar rooms, being asked similar questions.

What they had to to say wasn't half as interesting as Ron's narrative. He admitted to the murder of all the children Springer was supposed to have killed, and quite a few more, including Alicia Senna. He gave it all away, from the time he'd killed someone who wanted to adopt Springer, to his abuse of his daughter, and the car accident on Planetoid Three that almost killed Scott. The only problem was recording his statement as fast as he spoke. He tended to babble and laugh inappropriately, then turn his nails onto his own flesh, scratching at his face and ripping at his thick head of hair.

Jaguar and Alex watched the interview from the observation window, saw him put his electronic signature on the digital recording of the confession. Jaguar pressed her hand on the window and let her presence be known to him. He screeched as if scalded, and crawled under the interview table, mewling like a frightened child.

"Keep her away from me!" he screeched. "Keep her away!"

Jaguar looked to Alex, wondering if he'd scold her for this last move.

He didn't. His face was grim with satisfaction. "Thank you," he said quietly.

They turned away from the wreckage and went their own way.

* * * *

As always happened in an event this big, quite a few meetings followed. Jaguar was questioned closely, particularly about the video the whole world had seen, of her attacking Larry Engle.

"Dr. Addams," a Montreal lawyer said, "we do not allow empathic testimony in our courts, but it seems you used your psi capacities to garner information."

"No I didn't," she said.

"Detective Thei says otherwise. He says that you used the dog to gather information."

She laughed lightly. "You believe that?"

The lawyer looked abashed. "Then the video, of when you went after Mr. Engle."

"That was a whole different kind of contact," she said.

"Are you saying you didn't make empathic contact with him at that time?" he asked.

"Sure I did," she said. "But it wasn't about the case."

"Then what?" he asked.

"I wanted to find out if his prick was as small as I suspected. As it turns out, I was right."

After that, they asked her no more questions.

Paul Dinardo, present throughout the inquiry, offered his full support. He gave testimony to what Ron Schulman did during Springer's time on the Planetoid, and to his own part in assuring Jaguar had official status in the preliminary research regarding Alicia Senna's death. He might have gotten his hand slapped for any of that, but by then Ron, Didier and Francois had signed full confessions.

Didier's part in it was small, as it turned out. He wanted only to get Alicia out of the way so he could have a seat at Ferrari. When Detective Thei offered him a way to do so, he had no idea it would kill her. He didn't have the stomach for that kind of work, he said. But Detective Thei had more than enough stomach for both of them. He wanted Alicia dead. Wanted Jaguar dead as well. In fact, his only regret was that he'd failed to kill her.

"How the hell did Paul screw that out of my gentlemen callers?" Jaguar asked Alex when she had the chance to speak with him.

"They made a deal," Alex said. "Their testimony, in return for a sentence with any teacher except you."

"They got off easy," Jaguar said. "And who gets Ron?"

Though he was pretty much a wreck, he wasn't technically criminally insane because every murder he committed was with full moral and intellectual understanding, which meant he wouldn't go to Planetoid One. The choice was between Two and Tree, and Paul had already talked to Alex about that.

"He's going to two," Alex told Jaguar.

"Really?" she said. "After all my hard work, I don't get any toys?"

"You might have some fun with Didier or Detective Thei, but you don't want Ron."

A statement rather than a question, and normally she'd kick back at his presumption, but not this time.

"You're right," she told him. "I'd rather be eaten alive by fire ants than try and rehab Ron Schulman."

* * * *

After the official pronouncements were made, Jaguar and Alex found Rachel and Luna at her hotel, gave Rachel another two weeks off to go play with Meris, took the dog and rented an airrunner, which they flew to 13 Streams. Luna took the ride well and was waggling her rear end hard when they landed.

They went to the circle of adobe houses at the center of the village, Luna off-leash but staying at Jaguar's heel. When they got to Jake and One Bird's house they stopped, and Luna looked from one to the other, then planted her butt down on the dusty earth and waited further instructions. In short order a gangly twelve year old girl popped out of their house like a cork and came crashing toward them. Maya, who had also waited.

"Luna!" she screeched. Luna stayed put, but her tail batted back and forth, raising dust behind her. Jaguar looked down at her, moved a hand. "Go," she said quietly.

Luna made a beeline to Maya, who held her arms open and slid to her knees, engulfing her as she swathed her face with wet dog kisses. Alex took Jaguar's hand and squeezed it.

"Are those tears in your eyes, Dr. Addams?" he asked.

"So what?" she said crossly.

"Just wondering if you're happy to see Maya, or sad at losing Luna."

"I hate you," she said, with feeling.

He put his arms around her and drew her close. "She was your Nahuak," he whispered. "I'll miss her, too."

"Hell," she said. "Hell and rat fuck."

"All that. Let's go see our girl."

He released her, and they walked to where Maya sat with Luna.

"I guess," Jaguar said to Maya, "you two already know each other."

"Of course we do," Maya said. "She's *my* dog. Thank you so much!" She released her hold on Luna long enough to lunge at Jaguar in her version of an embrace, then returned quickly to ruffling the dog's head and squealing with delight.

As she continued in her ministrations, Jake and One Bird emerged from their house and walked over to them. Jaguar stood, lifted her face to them and smiled. Jake moved to her and smacked her hard on the shoulder, his own face full of fury.

"Ow. Jesus, Jake," she said. "What's that for?"

He spit some words in Zuni at her, and she answered in what Alex thought was equally clipped Mertec. They went back and forth rapidly, and the only word he recognized was Nahuak, but that was enough to tell him the jist of the conversation.

What the hell was she thinking? A Nahuak? Alone? Was she stupid, or crazy? Her grandfather would be ashamed of her if he knew. And from Jaguar, something to the effect that it worked, didn't it?

Jake pointed a finger at her face, but his scowl slowly transformed into a grin, and his growl became laughter, slow and certain. She laughed in return.

"I'm okay," she said. "I know it wasn't the smartest thing I ever did, but I had to."

"Next time, it wouldn't hurt to get a little help."

"I hope to hell there won't be a next time."

"Not this, but whatever crazy ass thing you try next. You promise me right now you won't go it alone."

"Okay," she said. "I promise. Really."

He pulled her into an embrace. Said something in Zuni. She touched his cheek, said something back.

Jake released her and turned to Alex. "Come inside. It's time for supper."

They went into the house with Maya and Luna, who looked completely content with her new situation. The table held a great deal of laughter, and Luna's tail was in almost constant motion, thumping against the floor, happy for every treat tossed her way. When they'd all eaten and Maya took Luna back to her adoptive parent's house, Alex and Jaguar went outside to admire the night time sky.

It was filled with stars, each one of them singing. They stood for some time holding hands and listening. Then, at last, Alex turned to Jaguar. "I caught everything but the last bit. What did he say?"

Jaguar knew what he meant. What Jake said to her when they arrived. "You want an exact translation?"

"Sure."

"He said, I can't lose you to the air, dark star. There's not another like you in—well, the phrase he used literally translates to the eye of all deer."

"That'd be the whole of time and space?"

"Pretty much."

Alex thought about this. "Dark star?"

"He called me that when I was a teenager."

"Dark star," Alex repeated. He turned her to him, caught her in his arms and held her close. "Not in any time, or any place."

EPILOGUE

Planetoid 3, Toronto City Replica

Alex and Jaguar spent another week in New Mexico, and when they returned they each went to their respective offices to clean up the final reports on the case. Alex was at it for some time when he felt the stir of empathic contact from Jaguar.

Still working? she asked.

Finishing up, he replied.

I'm done. You want company later?

Absolutely. I'll be home within the hour.

I'll meet you at your place. With Thai food.

That gives me two things to look forward to, he replied. As she exited contact, he felt the sensation of her finger, moving slowly across his face.

* * * *

He was glad to open the door on his apartment, glad to be home, glad to know Jaguar would be there soon. The first thing he saw when he entered was a box, sitting on his coffee table.

He stood staring at it. Boxes that appeared mysteriously were always a matter for concern in his job. He reached out a hand, testing the air around it for any sense of danger. To his surprise, all he picked up was Scott.

"Really?" he asked and approached the box. On top was an envelope, with his name on it, marked 'from Scott White.'

Something Scott had delivered, personally. He opened the envelope and read the note.

"Sir," it said. "This is material from the property room. It contains the personal effects of Springer Todd. As next of kin, it belongs to you. If you'd like me to take care of it, I'm available."

Alex dropped the note on the coffee table. He sat on his couch and glanced at his clock. Jaguar would be here soon. If he wanted, he could get rid of this before she arrived, look through it, toss it in the garbage, hide it in a closet for later. All choices were his. He continued to sit and stare, but not for long. In less than ten minutes, he heard his door open and was aware of someone standing next to him. He looked up. Jaguar.

She put the bag that held their supper on his coffee table, reached down and touched the box, then sat next to him. "I talked to Scott," she said.

"Mm," he said. "I was waiting for you before I opened it."

"I'm here," she said.

Here, he thought. By his side. He stood and started ripping away at the official tape. She peered into the box with him. They saw clothes— underwear, jeans, and a t-shirt. They smelled of blood and memory.

Alex ran a hand over his face. "Can you help me?" he asked.

They lifted the clothing out together, smoothed it with something like reverence and put it to one side. Then Jaguar reached into the box and removed something else. A thumb drive. She held it up, rolled it over in her hand. "I know what this is," she said.

"What?" he asked.

Their attempt to get Springer off the Planetoid had ended disastrously. On the way to the shuttleport, their car was hit by another driver, part of Ron Schulman's plan to kill him and Jaguar. They both survived, and Springer left the scene, made his way to the recording studio. Jaguar had found him there, singing.

She looked to Alex."When I got to the recording studio, Springer was singing. He had maybe fifteen minutes before I got there. I think he made some music."

Alex, white at the lips, gave a short nod. "Play it," he said.

"You're sure?"

"For fuck's sake, play it."

She moved to his music system, put the thumb drive in the appropriate slot, pushed some buttons. She turned back to Alex. "You might want to sit down," she suggested.

He did so, and she pushed one more button.

A voice spoke, raspy and rough, filled with self assurance bordering on arrogance. Appropriate, Jaguar thought. It was Springer, and he was about to sing. He'd earned any amount of arrogance for what his voice could do.

"If you're hearing this, and I'm not there, it means I'm dead," he said. "Also, if it's going like I saw, you're both alive, and you took care of Schulman. So I hope. Either way, this is for the two of you. You'll figure out the best way to use it. The first one is for the kids. Use a rock beat on it. Up tempo."

The song was about hope, and the need to nurture it in spite of fear. A major key, fast tempo. *Let it grow,* he sang. *Let it grow, let it grow. Hate has no teeth, and fear no breath. Only love remains. Let it grow.*

When he stopped singing, he laughed. "Jaguar'll appreciate that one. Not something I wanted to sing."

She remembered his reluctance to write a song for the children killed at his concert. She smiled, her face moving around the tears that stung her eyes.

"Okay," Springer said. "I think I got time for one more. I hope so. It needs keyboard—a rolling phrase. Lots of arpeggio. Also slide guitar and keep it really sliding. Gerry'll know what to do with it. I call it Daddy."

Alex's hand sought Jaguar's, and when he found it, he clutched her like a drowning man. She held on, her grasp firm and sure.

In your hands, Springer sang. *I'm in your hands. Time dances like the water of a storm. Time deals with us both, doing harm. But I'm in your hands, the safest place to be. And I see you, in my hands. I know you, in the words that try to heal. Hear you in the passion you can't help but feel.*

Alex's grasp on Jaguar tightened until her fingers went numb. She held on, listening. The phrases reminded her of the chant he'd recorded, but with more unleashed joy. His chant was the motion of his soul as it traversed worlds. This was the dance of the wolf on solid earth, celebrating a kill, rolling with his mate in pleasure, following paths that took him places where he could see forever. Wild to its core, it was a determined worship of the face of love.

When it ended, she looked to Alex, whose head was bowed. Springer spoke one more time.

"That's it," he said. "Listen, thanks. And I hope you two are fine. I hope you got him. Go have some fun for me, would you?"

Silence followed, and Jaguar would not break it before Alex did.

After some time he released her hand, looked away. "I'm not sure if that was one of my most painful moments, or the best gift I ever got," he said.

"Both, Alex," she said.

He shifted, stared down at his own hands.

"Y'know," she said. "You own these tunes now."

"Do I?"

"Sure. He gave them to you. So maybe we can sell them. Make some money for that horse ranch you went to. And we recorded some of his gigs with Moon Illusion. There's his chant, and a song he wrote for me. Well, ripped from my flesh, really, but that's another story."

Alex stayed still, his face stoney. "I'll have Rachel look into it," he said. "She'll know what to do." He spoke from a great distance, the space he occupied far from her. She touched his shoulder, then dropped her hand on her lap.

Where are you? she asked subvocally.

He jerked his head around to face her and seemed to see her for the first time. She hadn't yet shown him what she went through in his absence, but he understood. He'd been ready to die for her, but her choice was the harder one. The most active of creatures, she had to abide in stillness, let go of everything except love, seek only love, and a persistent will toward his life. For six months, her days were a creeping sorrow she consented to bear, and he wondered how she could. She was such a fiery woman.

"Didn't you say you were bringing Thai food?" he asked, speaking out loud.

"I was, but after I talked to Scott I had another idea." She put her hands to the bags on the table, opened one. Alex sniffed the rich, smoky scent.

"Chili dogs?" he asked.

"Springer liked them. A lot."

"I know." Alex moved his arm to pull her close. "I'm here," he said. "With you. Nowhere else I want to be except here. By your side."

She relaxed into him and let herself be held.

www.ingramcontent.com/pod-product-compliance
Lightning Source LLC
Chambersburg PA
CBHW020446270626
47155CB00022B/1680